Also by Maria Vale

The Legend of All Wolves

The Last Wolf

A Wolf Apart

Forever Wolf

SEASON OF THE WOLF

MARIA VALE

Published by Sourcebooks Casablanca, an imprint of Sourcebooks
P.O. Box 4410, Naperville, Illinois 60567-4410
(630) 961-3900
sourcebooks.com

Printed and bound in the United States of America.
OPM 10 9 8 7 6 5 4 3 2 1

do you know what it's like to live
someplace that loves you back?

—"summer, somewhere" by Danez Smith

Prologue

Constantine

In the forest stark and grim live unspeakable things.

My mother had never been one for bedtime stories. Never one for articulating much at all. Mostly she cleaned her tiny house—I never thought of it as mine or ours—with the fierceness of a woman who knew civilization danced on a razor's edge and a single misfolded towel or an undusted mote was enough to send it toppling.

To hold that eventuality at bay, she worked. Constantly. Touching up the bright-white paint. Washing the blue and purple floral linens. Tearing away the spiky fragrant bushes around the edges, chopping down the single shade tree in the yard. She gave it to a neighbor with a fireplace for nothing, a moment of largesse that made him trust our odd family even less.

Then she lay down rough green grass that came in rolls like toilet paper and was not to be walked on.

During the day, the house smelled pleasantly of cinnamon or chocolate and less pleasantly of ammonia.

There was a blue, onion-patterned curtain that shielded the window above the kitchen sink. It was always closed, except on laundry days, when the window opened onto a range of mountains, faraway and tree-covered.

Sometimes my mother would forget that the curtain

wasn't there. Then the faucet ran and the food burned until my father came home and turned everything off and put the curtain back on its brass rod and pulled his wife away from the window.

Those were the evenings when she told me, her only child, stories, cautionary tales about people who wandered into the woods, losing their way, their lives, their souls.

They all started the same way.

"In the forest dark and grim live unspeakable things."

One Christmas, when I was still very young—six, maybe seven?—I heard a noise downstairs in the kitchen. Convinced it was Santa eating the brownies my mother had made, I crept down the steps. I did not find Santa noshing on rich squares of chocolate and walnuts. Instead, I found my mother staring empty-eyed through the kitchen window toward the snow-dusted forests, bloody butcher paper on the counter.

Gnawing absently on raw beef tongue.

In the forest dark and grim live unspeakable things.

Chapter 1

Evie

In our stories, the forests were deathless. In our stories, they spread in endless protective waves across the land. In our stories, they could be hewed by disease or fire or woodman's ax, but each hewing left enough of the old forests to seed new ones.

In our stories, though, the old forests were not churned into a sea of mud and sawdust, herringboned by tread marks with iridescent puddles that smell sick-sweet, like venom.

This is not our land. Our land is beyond the gap between two mountains. There, a tree cracks, a beaver slaps its tail against water, and a loon gives out a long, haunting call.

Where are you?

Its mate calls back.

Here.

Here.

Here.

Our land is where my wolves wait for my own call. I try to clear the heartache in my throat then throw back my head and howl.

Where are you?

It starts out that way, though by the end of that long breath, it is simply *Are you?*

And from across the vastness of Homelands, the Great North call back.

We are, they answer, each voice reassuring me that all are safe and accounted for.

There are humans howling in a white windowless bus, who are not safe.

Tiberius slams the door on the injured would-be hunters, then bangs twice on the roof to signal Thea that she's good to go.

"Watch your tail," Thea says as Elijah Sorensson, the Alpha of the 9th Echelon of the Great North Pack, pulls his tail in and drops his muzzle on the shoulder of his human mate. She reaches across to pull the passenger door closed.

Victor, who had been our Deemer, our thinker about pack law, did not want to let this human who knew our secrets live. I knew he was angry that I refused to kill her, but not angry enough to stand by while human hunters decimated our pack.

Well, now you're dead, Victor, a noseless dog wandering hungry and alone forever, and Thea Villalobos, the Goddess of the City of Wolves, is smuggling those humans back into Canada.

When the Pack finally falls silent, one last solitary call floats down from Westdæl. It is hesitant, questioning, asking the hills and valleys of Homelands to help her make sense of her new life. It is nowhere near as loud or as certain as the wolf Varya once was, but then the Gray is no longer Varya.

For three days out of thirty when the moon is full and her law is iron, the Pack must be wild. However the Iron Moon finds us, she makes us wilder. If we are in skin, she makes us wild. But if we are wild, she makes us *æcewulfas*, real wolves. Forever wolves.

Varya and the Bone Wolf, the wolf she loved—loves—sacrificed their other forms to fight for us, while we writhed on the ground, neither wild nor in skin. Deaf, blind, paralyzed, and helpless.

The Alpha Shielder of the 12th Echelon had been made hard by memory. I choose to believe that she will be freed from those memories now.

As her call dies out, I throw back my head and answer. We may not be part of her pack anymore, but she will always be part of ours.

The Great North's runt hobbles up beside me, and as soon as she does, Tiberius lopes over, falling to his knees in front of her. Eyes closed, he buries his face in her fur.

One of the four Shifters sitting on rickety chairs starts to move. Without standing, Tiberius exhales, pivots, and fires.

Wild, Tiberius is a terrible hunter. Much worse than Silver with her bad leg and small size. In skin, though, his shot hits the burly Shifter, grazing his shoulder.

"I told you to sit down," Tiberius says.

"*Do you have any idea how much this suit cost?*" the Shifter says, plucking loose threads from the tear Tiberius's bullet left in his shoulder pad.

"It would be easier if I killed them now," Tiberius says without looking away from the Shifters.

I eye Silver. With Victor dead, the Pack needed a Deemer. There are older wolves and bigger, but no one who knows our laws and the needs of our wild selves better. Silver chuffs a long, disappointed breath, telling me what I already knew. Of course, it would be easier to kill them now, but if laws were easy and convenient, there would be no need for them.

The law says we can kill only for food or to stop an immediate threat to the Pack, and as much as I would like to get rid of these last Shifters, they did not side with the humans against us. One even fought on our side.

As for food...they smell like humans, and humans taste like plastic and mink and the grease trap at an all-you-can-eat mutton emporium.

Without moving my head, my eyes flicker toward the gun in Tiberius's hand. I wrinkle my lip back from a single fang, and he slides it back into his waistband with a sigh.

But just because I'm not killing them doesn't mean I will trust them. Shifters are different. They don't have to be wild so they never are. The Iron Moon means nothing to them. They don't have the same ties to Pack or land, and their wild is not sacred. It's just another resource to be exploited as they battle with humans to be apex predators.

"You can't trust them, Alpha," says Tiberius, and *he* is half Shifter. He is August Leveraux's *son.*

I lost my birth pack to Shifters. I have no intention of losing another.

Crystal shatters, and the solitary female Shifter screams.

She was cold, I suppose, so she'd tried to cover herself with the stained white length of damask, simultaneously knocking over a crystal flute and revealing the man with the hole in his forehead, centered like a third eye.

I'd forgotten about him. Another detail to be taken care of.

"That's Julia. She's August's niece. Cassius," he says, nodding toward the burly man, "is, I think, now engaged to her. She's spoiled, he's a fool. But Constantine's the one you have to watch out for."

I follow the direction of his eyes toward the two other men. I discount a smaller one who sits on a rock trying to hold back groans. He is frail and clearly in pain. The Shifter standing beside him, whispering too softly for me to hear, I recognize. He was here before, waiting for the blustering man to deliver August's ultimatum to the Great North. He'd said nothing, but I'd noticed him anyway: broad-shouldered, long and lean and tightly coiled, like a rattler made man.

Usually I appreciate Tiberius's terseness, but now I have too many unanswered questions and no way to ask them. What is wrong with the smaller Shifter? He looks sick, but I thought Shifters were like us, dying from bullets and traps and hooves, not from slow wasting disease.

And what is a niece? When he first said it, I'd looked toward Silver with a mystified blink, forgetting momentarily that as wise as my Deemer is in matters of the law, she failed Introduction to Human Behaviors four times.

Finally, Constantine fought for us, so what makes him dangerous?

The sick Shifter groans again, caging his face in his hands.

"Magnus, shut the fuck up," Cassius yells.

Before the last sound fades, Constantine's elbow cracks against Cassius's throat, fast as a rattler strike, which partly answers that question.

Julia sobs something about going home.

I slip into the sequestering trees silvered by moonlight, knowing they never will.

Chapter 2

Constantine

"I'M SORRY, MR. LEVERAUX. I DIDN'T KNOW WHO THEY were."

"August," he said. "Call me August. You misunderstand me. I could not be more pleased." He gestured dismissively toward the man with his arm in a sling and the other with the swollen jaw. They had handled me roughly, pushing me into a car. That much I remember; the rest, not so much. "How old did you say you were?"

"Nine. Ten in..." I couldn't remember how many days it was supposed to be. "Soon. My mother knows. She is making me brownies. Where is she?"

He didn't answer my question but instead asked one of his own.

"Do you know how we came to this land?"

My mind had been fragmenting, all certainty gone.

"Focus," he said.

I hadn't been able to focus on anything. Nothing large anyway. Tiny details were there: The squeak of the oven door. The tear of a paper towel. The running water. My mother's distant expression. The way she lay down on the floor. My math homework floating from the table, landing on the linoleum beside her. Her thumbs shriveling. Migrating up her wrist, her nail twisting and darkening into a claw. Calling down to the basement where my father had his workshop.

"Something's happened to Mom."

My father's step fast and loud up the stairs. His pump-action rifle in one hand, a scrap of paper in the other. I wobbled helplessly as he shook me, repeating something over and over. "Focus," my father said. "Call this number and tell whoever answers that you are Constantine, Maxima and Brutus's son. Someone needs to get you before the humans do."

I stared at the frayed and discolored piece of paper while my mind circled in helpless fugues. I wasn't Constantine. I was Connor. The brownies were burning. Her thumbs. Who were Maxima and Brutus? The guns. Police sirens. *Before the humans?*

"Run," the man on the other end of the line had said. "Stay hidden. We will find you. We will always find you." As the handset left his mouth for the cradle, he yelled to someone. "Get August. Maxima and Brutus are dead."

Click.

True to his word, men did find me and handled me roughly.

"Do you know," August started again, his limited patience gone, "how we came to this land?"

My unraveling mind landed on my father's advice that when conversation falters, turn to cars. Cars were always a safe topic.

"Chevrolet?"

"No," August said, his face closed.

"Where are my mom and dad?"

"We'll get to what happened to Maxima and Brutus in a minute."

"Their names are Maxine and Bruce."

He studied me with those bright, terrifying eyes that

sought out dissimulation so often and so well. "Whatever else she was, your mother was *not* Maxine."

I would have argued that he could look it up in the minutes of the Rainy River Elementary School PTA, except that there was something about his repeated use of the past tense that had broken my ability to speak.

She was.

She was not.

"*Nous sommes* Lukani," he said. "*C'est notre devoir de dompter le sauvage qui nous entoure, comme nous l'avons dompté en nous-mèmes.*" August looked at me again for signs of comprehension, and finding none, he translated. "We are Lukani. It is our duty to tame the wild without, as we have always tamed the wild within."

He stared off into the distance, rubbing his finger along his lower lip. "It makes us strong," he said. I should be proud, he said. Ever since Romulus and Remus left the woods, the Lukani have been *domitores terrae*, the subduers of lands. Our *happy* group—he called us that, "Our happy group" or "Our merry band," as a way of mocking the fact that we were anything but—arrived from France as *défricheurs* to tear down the great forests of Canada. Not to build ships or houses, but simply to clear the trees, extirpate the wild.

To make, he'd said, the New World safe for cabbages.

"Now, sadly, there is so little wild left that you will never understand the pure joy of taming it." Then he added with a theatrical sigh and a hand to his chest, "So we have to make do with harnessing the darkness in men's souls. It's...a poor second."

He laughed at that, and though I was young, I understood there was nothing pure or joyful about it.

"Cookies?"

"Thank you, Mrs. Leveraux," I said, though I didn't like oatmeal and hated raisins.

"Drusilla. Call me Drusilla." She reminded me a little of my mother. Tight and neat, her head a mass of symmetrical gold coils. "Leveraux is for humans."

"Thank you, Drusilla," I said, gagging on the name and the raisins.

"So this is the one," she said, touching my shoulder and pinching my arm, not in the way of someone giving comfort to a lost boy, but like I was horseflesh or a prize fighter.

"Lovely. I think we can make something of him," she said to August before turning to go.

August watched her, all ruffled apron and tight skirt and stockinged menace.

"Mr. Lever—August? My parents?"

"Oh yes, of course. Well..." He clapped his hands together, brushing away crumbs of oatmeal. "Your father shot your bitch mother and then drove them both off a bridge where they conveniently immolated. So." He held the plate toward me. "More?"

With a clap and a cookie, my childhood, my family, and my humanity were gone, and my career of making the world safe for cabbages began.

Magnus has never been this bad. He's always been unwell. It started with toothaches that would come and go, but now they come more often and go less frequently.

Because we are not human, I couldn't take him to a doctor. I'd tried, dragging Magnus on a lengthy car ride to visit a dentist in Ottawa. Dr. Spassky'd been skimming from August and would be dead in the morning, so what was the harm in having him take a look at Magnus's teeth in the afternoon? Except that shit Lucian killed him before I even got Magnus in the chair, so that was the end of that.

Now the pain is spreading to his joints, his stomach, even his skin. Now he clings to the side of the car, whimpering with every thump.

"Where are we going?" Cassius asks, his voice still rough from my elbow to his trachea.

"When the Iron Moon is done," Tiberius says, "the Alpha will decide what to do with you."

After passing through a huge slatted gate, we arrive at what looks like the parking lot on the last evening of the county fair. The ground is churned into mud, and cars are crammed in haphazardly as though deserted by fairgoers afraid they are going to miss the fireworks.

"She can't walk on this," Cassius says as soon as he gets out. "It's going to ruin her shoes."

Tiberius's arm darts forward, jamming the muzzle of his gun into the soft V of Cassius's lower jaw.

I move Magnus behind me. Bullets in skulls make for unpredictable trajectories.

"Look up," Tiberius commands. "What do you see?"

"Trrs?" Cassius hazards, unable to move his jaw.

"The moon. And not just any moon." His mouth is close to Cassius's ear. "That," he growls, "is the Iron Moon. For three days out of thirty, when the moon is pregnant and full and her law is Iron, the Pack must be wild. *I* should be wild, but I'm *not* because I have to fucking babysit you. So whatever it is, figure it out yourself and do not make me speak to you again."

His head snaps up, his nose twitching, his eyes abstracted, distant. He swivels toward the trees and a pale shadow in the woods that coalesces into a light-gray wolf. It moves closer with a quick lurching pace, one hind leg curled up against its torso.

Tiberius must have smiled when he was an infant, though I don't remember. Certainly he hasn't for twenty-five years or more. Not since he lost his baby teeth and his father watched in horror as the needle-sharp canines peeked out of his gums and kept growing longer and longer. August made sure his son didn't smile again after that.

Now, though, he smiles, broad and bright for this gray runt. This was clearly the wolf August meant to take when he arranged to have his grandchildren kidnapped. Instead of this small, light-furred wolf, the dim-witted human Lucian recruited had drugged and abducted a monster and brought her to our compound.

When Varya woke up, she became a tall woman with black hair, eyes the color of granite, the grace of a raven, and a look of death about her.

"Follow her," Tiberius commands. The wolf turns with two rapid hops and slides into the woods, dissolving between the trees like a shard of moonlight.

In the forest stark and grim live unspeakable things.

My mother's voice has faded over the years, but the warning is still there and I hesitate at the boundary. One more step and I leave this borderland where there is at least enough sky to coax out a rim of flowers and head into the realm of unspeakable things. Then Tiberius pushes me and I stumble in.

"Hey, Ti, ease off. Remember, I was the one who called you. I was the one who warned Varya—"

"Stop," he says. His eyes glow green and creepy in this low light. "How do you know her name?"

"Varya's?"

"Yes, how do you know her name?"

"She told me."

"Why would she tell you?" he asks again with increasing urgency.

"Because I told her mine? I don't know. You'll have to ask her." He flinches, jabbing his gun sharp into my back. "Careful of the kidneys, Tiberius, and for fuck's sake, put the safety back on."

He looks into the pitch-black woods with an unreadable expression and shakes his head.

I see nothing but the forest stark and grim where there are unspeakable things.

August's compound was on the coast. Aside from a few scraggly plants, there was nothing but the wide sky and rock ground flat by the pounding ocean. It felt light and open. Not dark and secretive. Here I can feel the insistent moving and growing and living and dying. Leaves shake overhead. Liquids dribble. Branches crack dry as old bone or bend almost in half before slicing through the air and hitting whoever is behind in the face. Things stalk us through the canopy as fast and quiet as secrets. Whatever moonlight manages to leak through the leaves moves in dappled waves, making the forest floor shift, precarious and uncertain, and for the first time, I truly understand August's obsessive need to chop it all down.

I'm so focused on keeping Magnus from falling that I miss the fact that we've arrived at an opening that's more than one tree in diameter and I can actually see the starlit sky and ground and a long log cabin sitting atop stone footings.

The pale-gray wolf stands to the side of the stairs leading to the porch. In the dark, Cassius misses a step and trips forward.

"Watch it," he snaps when he sees Julia watching. As though he thinks she is somehow to blame.

"Sorry," Julia answers miserably. As though she thinks so too.

Tiberius signals for us to go in and then slides down the length of the peeled-log support, his gun held loose between cocked knees.

Holding the screen door open for Magnus, I take one last look back toward the spiked fringe of trees. That's when I see her.

I'd seen her once before when I came with Lucian to lay out August's proposal. Join with us—become like us—or die.

While Lucian made threatening noises at a bush, my eyes wandered to eyes glaring in the dark. They were gold… No, not gold: gold is all glitz and surface. They were like amber, like fire. And when she stepped out from the tree line, fire eyes glowing against black fur, I already knew that we were wasting time. This was the beating heart of the pack, and we had nothing to offer her.

August talked about the Great North with disdain, claiming that the Pack were throwbacks, refusing to acknowledge that there was no longer room for the wild.

But when I looked into those eyes, I knew that she, at least, understood exactly how the world had changed, how tenuous their existence was. And that she would fight for it anyway.

"Close the door," Cassius says. "You're letting moths in."

The latch snicks. I lean against the frame, looking

one last time across the dark to the unblinking fire of her eyes.

There are moths gathered around two dim flame-shaped bulbs that do little more than make the shadows darker.

Magnus is already collapsed on one of the bottom beds of the bunks arrayed against the long walls on either side. The mattresses and pillows are bare, but sheets and plaid blankets are draped over the railings at the end. He stares sightless at the exposed ticking of the mattress above him, his feet hanging over the edge. I begin to pick away at his knotted, mud-encrusted laces.

He had none when I first saw him in the visiting room of the juvenile center. I was checking in on Sergei, a human kid who'd worked as a lookout for August. I'd been told he was talkative, so I wanted to remind him of the very real consequences of saying...well, saying anything. That was when the bone-thin boy came in, haunted and hunched, his laceless shoes flapping loose around his feet.

He sat next to us. A woman—legal aid? Child Protective Services?—started chatting amicably, trying to get answers. The boy said nothing, just wrapped his arms around his waist and stared without seeing.

I'd said what I had to say to Sergei, but I kept him there. He always felt he had to fill the silence with words, though his words weren't worth the sound it took to form them and I told him so.

"Excuse me, do you have a pen?" the woman asked. I remember her looking through her vinyl briefcase, the plastic cracking over the webbing. "I can't seem to find mine." The boy was looking at some piece of paper the woman wanted him to sign. She had set it on a legal pad because the table was made of metal mesh and was impossible to write on.

I gave her a pen. The boy's right hand was fisted shut around his thumb. When it came time to sign, he didn't unfurl his fingers, instead jamming the pen into his fist and scrawling awkwardly.

When he returned the white ballpoint to me, it was covered with blood. He grabbed it back, wiping it on his orange pants, smearing it more. He looked at it, then at me, and I felt his despair.

"It's okay." I took back the pen, waving it in the air in front of me to indicate that it was meaningless. The guard came and took him away, handling him too roughly.

He was already gone by the time I realized that the smell he had left on the pen was not human.

"Who is that?" I abruptly asked Sergei, who was at the top of the pecking order and knew everyone, but not this boy.

"John Doe," he'd said. "No home. No family. No name." Then he sliced his finger across his neck. "A born vic."

It made me angry. That finger and that word. I knew what it meant to lose my family and my home and my name, but I was no vic.

I told Sergei that I didn't want this kid to be one either. If Sergei wondered why, he knew better than to ask. He was nothing, a tool guarded by August's name, but he knew how hierarchies worked. He knew that the guy at the top could be as arbitrary as he wanted. I was close enough to the top and arbitrary enough to make Sergei's life immeasurably harder and very measurably shorter.

Sergei let the word out that John Doe was my brother. And when he got out, I called him Magnus and kept the lie. No one ever questioned me.

Not even August.

"Blanket, Mags?"

He blinks at me. "You feel them, right?" he whispers, pleading. "Tell me you feel them."

Pursing my lips, I hush him like I always have so that no one would know that his mind's not quite right and he sees a world that doesn't exist.

He turns toward the wall. Then I spread the blanket over him and sit on the floor, boots still on, hands propped loose atop my knees. I don't trust any of them. Not Cassius, not Tiberius, and certainly not any of the unspeakable things that live in the forest making noises like the clawing of broken fingernails on nylon or the rasping moans of dying lungs.

When I wake up, my leg is lead and my ass is cramped tight, a hazard of falling asleep seated on the hard wooden floor. I pull myself up, checking on Magnus, whose breath is sour but steady. Shaking out my leg, I check on Tiberius. He's still on the porch, but he isn't alone. Leaning back, he offers up his neck to the pale-gray wolf above him. She has her fangs at his exposed throat, and in the glow of the full moon, her white teeth scrape against skin the color of midnight. His hand spreads across her shoulders, his eyes are closed and he exhales, relaxing into her jaws.

Her eyes catch mine, and I feel like a pervert watching something unbearably intimate. I look away, catching the burning eyes of someone who knows what she's fighting for.

A creak starts across the room, then stops, waiting for Cassius's snores. In fitful starts and stops, Julia creeps across the floor.

"Constantine," she whispers. "Are you awake?"

"Hmm."

"Shh. I don't...I don't want to bother Cass."

She creeps closer, pausing with every step to make sure that Cassius is still snoring.

"They're going to let us go, right? Cass says so. We didn't do anything to them, so they have to."

Julia was always protected from everything. She was never told and never asked where the money came from that had been laundered and rinsed and fed into her seemingly endless account. ("Import-export," August said.) At her father's funeral, we were told not to mention how he died. ("Heart attack," August said.) She seemed utterly unconcerned with how a healthy, middle-aged man came to die of a heart attack, or why a healthy, middle-aged man who died of a heart attack warranted a funeral with a closed casket.

Afterward, when we went out to eat, the table was rearranged so that Julia wouldn't have to see the crustaceans getting fished out of the tank when she ordered lobster.

Something about it has always bothered me. Not something. I know what bothers me. It's that Julia was still being treated as a precious innocent when she was thirty while I was forced to fight adults for food at the age of nine.

"You mean aside from the killing, arson, and kidnapping, we've done nothing to them."

"I don't believe you for a second, and anyway, *I* never did anything," she says, her voice simultaneously hushed and indignant.

"You drove a van of guns and hunters to their land."

"That wasn't *me*. Cassius was driving. I was just supposed to be entertaining. We were supposed to go to New York. *I* didn't know anything."

"What do you want, Julia?" I'm tired and she's grating on my last nerve.

"Is Uncle August really dead?"

"A werewolf put a metal slat through his throat, so yes, he's dead."

"Did you kill him?"

"Who?"

"The *werewolf.*"

"No. I gave her a car."

I feel the fringe of her blanket brush against my hand.

"Baby?" Cassius says groggily, snuffling around in his pillow. "Julia, what are you doing?"

She jumps away from me.

"I'm just trying to find the bathroom."

"Hold on, I'll be right there." The dull *thunk* of skull against wood is followed by a muffled "*Shit!*"

"Sorry," she says again and stands sniffling in the middle of the room until Cassius shuffles over to join her. Her voice is faint against his shoulder.

"Cass, we're going to get out of here, right?"

He makes all sorts of reassuring promises about plans to escape, none of them true. We have no guns, no phones, no families, and with August gone, nobody who cares whether we live or die.

The difference is I don't care. I had asked for one thing from August. Maybe if I'd asked for more I might not have been so surprised when he reneged. Anyway, I spent several weeks trying to figure out how to get myself and Magnus far enough away fast enough and with sufficient funds that even August Leveraux couldn't track us.

That was when it started to dawn on me that following elaborately laid-out directions was not the same thing as having a plan. I scrapped all my half-baked ideas when Lucian abducted Varya. It didn't matter whether my lupus ex machina had a plan, because she had something better. She had purpose. It radiated from her in wave after dark wave. She refused to give August anything—fear, respect, anything—until she whipped out the steel slat she had torn from its soldering under the bed in the room where we'd kept her and, with a graceful pirouette, pushed the bar still dripping with Romulus's blood through August's throat and gave him death.

Why did I warn her about the hunters coming to the Great North?

I think because I couldn't help but wonder what it was that inspired so much devotion in such a brutally hard woman. After she had gone, I stood looking at the dead men who had defined my past. Just for a few minutes. Nothing morose. Then I called Tiberius on his old number, and on the third ring, he answered.

It was warm during the day so we opened the windows, and when the drops hit the screens, they explode into cool mist. We pull the windows shut, fastening them by hooks and eyes so the sheets and blankets won't get wet. When I go to close the door, I find Tiberius still sitting there, the rain streaming down his face.

From the tree line across from the door, a dark wolf-shaped shadow watches with flaming eyes.

Chapter 3

Evie

It always takes me time to come down from the Iron Moon, to coalesce and shove myself back into the outline of this two-legged form that is so much lonelier than being wild. John never complained about it, but he'd been Alpha longer. Trained to put his needs aside younger.

Through the open window of the Meeting House, I catch those last shirred breezes against my skin, hear the rustles of the summer canopy, smell the tangy musk of the deer leg the 8th brought for the pups. Holding on as long as I can to senses that dull with each passing moment.

Outside, Adriana bangs a sledgehammer against the dirt in the deep cleats of her boots, first one, then the other. She does it to warn the wolves inside that the Shifters are coming, as though they haven't been loud enough slipping and tripping and falling and complaining the whole way from the dormitory.

They've scared off everything edible, and any wolf hoping to chase down a snack after the morning's formalities will have to settle for a carrot muffin.

The stairs groan under their heavy steps. The largest one is moving fast. The female limps behind him, her steps having a sharp staccato like an ingrown claw. The tall one walks behind, shortening his stride to stay apace with the one who is sick.

Cassius, Julia, Constantine, and Magnus.

Cassius, the big one, falls on the table holding plates of food meant to fuel the Alphas who are missing the Iron Moon Table. He takes the lids from chafing dishes filled with eggs and barley soup and curd-cheese pastries and scones and my own favorite: hasty pudding with cream and the end of last year's preserved gooseberries.

Probably looking for carrion, like Tiberius did when he first came. He complained steadfastly about the lack of meat until Silver explained that meat was what a wolf hunted and devoured still warm from snout to tail. Carrion, she said with no little disgust, was vacuum-packed roadkill.

Finally, he chooses something. Eggy cakes by the smell of it. Julia takes a small bowl of strawberries. She shows it first to Cassius, who raises a dewclaw. No, not dewclaw. Thumb. He raises his thumb. I bend my own against my fingers, reminding myself of the feel of its opposability.

Leonora, the Great North's human behaviors teacher, arrives late. Something about the sick one, Magnus, attracts her attention, but before she can get closer, Constantine pivots, making his body a shield against her. He seems to have only two modes: striking or coiled to strike.

Now Leonora cups her hand to her face. Sniffing at it with a worried expression, she looks toward me, her mouth open.

"Alpha?" says Cassius, and Leonora immediately forgets her question. Cassius's voice is now smooth and healed. The Pack looks to me for guidance, but with a quick dip of my eyes, I tell them to wait. Wolves are watchers first.

The Shifter brushes the crumbs first from his mouth and chest, then from his hands. He combs his fingers through his hair, then holds his hand out to Elijah Sorensson, Alpha of the 9th.

Elijah's eyes shift toward me. Without turning away from the window, I lift a lip over my right canine. The prey wants to play. Play with him.

Elijah is a lawyer and spent decades Offland before coming back home this winter. It has made him a consummate practitioner of human customs, and maybe that's what fools Cassius into thinking that the one who looks the most human, the one with neatly combed hair, with no traces of burrs, with no patches of molting fur stuck to old blood, must be in charge.

Or maybe it's just that Elijah wears a shirt with buttons, the kind of additional obstacle to being wild that Homeland wolves have little patience for.

"Alpha?" Cassius says again, holding out his hand. "Name's Cassius. I'm what you might call the Alpha of our merry group."

Two of the Shifters anxiously follow Cassius's interaction with the "Alpha," but the fourth one, the dangerous one, watches me. He is tall enough to see even over a roomful of wolves. To make sure he's not looking out the window, I step to the side. He doesn't move, but his eyes track me. It's an old Alpha trick: to watch without watching, because wolves who feel their Alpha's gaze on them become stilted and unnatural.

Constantine is the dangerous one.

What makes you dangerous, Constantine?

I watched our "guests" during the Iron Moon. Magnus is too sick to be dangerous; Cassius, too stupid; Julia, too afraid. Constantine has never seen me in skin, but I get the uncomfortable feeling he knows who I am anyway.

"As one Alpha to the other," Cassius says, "I wanted to find a way out of this misunderstanding so that no one has to get hurt."

Elijah scratches the corner of his eye. "What do you think has been misunderstood?"

"This whole..." Cassius waves his hand vaguely in the air, indicating the general disastrousness without admitting to anything in particular. "Julia and me, we came here for a *dinner*. You can tell... Come here, baby."

They look like they could both be in the same echelon, the same age group, so why would he call her "baby"?

Julia puts down the empty bowl and teeters over to Cassius, a hand clutching one of our blankets around her bare shoulders. He puts his arm around her waist. "Look at her. Look at me. You can tell by the way we're dressed that we were just coming to party."

"So nothing about the ATVs and rifles and jacklights at the edge of our land made you suspect that this wasn't just a dinner?"

"I knew it wasn't *just* a dinner. But I didn't know it was *your* land. Before he got shot, August hosted hunting parties all the time. You know, get a bunch of rich guys together, drive them out to some piece of land all stocked up with game. He always said nothing lubricates business like shooting at exotic animals wondering how the fuck they ended up in Canada."

He laughs and looks around at the silent faces surrounding him. He has mistaken his audience if he thinks we would appreciate the uproarious confusion of tropical beasts trembling in the cold while guns explode around them.

Yes, we are hunters. But our hunts are not from a safe distance; our hunts are intimate: teeth against hide, tongue against blood. The *Gemyndstow*, the memory place, is filled with stones bearing the names of wolves who have taken a hoof to the head or a claw to the throat. Soon hands go to seaxs, the daggers that are a poor substitute for the lost sharpness of fang and claw when we are in skin.

I shake my head once and they drop their hands, but I know they are not happy about it.

"Anyway, when August tells me to pick up these rich guys at Saint-Hubert Airport and drive them here, have dinner, be entertaining, then wait around until they've had their fun and drive them back, I did it. That's the way it is with him. He tells you what to do, and you do it. It wasn't up to me to figure out why.

"I honestly had no idea he was hunting you," he continues. "Look, if August really is dead—"

"He is dead," says the tall Shifter, in a voice that is deep and fluid and quiet, the kind of hissed quiet that is meant to make humans listen.

"*If* it turns out that August really is dead," Cassius snaps back, "which I still can't hardly believe, then it's over. I've got no beef with you."

"And what makes you Alpha?" I ask.

Cassius stills as the gathered Alphas of the Great North turn toward me, their heads lowered. He looks between Elijah in his wool slacks and white shirt and me in my torn jeans and ivory waffle-knit shirt with rust stains across the front and wonders if perhaps he has made a mistake.

My wolves part in front of me like water.

"Ah." Cassius's mind grapples with the new

development. "Of course. Alpha." He holds out his hand to me this time.

Now that I am Alpha, I have had to deal more often with the proffered hands of humans and know that I am expected to touch it, but here in Homelands, I do not have to pretend to be other than I am and will not shake this appendage that stinks of steel and carrion.

"What," I ask again, "makes you Alpha?"

His empty hand drops. "Not really Alpha exactly, but my fiancée?" He points to the female. "She is August's niece. By marriage."

Fiancée. Niece. Marriage.

"Leonora?"

Leonora pushes forward. She has a little brown bag that makes a hard snap when she opens it. Pulling out a tiny mirror with a tinny shine, she dabs at her face with a damp towel.

"He is saying"—she looks into the mirror—"that he is the bedfellow"—there is a streak of pine sap at her lower jaw—"of the offspring." It bristles with the sticky remains of owl feather. "Of August's mate's littermate?" Even Leonora seems uncertain about her interpretation.

"And this is a thing?"

"Humans put great importance on blood lineage regardless of suitability."

"But if it's about blood lineage, then why is 'the girl' not the new Alpha?" I indicate a spot behind Leonora's jaw. Owl blood.

Leonora pauses in her cleaning to shoot a questioning look over her mirror at Cassius.

"Well, because she's..." Cassius starts.

"Yes?"

"Because she's not interested, that's why. She doesn't know anything about import and export and stuff like that. Fuck, she doesn't know how many grams are in a kilo. And she doesn't *want* to know. Right, baby?"

Julia nods without looking up from the slow process of chipping away the nail polish on her thumb. I'm not sure she heard the question, just that Cassius has said something to her that requires an affirmative.

The screen door opens. I can't see who it is over the heads of the Alphas, but as soon as I see the big wolves jump away, I know it's Silver. Silver who was born a runt and stayed a runt, but it doesn't stop her from pushing her way through with that rolling gait that is wild even in skin.

I have known Silver since she was ripped tiny and weak from her dam's belly. Packs have no tolerance for weakness, and not only is she a runt, but her leg curls tight against her torso when she is wild. Still, there is no one in the Great North who is stronger of marrow or who loves the land, the Pack, and the wild more. No one who knows our stories and our laws better.

So when our last lawgiver betrayed the Pack, I called her to be Deemer. Her role is to clarify, arbitrate, mediate, and finally to offer a decision to the Pack.

Respect for the law starts young and continues. This morning, too, we started the Iron Moon Table, that one time when wolves are all together and in skin, with the familiar call and response.

In our laws are we protected.

And in lawlessness are we destroyed.

They've been through a lot, the Great North, and maybe it would have been better to choose a bigger wolf as Deemer. Someone with strength and size to handle the anxiety and skittishness that can make wolves hard to control.

Too late. An Alpha cannot afford even the appearance of doubt, so I school my face to confidence, staring unseeing into the middle distance as though there is no chance that the Alphas of the various echelons will fail to offer Silver the deference due her position.

Most lower their eyes, though Poul, Alpha of the 10th, hesitates. I pray to the moon that I have not made a mistake and that Silver is not too young or too weak to fight for herself, but I feel my body tighten, already preparing to enforce my decision in case she can't.

Silver leaps, scrabbling past other wolves, her silver hair tangled with burrs and dried grasses, a cut on her forehead, her upper lip curled back from fangs that are too feral and long and sharp ever to be mistaken for human.

A low, long rumble runs through her chest, Poul bows his head, and I finally exhale.

"Deemer," I ask. "Does the law allow us to kill the Shifters?"

The tall Shifter's eyes flit to the door, to the wolves closest to it, to their seaxs, to the sick young man behind him. Maybe he could get some distance, but not with Magnus. And while I believe Cassius would leave his bedfellow, everything that I saw over the Iron Moon made me think that Constantine would not abandon Magnus.

Besides, I watched them. Not a single one knows how to read the forest.

"If they are not a direct threat," Silver says, "we cannot by law kill them."

"Thank god for small favors," Cassius snaps.

Wolves say what they mean and find human things

like irony and facetiousness difficult to understand. Still, Silver seems to grasp that Cassius is not offering up thanks to his deity. She moves toward him, standing close, her eyes unyielding.

"Unless, of course, we eat them," she says and sucks at her front fang.

Cassius moves closer, and though he is taller and larger by far, Silver does not back down.

"Bite me, bitch," he says, and because wolves say what they mean, Silver does.

Before he finishes drawing his fist back, I pin him to the wall, his feet dangling in the air, clawing at my forearm pressed under his chin, so that now this Shifter will have no choice but to listen.

"I lost my birth pack to Shifters," I growl against his face. "I will not lose another. A hundred years before the United States had any 'founding fathers,' our founding Alpha came to this country. The last thing she did before departing the Old World was to eat a Shifter, a loose end that needed to be clipped off before they left. If you so much as inconvenience a single one of my wolves, I will follow Ælfrida's example and eat you—eat all of you—myself."

Cassius falls to the floor, gagging, the side of one hand bleeding from the deep puncture wounds left by my Deemer's teeth.

A murmured sound of disapproval circulates through the room. "No, Alpha," says Eudemos, Alpha of the 14th, Silver and Tiberius's age group. "That cannot be." He puts his hand on the hilt of his dagger. "You will not eat alone. The 14th will join you in the taking of their foul flesh."

One by one, my Alphas repeat the pledge. Wolves are not particularly imaginative, so most repeat it verbatim, though Esme, perhaps remembering the taste of the state trooper some years back, opts for "rancid tallow" while Orvin, the fusty Alpha of the 1st, vows to partake of the "loathsome thews."

Gea-la. Gea-la, they yell, a kind of general affirmation of togetherness that is as close to a howl as we have in this form.

Although I know she can't, it is almost as though she hears us, and the Gray's howl echoes down from Westdæl. The Alphas fall into a respectful silence, listening to the *æcewulf*, the forever wolf, as she sings her long and curious song. The only sound comes from the sick Shifter. From Magnus, whose red-rimmed eyes look beseechingly through the window toward Westdæl.

"Please. Someone answer," he croaks through cracked lips. It's the first I've heard him speak in the days he's been here. Constantine shakes his head, telling him to be quiet. Telling him that *no one said anything*, but that's not true. The Gray spoke and Magnus heard. He looks at me, a hopeless expression in his eyes. "*Please.*"

I size him up, this sick young man, trying to figure out what is niggling at the back of my brain. What doesn't belong.

But he's right, the Gray must always be answered. I clear my throat and start to speak, not with the voice that is the familiar one I have used since I came into adulthood but the other one. The one Alphas have always used to compel their wolves' innate debt of obedience. I asked John, when he first became Alpha, how he'd learned to use it. "I didn't learn it," he said. "It was always there. Waiting to be needed. It's like when a queen bee dies and another arises because it is needed."

I didn't think about it again until John died and the wolves of the Great North looked to me. Even though I was drained by my lying-in and heartsick, they looked to me and I had no choice but to lead or watch the Great North fall apart. That first night when decisions had to be made, I made them. And I made them using the voice of an Alpha, the voice that had always been inside me. Waiting to be needed.

Now, it vibrates through my chest and throat and the cavities of my face, and when I finally let it loose, it resonates like a wave through the assembled Alphas.

"*Sona hy æcewulfas andwearde.*"

The wolves lower their heads and murmur their reply. "The forever wolves will be answered, Alpha."

Magnus slumps against the wall.

Chapter 4

Constantine

There is something about what she said. Or not *what* she said—I don't know what it was—but how she said it.

Her head held high, so I could see the vibration along the deep ochre skin of her throat, a sure sign that I'm looking too closely. Her voice is like a physical thing unfurling from her and embracing everyone. The werewolves lean in like they are trying to lick up that last syllable before it fades away. Only after she has lowered her head do I realize that I am leaning toward her too. Now I see in the cloud of her hair a single parachute of a single seed sparkling among the black, like a lone star in the night sky.

There are holes in her jeans. Not the expensive, purposeful kind. These are free and come with age and wear. Muscles curl, sensuous and strong just underneath. Something ripples across my skin and every nerve ending tingles and stings and something happens that hasn't happened since I was a fourteen-year-old virgin. My cock is so hard it aches, the tip rasping against my mud-stiff jeans.

She catches me staring, with her amber eyes. I hold my wrists over my crotch, grateful when the door opens again and Tiberius's enormous body fills the doorway.

The woman with the silver hair moves to him quickly. His hand slides around her back, pulling her close, and he whispers into her ear. When he's done, she nods and rubs her cheek against his, putting her hand to his heart. This, then, is Tiberius's pale-gray wolf in human form.

"Alpha, I will change now," she says. "Offlanders have times written in calendars that require them to do…things."

Then she smiles a sad smile full of long, sharp feral canines.

Are they all like that? I wonder, staring at the Alpha's mouth, wondering if hidden beneath her soft lips, there are fangs. Wondering just how dangerous her mouth is.

"And the Shifters?" the Alpha asks.

"A *Clifrung* must be witnessed by the entire Pack. They will have to come along."

"Hurry it up, and *stick to the path,*" Tiberius barks. The other werewolves slipped past us long ago.

"*There is no fucking path,*" Cassius yells back.

Not that I'm going to make a habit of it, but for once, I agree with Cassius. Even in the daylight, there is no path. No markings or clearings of any sort. The only "sign" at all is the eye-height recoil of branches that indicates Tiberius's passage.

The forests of my mother's stories were always winter forests, with their long nights, skeletal trees, sharp ice and snow beckoning pilgrims to eternal sleep, but give me a winter forest anytime. Here, there's too much fucking life flapping, screeching, eating, slithering, defecating… I can almost feel the sap oozing up and down the trees, life sucked from both the earth and the sun.

And so much green: hunter-green leaves overhead, gray-green lichens, emerald ferns, tea-green bushes—it's like we've been consumed by some enormous chlorophyll-sodden entity and are being squeezed through its entrails.

Vines sprout up from the ground and reach for our feet like the thin green fingers of a sentient being rather than some goddamn plant. Magnus trips on one and falls, twisting his ankle. He sits down on a moss-covered trunk, his arms tight around his waist. Cassius eventually arrives, complaining about the path and his hand. When Tiberius asks him where's Julia, he turns around with a sour expression, as though annoyed to find out that all his high-quality grousing had been directed toward an audience that wasn't there.

"Stay here," Tiberius shouts as he heads back the way we came.

Rubbing his throat with one hand, Cassius glares at the bite mark on the other. "He took my phone," he says as soon as Tiberius is out of range. "Julia's too. Did they—"

"No phone, no wallet. Nothing." I drag a handful of chartreuse seedlings from the ground, their tiny roots naked and exposed, still clasping the ball of dirt that birthed them.

"Fuck. We got to—"

Tiberius pushes through, half carrying Julia. "Where were you?" Cassius asks irritably, pushing Tiberius's arm away.

She lifts her glittering red high-heeled sandals by the ankle straps and mewls something about blisters.

"You should have told me," he says. "What were you doing?"

Julia doesn't answer, just looks bleakly at her muddy

feet before taking a seat beside Magnus. The wool blanket she grabbed from the cabin slips down from arms that are purple-splotched and pimply with cold.

I begin tossing the seedlings one by one into the forest beyond the arthritic reach of their elders until Tiberius snatches the bouquet from my hand. "What do you think you're doing?"

"Clearing a path, because what you've got here, my friend, is not a path. It's trees fucking other trees and making baby trees."

"Just because you can't see the path doesn't mean it doesn't exist." He squats down, putting the seedlings back into the holes, and taps them gently with his fingers. "The Pack cannot survive without its territory. We will not tolerate its destruction."

August would be spinning in his grave.

Julia sobs, though no tears leave traces down her days-old makeup. Everything about her is a mess—from the dark capillaries of mud creeping up the white silk of her pants to the silt squelches between her chipped bloodred toenails and around her blisters.

The forest ahead of us parts, revealing another werewolf. One who wasn't there this morning. He is not burly like most of them, rather tall with a slim, elegant body, carved cheekbones, wide-set eyes, perfect curved lips. His wavy dark-brown hair brushes his jawbone.

"Arthur," Tiberius says and lowers his head.

August said that the Pack only respected physical strength. That they were like dogs that way. I'm not sure he was entirely right about that. I have seen werewolves defer to the Alpha but also to the woman with the silver hair, and now here is Tiberius, who is as big and strong as any of them, lowering his eyes to a man he could snap between his fingers.

"The Pack is already in the Clearing," Arthur says. "But the Deemer can't start without you."

"Can't start without you either."

"No," he says with a quiet smile, "I suppose not."

"Tell her I'll get them moving as fast as I can."

"Wait a minute," Cassius protests. "She's got a blister, and look." He flips his hand up, showing two long puncture wounds in a semicircle of smaller abrasions.

The new werewolf looks at it with one cocked eyebrow. "A flesh wound," he says.

"*It is not a flesh wound,*" Cassius insists, affronted, and pushes his hand in front of Arthur. "It's swelling. What if she's got rabies?"

"Our Deemer does not have rabies," Arthur says, squatting down to look at Julia's feet. "If it does not shatter bones or damage internal organs, it is a flesh wound." He gently wipes at them. With the mud gone, I can see that the bloody flesh of her ankles and toes looks so much worse than Cassius's hand.

"We cannot keep the Offlanders waiting." Arthur begins to untie his boots. "You will take these."

Julia doesn't answer, looking instead at Cassius.

"She *has* shoes. Nice ones." Cassius points to the strappy red stilettos hanging from her fingers. "They weren't made for hiking."

The young man leans over, pushing his hair behind his ear as he pulls off his boots. He hesitates a moment, looking at his stockinged feet.

"I forget how humans feel about socks. Is it like sharing underwear?"

Julia stares at him, dazed. "I…" Then she focuses on the boots and the socks in his hand, and her voice breaks.

"I will tell the Deemer that you are coming," Arthur says and pushes himself up on pale bare feet crisscrossed with scars. Then he is gone, leaving nothing to mark his passing but the shuffle of leaves and the boots on Julia's feet.

Tiberius pushes us faster until we finally break through the trees and he doesn't have to. Here, we move on our own, grateful to trade the murky uncertainty for the sunlit clarity of long grasses with nothing above but broad blue sky, sun, and swallows.

At the far edge of the ocean of grass is a single enormous boulder shaped like an anvil and surrounded by hundreds of werewolves. Some are wolves but most are in human form, dressed in some combination of lumberjack light and ex–student athletes of multiple alma maters, but there is also a hefty sprinkling of werewolves dressed as bankers and lawyers, except they wear their suit pants rolled up above their knees and their shoes tied flopping from the straps of their backpacks.

They stand too close together, these lawyers and bankers and lumberjacks, all clinging to one another, curling around one another, touching, nipping, sniffing. A man in a black pinstriped three-piece leans against a woman's breasts, his head tucked under her chin, while she reaches under his collar, scratching beneath his ear.

Only the puppies running through the forest of legs make any noise. Everyone else is silent. The Alpha too. She sits on top of the enormous slab, her bare feet swinging against granite that glitters in the sun. Next to her is the pale-gray wolf with the bent hind leg, waiting.

As soon as she sees us, the Alpha rises, brushing off her pants.

"What's happening?" I ask.

"You're here because we cannot leave you alone," Tiberius whispers, "but it has nothing to do with you."

As before, the Alpha speaks not as a woman, or not as just a woman. Her voice is complex, a conduit for generations of command, and though I don't know what she is saying, I feel it penetrate me as raw as new heartbreak.

"*We earon twisælig*," she says.

A murmured answer ripples through the Pack. "We are twice blessed."

"*We cnawaþ nydriht frignes.*"

"We know the price of freedom," the Pack responds.

"*Ond geweorþ pleos.*"

"And the worth of responsibility." A woman with a string of pearls and a gray silk shirt dress tucked up into a belt buries her hand in the pelt of the wolf standing next to her.

"*We earon*," the Alpha says in a whisper that I feel against my face even though she is far away, "*twisælig.*"

The Pack stands motionless, heads down, except for that pale-gray wolf, who stretches out her front legs and jumps from the rock, stumbling hard onto the ground. Next to me, Tiberius hisses out a low breath, strain written across his face.

Otho used to say that cemeteries are filled with people who didn't know what was coming next. I think he got it from someone else, not that I cared about the provenance, only the importance of reading ahead. Men, I know. Men, I can read. Werewolves? Not so much. The only thing I am certain of is that I don't want to be here when whatever is coming arrives. I signal for Magnus to get behind me, and I begin to back up.

"Don't think about it," Tiberius says without turning his head. The gun that had been in his waistband now peeks under his elbow, aimed directly at me.

The Pack churns and ripples, making way for someone. Finally, he emerges in the space below the boulder. It's Arthur, the same tall, slim werewolf who gave his boots to Julia. Now not only are his feet bare, but his whole body is too. He carries a thin folded pile of clothes awkwardly in front of him, looking around until a woman in a red suit and bare legs takes them with a whispered word. He smiles.

"Julia! Baby! Get back here!" Cassius calls after Julia, who is pushing blindly through the big bodies, the oversize boots on her feet making sucking sounds each time she pulls them out of the damp ground.

"Dammit." Tiberius signals for the rest of us to follow him through the gap in the Pack to the very front where the man has taken a seat on the long grass.

He lies down, reaching under his back and removing a small, tight green pinecone, then he stretches his arms out wide at his sides. Turning his head, he trains his eyes on the bald mountain to the west.

The dirt on the outer rim of his feet marks a dark contrast to the pale skin at his arch.

A man with blond hair pulled back in a messy ponytail bends over Arthur, whispering. I recognize him as one of the werewolves who put hand to knife and promised to eat us, should the Alpha decide we were on the menu.

Arthur nods quickly and pushes his long cock between his thighs before clamping them shut. He stretches out again, holding the pinecone tight in his left hand. Once again, he looks toward that distant mountain and the sketchy clouds running across it.

Maybe he recognizes his borrowed boots standing next to him; he peers up at Julia and mouths something to her.

I think it was meant to be reassuring, though nothing about this situation seems reassuring. Confused, Julia moves back when the ponytailed werewolf is joined by two others who kneel at either splayed arm while Ponytail kneels at his ankles. Arthur looks up toward the Alpha standing tall over the Pack.

"Alpha, I can do this myself."

The Alpha blinks once, then waves her hand to the side. As soon as she does, the werewolves who were holding his extremities stand back, making way for the small lame wolf, who rests her muzzle beside Arthur's face.

The Alpha lowers her head, and the silver wolf places her paw on the upper quadrant of his chest right below his shoulder.

Julia's scream slices through the quiet. Werewolves back up, their hands, if they have them, over their ears. If they don't, they stumble away fast.

Julia drops to the ground next to Arthur, sobbing. She still clings to the stilettos gleaming just as red and bright as the blood pouring in rivulets across the man's chest and down into the earth.

She throws the shoes at the silver wolf, who blinks once before going back to licking her bloodstained paw. Tiberius grabs Julia's arm. For whatever reason, he seems to be having trouble controlling her, and Julia breaks free of Tiberius's hold only to be grabbed by Cassius. He wraps his arms around her, babbling "Babybabybabybabybaby. Caaalm down. Caaalm down" over and over again.

Babybabybabybabybaby. Caaalm down. Caaalm down.

Then this woman who has always been so contingent—Otho's pretty, spoiled little girl; August's pretty, spoiled ward; Cassius's pretty, spoiled girlfriend—pulls back her hand and slaps him, hard, by the sound of the crack reverberating through the empty space. His head whips around and he lets go, the jolt as bright in his eyes as the pink hand mark is on his cheek.

She tries to clamber up the Alpha's rock, a futile assault on a stone that is too high for her.

"*You killed him,*" she screams, falling back, blood and broken nails indistinguishable at the tips of her fingers. "*The only decent person in this hellhole, and you killed him!*"

The Alpha cocks her head to the side as though seeing her for the first time. Then she jumps down lightly, landing on the grass near the man's head. "He's not dead," she says, toeing him with her foot.

"Breathe, Arthur."

And he does. As his chest expands, something pulses and glistens through the rips in his skin. The muscles at his jaw are working overtime, and he swallows convulsively. His left hand raking through the grass, retracing the same area as though he is looking for something.

Julia falls to her knees and pats the ground like she understands. Like she knows what he needs. Finally, she finds that little green pinecone and puts it back in the palm that is marked with the sharp imprint of it. Arthur balls his hand into a tight fist. Perhaps the small pain he can control helps him bear the much larger pain he can't.

A man behind me offers someone a ride as far as Boston,

saying something about detours and the HOV lanes on I-93. Turning, I realize that most of the werewolves have already disappeared back into the forest, taking with them their observations about traffic and bosses and missed breakfast, all of which would sound banal in an office building around a box of doughnuts but are disconcertingly cold-blooded in a swampy clearing where a man lies eviscerated.

"He needs help," Julia whispers to the disappearing Pack. "*Why won't they help you?*"

Arthur shakes his head, then touches her hand, pressing the pinecone into her palm as though it were something precious rather than another seed for another tree in a place that already has too many of them. She wraps her fingers tight around its thorny shape as though she thinks it's precious too.

The werewolf turns his head away with a strained smile, looking back toward the bald peak of a mountain far to the west. Julia stares at him, helpless, before taking off the maroon blanket. She holds it in midair, trying to decide where to put it so that it will not touch his shredded skin. Finally, she shakes it out and wraps it around his hips and legs.

Chapter 5

Evie

"Beta," I say to Tara, who follows somewhere in the silent dark. "Send Lorcan, Eudemos, and...and Elijah to my office."

At the Great Hall, pups play in the corner where Tiberius lies changing behind one of the Adirondack chairs. Usually Tiberius would have found an isolated spot, but I have smelled his temper and know how hard this Iron Moon spent in skin has been for him. I avert my eyes, a kindness we give each other during the change when we are neither in skin nor wild, when our faces contort and drool, when our hips narrow and shoulders thicken and fur sprouts out in strange places.

John runs to me, his forepaws on my calves. I pick him up and mark him. Like all pups, he takes the belonging he needs before struggling away, back to clamber over his sire's writhing body.

John.

Wolves don't have time for regret, but sometimes anger bubbles up and I feel myself growing angry at Ronan, the wolf who brought the Pack to August Leveraux's attention. Angry at John for letting Tiberius come. Angry at Tiberius for staying. Angry at myself for being weak after my lying-in. Unable to move quickly enough to get away when August's men came. Angry with John, my mate, our

Alpha, who distracted them and got himself killed, leaving me to deal with everything that came after.

The screen door slaps closed behind me. There were two things John dreamed of fixing. One was the junkyard, that five acres of land that sits like a carbuncle in the middle of our territory. The owner had refused every offer of payment out of spite, and then out of spite, he sold it to August, who promised we would never have it.

The other thing John wanted to fix was the Great Hall itself. "It's not so much a Great Hall," John had said, "as a Fair-to-Middling Hall that will never change because wolves like the way it smells."

Would he approve of it now? Now that the ash smell of the hall the Shifters burned is gone. Now that the whole Pack could gather together. Now that it is tall enough for adult wolves to stand without cracking their heads on dormers. Now that it is big enough for them to move about without knocking over lamps in cramped rooms.

"Alpha." Joelle, Gamma of the 10th, stands at the entrance to the Alpha's office—my office—shaking out a sheaf of multicolored papers.

The requirements of the Iron Moon—disciplining an echelon, helping with a hunt, teaching a juvenile—are so radiantly clear and necessary.

In skin, the requirements of an Alpha are tedious and in triplicate.

"Do it again without the two-by-fours." I pass the purchase order back and run through the work schedule in my mind. "Send the 4th and 8th and 13th to take what the Shifters left on the lands north. Whatever we can use. There is good wood there."

Trevor approaches to ask about next year's education

plan, and I search through a canvas bag for the sheaf of papers bristling with multicolored stickies. I'd almost finished, but then came the time when I lost the fingers and thumbs I would need to hold a highlighter.

When Lorcan, Eudemos, and Elijah come, they join Trevor next to the open window, tasting the news on the air, while I finish my paperwork.

What happened to the Transcendentalism class? John taught Thoreau and Emerson and Whitman. I will not have that gone. I finish writing in the margins of the teaching plan and hand it back to Trevor. Tara's claws click on the front stairs.

Elijah cranes his head to look through the door. "They're coming."

Heavy footsteps oblivious to everything thud up the stairs, and the front door opens.

"*Take off your shoes!*" shouts one of the juveniles who had been sweeping the floor.

Tara stops in front of my office and bends her head toward the mudroom.

We wait, my foot tapping impatiently on the floor.

How long does it take to take off shoes?

"Did anyone check the Spruce Flats?"

"Poul did," Lorcan says. "The bodies are still there. The coyotes aren't eating them. The deer who fled the land to the north have made the coyotes picky."

"And the dog?"

"Not the dog either." Lorcan's chin droops down to his chest. He had called Victor Deemer, as we all had. And when Victor had used the excuse of Elijah's human mate to divide the Pack, Lorcan had followed him, as had so many of the younger echelons. Then he discovered that

Victor intended to replace me and hand over the Great North to August. Now Lorcan cannot look me in the eye.

The smell of steel and carrion wafts down the hall followed by the loud tread of the Shifters who stink of it.

"Lorcan," I say to the bright-pink line of his scalp at the part of his hair. "Wolves do not have the luxury of regret. *Cum, agna in rihtum.*"

Come, claim your right.

And Lorcan, broad and powerful, bolts for me like a pup, his eyes wide with the fear of loss and the need for belonging that only the Alpha, the symbol of Pack unity, can give. Slowly, slowly, I pull the strands of hair away from his face so nothing will come between his skin and mine. I rub one cheek against his, then repeat it on the other side.

The Shifters stand watching at the door, but I will not hurry Lorcan as he takes my scent. He has spent the whole moon angry that he allowed Victor to mislead him, fearful of losing his connection to the Pack. I give him the time he needs to breathe in that belonging again, and when he is done, his head is higher. As soon as I am done with the Shifters, I will mark again all the wolves of the echelons misled by the traitorous dog.

I have decided to divide the Shifters among the Alphas I trust the most, so Julia will go to Lorcan; Elijah will have to handle Cassius, who after all his loud complaining stands oddly silent, glaring into the distance. Julia, who had said almost nothing, now pleads incoherently, holding out her red and ridiculous shoes to Cassius's retreating back as though they are explanation of something. Lorcan takes her wrist and pulls her toward the door, still endlessly babbling *sorry, sorry, sorry.*

"I'm sorry. I don't belong here. I'm sorry, Cass. I don't know why. I wasn't supposed to be here. I was supposed to be in New York. I'm so sorry."

As her "sorries" retreat down the hall, I look at the two remaining Shifters. Eudemos, Alpha of the 14th, will take Magnus while I—

In the distance, the gray wolf calls.

As soon as her voice has had time to reach all the way from Westdæl to Endeberg, whatever wolves are wild respond. Even a few of the pups add to the chorus with their little *Orrroos.*

Magnus slides down against the wall, his hand to his mouth, his breath coming in hitched groans. His brother squats next to him, his hands tucked under his arms.

"What's wrong with him?" I ask.

"*I don't know,*" Constantine says. It's curious. He sounds angry, but he doesn't smell like it. Anger has a bright burn to it, but he smells like carrion and steel and soot, like anger has burned through him so often that only ash remains. It's overwhelming, which explains why I didn't understand earlier what had bothered Leonora, what itched at the back of my brain in the Meeting House. I collapse to my knees, my hands on the floor on either side of the young man, getting close enough so that the weak senses of this form can sort through all the human smells to the bitterness of black walnut and juniper, a wild stronger than any Shifter has a right to be.

"What is your name?" I whisper, trying to keep the frantic edge from my voice.

"His name is Magnus."

"*I'm talking to him.*" I raise my hand stiff in the air, commanding quiet. "What is your *real* name?"

"His name is *Magnus*," Constantine says again. "*And he is my brother.*"

There is a dark, sharp edge to his voice like chipped obsidian, but his eyes are green like Clear Pond in the summer when the light streams through at an angle, making the water glow pale green, streaked with the shadows of trees.

"He can't be," I say, turning back to Magnus. "He's not even a Shifter."

Something chases across Constantine's face but then it tightens. His hand searches the back of his waistband like he's looking for something that he doesn't find. "He's not *human*."

I wave my hand dismissively. "Of course not," I say. "He's one of us. He's Pack."

The Shifter takes a step back, his brow furrowing a moment in disbelief before he laughs. "How? He's never changed. In twelve years. Not once. Tell her, Magnus," he says, reaching out for the young man. "Tell her who you are."

He pulls his hand away when Magnus whimpers.

"*Gea, wulf,*" I say in the Old Tongue. "*Ge mé secgon. Hwa eart þu?*"

Yes, wolf. Tell me. Who you are?

The young man begins to rock, his breath a torment.

"I don't know," he says quietly.

"Where are you from?" I ask.

"I don't know."

"What is your Pack?"

"I don't know anything," he whimpers, but he doesn't deny the possibility of a Pack. Now he looks toward Constantine, pleading with him. "Con? I can't. I…"

I move my hand toward his face.

"*You saw,*" the Shifter snaps. "He doesn't like to be touched. Not when he's like this. His skin hurts. Everything…hurts…"

His voice fades as I tilt Magnus's chin up, doing for this wolf what I did for Lorcan, what I have done for every member of the Great North Pack over and over again. I set my face next to his and leave a little bit of myself on his skin. His dark hair moves with my breath, but he doesn't stiffen or move away. He relaxes into my touch.

I have you, wolf. I have you back.

I whimper a little because the wild, while easily lost, is so rarely found. When I pull away, I take not only the faint trace of his mark. Blood oozes from my palm and down my wrist. I wipe it away from the corner of his mouth, but more bubbles out.

"*Eudemos,*" I whisper without turning. "*Get Tristan.*"

Eudemos runs for the door, the sturdy floorboard creaking beneath him.

"What hurts, wolf?"

Magnus pinches his eyes closed.

The door opens again, readmitting Eudemos accompanied by Tristan, whose teeth are buried in an apple. He is wearing jeans and a gray T-shirt with a blue police box that says *My other car is a TARDIS*. It is a joke, our doctor explained to me once, but it was too complicated. Leonora has reassured me that I can still interact with most humans without understanding it.

"Tristan. This is *Magnus.*" His name comes out like it's in quotes, but that can't be helped. "Heal him."

Tristan pops the last of the apple into his mouth and wipes at the juice that runs down his chin. He dries his fingers on his thighs.

He kneels down. "Hello, Magnus. My name is Tristan. I'm what passes for a doctor in these parts."

"What do you mean 'passes for'?" Constantine surges forward, instantly protective.

"He did his residency at Massachusetts General," I say, "where he specialized in internal medicine and sarcasm."

"It's really more facetiousness than sarcasm, Alpha."

"That doesn't matter: it's a human habit and it confuses the Pack."

"Well, wolf," Tristan says, taking a few quick diagnostic sniffs. "What seems to be the problem?"

Magnus looks warily at Constantine.

"Let him see, Magnus. If he hurts you, I will kill him."

"Ahhh, hyperbole." Tristan peers into the narrow opening of Magnus's mouth, then pulls a pen light from his shirt pocket. "That's another thing we don't get nearly enough of at Home...lands..." His voice falters and he purses his lips, looking at the crooked teeth stained with blood. At the drop falling from a canine.

"I need him in Medical," says Tristan, standing once more, all sarcasm and facetiousness gone.

"Eudemos, help him."

The Shifter starts after them before I manage to raise myself from the floor. I shoot out my hand, grabbing his ankle, and he freezes as I feel the ridged skin under my fingers, then look for the brown and burgundy scars around his ankle that I know will be there.

"I fell," he says, pulling away from my hand.

"Hunters have set enough snares on Homelands for me to know a ligature mark when I feel one."

With his toe, he nudges the hem of his jeans down, and at that moment, Magnus groans, the sound carrying both through the open window and from the connecting wall between my office and Medical.

"You have to believe we are trying to help," I say. "There aren't enough wolves in the world for me to be careless of even one."

"Really? How about the 'wolf' you ripped open and left to die? Or was that too deliberate to be careless?"

"Arthur," I say coldly, "is paying the price for *your* interference in the Pack." Our former Deemer, the dog who betrayed us to August, would have been found guilty under the law, but the Iron Moon was almost here—hunters were almost here—and we didn't have time for for-speakers and against-speakers and the casting of stones into the Thing, the way of our law. So Arthur took it upon himself to kill the Deemer, knowing the penalty was death.

I pick up my cup, holding it tight as though I'm trying to warm my hands, even though it is, as always, cold.

"Humans say even a wolf's kindness is cruel. We say even a wolf's cruelty is kind. Silver had just been made Deemer. Killing Arthur would have been the easy way out; it would have followed the letter of the law. But…" I take a sip of frigid coffee to disguise the break in my voice before I start again. "But the law required he be punished, so Silver found a way that satisfied the law and allowed him to live."

When I set down the mug, he looks at the cartoon deer and the words *The buck stops here.* Maybe he will find it funny. Erika had written me a note explaining the joke—*dollar = buck, male deer = buck*—but I have never quite understood it. Wolves are not known for their sense of humor.

"How old is he?"

"Magnus? I don't know. Not exactly. He hasn't grown much since I found him in the youth center."

"What is a youth center?"

"A detention facility," he says. "In western Canada."

Leonora has a whole pamphlet translating the words humans use to protect themselves from uncomfortable ideas: Passed away. Downsized. Enhanced interrogation. Detention facility. "So he was in a prison for children?"

"He'd been living on the streets. Stealing. They had to put him somewhere."

The pups have found a spool of garden twine and are chasing it around the grass, unwinding as they go. This close to Home Pond, there is no need for supervision but they are never truly alone. No wolf would allow one of their own to end up in a prison for children, so it can only mean that his pack is dead.

"Has he always been sick?"

"Yes," Constantine starts, then hesitates. "No, not like this. At first, it was his teeth. It would come for a few days but then subside. Now it's spread to his stomach and his joints. His skin sometimes. It's hard for him to eat."

He looks at something on my desk.

I can see the muscles along his jaw working. "August called him a pet. A child grows up, he said. Leaves. Not a pet."

There's a dull silver disk next to the juveniles' practice SATs. He stares at it, turning it slowly.

"I don't know what that is."

"This? It's a... It's a compass," he says, picking the thing up. "It tells directions. So..." He holds it on the flat of his hand. "So, that's north."

I look down at his hand. "What's north?"

"Where the arrow is pointing."

There is a circle with the letters and an attenuated diamond. Half of the attenuated diamond is painted red. We can smell north. Hear north. Feel north. Taste north. "Why would someone need an arrow to tell them *north*?"

"In case you need to go north. Or south or any other direction."

I need to go toward prey, away from hunters. To water, away from fire. To my wolves. I don't need to go *north*.

"Hmmph."

"So why do you have it?" he asks.

"A hiker dropped it last moon."

He turns it around, examining a dark smudge on the back.

"We didn't eat him if that's what you're thinking. We watched him until the Iron Moon was over and then when we had thumbs and Wi-Fi, we filed for injunctive relief."

"Alpha?" Ove sticks his head in to remind me about the divestiture meeting but as soon as the door is open, wolves start to crowd in with questions about discipline and firewood and insurance premiums. Some I can answer immediately, others I need to think about, but wolves need decisiveness, so I simply tell them they will have to wait while I take one of the awkwardly cut pieces of scrap paper the Year of First Shoes make as they practice using fingers.

I pull out the pencil from behind my ear.

The Shifter stands, his hand stretched in front of him, staring at me.

Chapter 6

Constantine

Many years ago when I was a boy living on a cul-de-sac, I got a toy compass in a cereal box. This was back in the day when children could be trusted not to eat toy compasses in cereal boxes. There was something wrong with it. The needle didn't have the magnetic paint that would have made the end point feebly north so my mother threw it away, saying she would not have broken toys cluttering up the house. I retrieved it, though, because it pointed in whatever direction I tilted my hand. It pointed me the way I wanted to go.

This one—this tool of an outdoorsman who is probably even now wondering why six lawyers are harassing him for simple trespass—points toward a woman. Tall and ramrod straight with eyes the color of amber and honey.

I know it doesn't really, not any more than the arrow points to her desk or to the window or to the mountains that August thought he could breech like Hannibal. Except standing in his way was this woman.

The door opens and a man sticks his head in. "Alpha?" he says and tells her about some meeting but as soon as werewolves see that the door is open, they flood in asking for her to decide, to tend to, to care about, to be responsible for.

She pulls a pencil from behind her ear. A spiral of black

hair catches on the metal cuff holding the eraser, and when she yanks it loose, the hair bounces back, framing her eye and her cheekbone. She lifts her eyes to mine, and for one moment, I see the woman beneath and I wonder when was the last time someone tended to her.

"Alpha?"

The woman disappears and the Alpha is back. I return the compass to her desk because it is not going to tell me where I need to go.

Across the hall from the Alpha's office is a wide doorway that opens onto a kitchen with slate floors, an enormous stone trench sink, an industrial stove, and a refrigerator. Three werewolves sit frozen at a big sanded table before mountains of chopped carrots and onions and celery. Another stops, a huge pot of water in midair.

As soon as I turn away, the cleavers thump against wood, the pot hits the stove with a clang and a splash.

The hall ends in a back door leading to a cleared area filled with vegetable gardens and cold frames and puppies playing with a dead squirrel. One tosses it into the air with a quick flick of his neck while another grabs it and springs away. Others wait, their little legs shaking and shivering for a chance to pounce and squeal and bite and tussle.

It's like watching children at a game of keep-away, except in the end, someone eats the ball.

When I put my hand on the lever, an enormous wolf comes out of nowhere and leans heavily against the door, fur squashed against the metal mesh. He licks his paws, but the meaning is clear.

In the other direction, past the kitchen and the Alpha's office, is a big room that I had noticed before. Lined with half-empty bookshelves, the room is occupied by a group of small children nestled together watching a man with colored and numbered tongue depressors as he tries to extract a blue stick from a boy's teeth. "Soft mouth, Edmund," he says. "Soft mouth." Seeing me, he kicks the door closed with his foot.

The hall opens onto an enormous space with raw beams above broad floorboards dappled by the jade light leaking in through the trees outside. A breeze blows through the open windows, bringing the whisper of rustling leaves and tussling birds. It's huge but not in the way of August's cavernous cathedral ceilings and double-height windows that had nothing to do with need and everything to do with signaling that he had the money to build and heat more space than he needed.

This is huge in the way of a place that is meant to accommodate very many very large people.

The far end of the room is occupied by long, heavy tables that smell of beeswax. When we first arrived, they had been surrounded by flimsy metal chairs, but now those are all folded against one wall.

At the near end, a huge fieldstone fireplace is surrounded by a mismatched trio of worn and clawed sofas and secondhand lamps. A well-chewed shoe drops to the floor, narrowly missing my head. Above me at the top of a set of stairs, a little furry head pops out from a birch-branch balustrade. The puppy looks at me and then at the shoe and barks. I pick up the shoe. The puppy barks again. I draw back my arm and throw. With a quick flick, the head disappears, followed by a thump and the scratching of claws on wood up above.

Then Magnus screams.

Doors that had been closed now open as werewolves

turn alarmed toward the room with the closed door just past the Alpha's office.

When I crash through the door, Tristan turns toward me, his latex gloves coated in blood. Magnus's eyes are huge above his gore-smeared face. I hear his garbled voice behind me as the doctor's body slams into the floor, his head between my hands, until someone enters the room and gathers me up in arms like iron.

What are they doing to Magnus?

"I am *trying* to help him," the doctor says, feeling the back of his head.

"Magnus," the Alpha grunts, "tell him."

"He can't, Alpha. He's got film in his mouth."

"Get it out. While I still have him." She holds me so tight, my shoulder blades rub together.

Trapped between her hardness and her softness, I strain when the doctor reaches into Magnus's mouth. Magnus whimpers as Tristan pulls out a white tab covered with blood.

"That's it, Shifter. I needed an X-ray." He turns his laptop around, dislodging a pile of heavy stationery embossed with TRISTAN RASMUSSON, MD, FACS, which slides to the floor.

Dr. Rasmusson clucks with annoyance, stepping over the puddled pages to retrieve a damp cloth. He gives it to Magnus, signaling for him to wipe his face.

Magnus dabs weakly at his mouth, then falls back, the white paper lining the bed crackling under him as he turns on his side, the cloth to his mouth. All the fight seeps out of me.

"Alpha?" The doctor picks up his laptop, bending his head to the other side of the room, away from Magnus's racked body.

I pull a blue cotton blanket up to cover Magnus's distended shoulders and his swollen joints and bony vertebrae, the guilt I feel is almost nauseating. I can't pretend this is anyone's fault but mine.

"Shifter?" the Alpha says.

I pull the blanket up farther, less for Magnus's sake than to hide the unpleasant truth that having promised to protect him, I had let him become this.

"Shifter?" she says again and I head numbly to where the two of them stand over a cart with shallow drawers and a small tray of metal instruments.

Balancing the laptop next to the tray, Tristan pulls up a complicated patchwork image of black and shades of gray.

He patiently points out the flat ridge of Magnus's teeth and the jagged roots. Then the second set of roots on top of them that are sharp and high and curving deep into the line of his upper jaw, a bare millimeter from a charcoal-gray cavity. I try to blink away the image, but I can't.

"He's always had toothaches," I finally manage to say, knowing full well how inadequate it sounds.

"*This* is not a toothache," the doctor says. "*This* is a face on the verge of disintegrating." He closes the computer and opens one of the shallow drawers, dropping what looks like an oversize wire stripper on the paper-lined surface.

"What happened to his claws?"

"Claws? I told you. He's never changed, so he has never had claws. He's got some kind of genetic condition with his nails?" I can't stop my voice from raising up in a question.

Tristan closes the drawer and holds it shut for a moment, then he turns around, arms crossed in front of him, assessing me.

"There's nothing genetic about it. Someone wanted to stop him from changing, so they pulled out his claws until he did. Stop."

He keeps looking at me expectantly, like he's waiting for a denial but he knows all the facts are lined up on his side. I don't bother. Somehow, I've always known. Not that his claws were pulled out, but that I'd been lying to myself, pretending that the troughs on the bare skin of his nails and the blood on that white pen I'd lent to the haunted boy in Burnaby could be explained away by a rare human ailment found on Google.

Everyone thinks—thought, they're all dead now—that I must remember the day my mother changed. Who wouldn't? One day, she's the reserved, OCD but otherwise unexceptional Maxine Brody of Evergreen Terrace. Recording secretary for the baked goods committee of the Rainy River Elementary PTA. The next day, she's a wolf the size of a VW.

I didn't remember.

I remembered the smell of burning brownies, the homework on the floor around her, but nothing else. Nothing except for her thumbs. The way the nails grew and thickened and darkened, folding to a point. The way the digit migrated up her wrist.

Someone tore that claw out of Magnus's living flesh.

"Tristan, give us time."

The doctor looks at me warily, all smart-assery gone. He bolts away, his laptop clutched to his chest like a breastplate.

Something touches my hand, my skin. "Let it go." Gentle and secure and strong. "See what you're doing and let it go." I don't feel the blood itself dripping down the side of my hand or the bent and broken steel jammed into my palm.

"I didn't do it." I pull the long, sharp tweezers out and drop them to the tray, flexing my hand.

"I know you didn't," she says. "I've dealt with enough humans to know what a lie smells like." She picks up the broken metal and wraps them in a paper towel.

"I didn't even know he looked so...sick. He always wore thick clothes and... I don't know."

She heads over to a bin in the corner of the room. When she puts her foot on the pedal, the cover thumps against the wall, then the broken tweezers hit the bottom of the bin.

"It's so weak," she says, straightening out the blue paper liner on the cart. "The word 'change.' Makes it sound like putting on a costume."

She rubs her shoulder.

"In the Old Tongue, the word is *eftboren*. It's..." Across the room, metal scrapes on metal as Tristan draws the thin curtain around Magnus. "Again born? No, reborn. It's why we live so long, because our bodies are constantly dying, and with each change, they are renewed. Reborn.

"Without the change, Magnus is not being reborn. Without the change, he is only dying."

Chapter 7

Evie

I DIDN'T SLEEP MUCH LAST NIGHT. I SPENT MOST OF IT in a desperate triangulation. How close was close enough for the Gray to get used to my scent? How close was too close? I didn't know what might make her leave her mate's side, the fur on her hackles high, her lips pulled back from sharp teeth.

Or worse, go Offland.

I'd immediately discounted Tristan's suggestion that the Shifter had been responsible for what had been done to Magnus because I was the one watching him from the woods during the Iron Moon. I'd seen him stand—or rather sit—guard on the floor beside Magnus's bed, his hands propped loose on his bent knees, staring ahead, unsure what to do with the fragile life in his care except stand guard.

Like me. I know how to deal with Pack. How do I deal with forever wolves? What will keep them here where I can at least try to stand guard?

I've also spent enough time Offland to know the shrill, staccato sound of hype, the sour sweet smell of a lie, the look of a short con, and the greasy taste that self-delusion leaves on the tongue. When I told the Shifter what was happening to Magnus, there was none of that. No denial or protestations, as though it wasn't news at all. As though it was simply the confirmation of something he'd always dreaded. Now he walks silently beside me.

When the Great North bought the camp from the executors of Hiram Cheeseprunt, ruined suicide, in 1931, there had been four dormitories built to accommodate the enormous staff that Mr. Cheeseprunt required to service himself and his guests during the summer months. Three are normally used to house those Offland wolves who feel the need to sleep in skin, juveniles acting out "sleepover," and now the motley of Shifters we are saddled with. The woods wanted the fourth so we salvaged what we could and let her have it. It is now an unstable hillock of green north of the Bathhouse.

The Shifter collapses on a lower bunk to one side and stares blankly at the distorted rectangle of late-afternoon light creeping hesitantly across the wide wooden planks.

He leans over, plucking something from the floor, and looks at it carefully before handing it to me. It's nothing, a shirt button. We have a huge box filled with them in dry storage. Holding it to my nose, I scent past the carrion and steel to the juniper and black walnut.

"But he's not going to die." Half question, half statement of intent, it is the first thing he has said since we left Medical.

"No."

He falls onto the mattress, his back to me, his arms wrapped around his waist.

I slide the button into my shirt pocket.

He must have heard me from the shower because when I come through the door the next morning, he is standing in the middle of the room soaking wet, a small towel wrapped around his waist, his legs coiled like a wolf ready to pounce. He is armed curiously enough with a curry comb in one hand and a rolled-up copy of *Corporate Counsel* magazine in the other.

Pulling the screen door closed, I drop a pile of clothes on the desk near the front. I twirl the desk chair around and settle in facing him, my legs straddling the chair back.

"How do you know Varya's name?"

Water drips into his eyes. He wipes at it with the back of his wrist, then holds out his impromptu arsenal.

"Do I need these?"

"Not unless your fur is matted or you have a need for alternative dispute resolution, no."

Smiling weakly, he tosses them onto one of the low bookcases where some Offlander must have left them and holds the unraveling ends of the towel.

Tiberius said he was dangerous and he is. Tiberius was afraid he might be dangerous to the Pack, but I don't think he is dangerous to the Pack or even to the Alpha I have become.

But when he looks at me, I am afraid for the terrified, lonely self I packed away in mothballs the night John died.

With all his hardness and sharpness, this was a man I could cut myself on.

I reach back to the desk and throw him jeans and a long-sleeved T-shirt. His hand shoots out to grab them, and the towel falls with a damp plop.

Like that, I think, annoyed with myself for dropping my eyes as though I were some human unnerved by nakedness. *Look up, Alpha.* There's nothing special about the way the early morning light catches the water beading across his skin before it gathers into small rivulets and swirls down the muscled fissure of his chest. Nothing unusual in the way they tremble among the dark hairs at his nipples or nestle in the curled thicket gathered around skin that is dusky and veined and muscled but not in the smooth and prosaic way of that hard chest.

Shit. I wrap my arms around the sturdy wooden ladder-back as though it will shield me from the distraction and slow the pulse that beats fast and hard at my nipples and puddles warm and slow at my core.

Except when he pulls on the jeans and I see the thick brown and burgundy scars at his ankles.

"She told me," he says, the stiff line-dried denim rasping against his skin.

It takes me a moment to remember my question.

"Here's my problem." A strand of hair has come loose from the band. I tuck it under and cross my arms across the back of the chair. "When she first arrived years ago, Varya Timursdottir told one wolf her name. The Great North's Alpha. She never told anyone else. The rest of us found out eventually, but not from her. So why would she tell you? A complete stranger? A *Shifter*?"

He starts to pull the T-shirt over his head.

"I'm going to tell you what I told Tiberius. You're going to have to ask her."

Chin propped on my arms, I look toward Westdæl.

"I can't," I say, turning back to him. "She will never have the words to tell me."

His head emerges slowly from the collar. "She's dead?"

"You really do think like a human. Just because a life has no words doesn't make it less alive. She is very much alive, but she is an *æcewulf*, a real wolf. A forever wolf."

He arches his back, reaching behind to the fabric scrunched up high against his damp skin. The jeans hang low, framing the hollow of his hips and a gash of dark hair right down the middle.

"So she will never be human again?"

"She was never human, but no, she will never have thumbs or words again."

He stands near me, bending down to follow the path of my eyes through the window, past the billowing crown hardwoods, past the sharp tops of pines toward the dawn glow of Westdæl's bare top, home to the one other wolf who knew what it was to be an outsider, a teeterer on the edge of annihilation.

"How did it happen?" he asks in a quiet tone that almost sounds as though he wants to know. I've forgotten what that feels like, the give and take of conversation. John had me to talk to, but I have a Pack of worried wolves, and with them it's all *Alpha, reassure us, Alpha, decide for us, Alpha, direct us.*

"The Iron Moon takes us as she finds us and makes us wilder. If she finds us in skin, she makes us wild. If she finds us wild, she makes us *æcewulfas*. Forever wolves. Varya became a forever wolf so that she could protect us when we were at our most vulnerable. So." I squeeze my hand, feeling the thick scar at the base of my thumb. "I really can't ask her."

Plucking the towel from the floor, he shakes it out and heads to the bathroom.

"You said Shifters had done something to your pack," he says, watching me in the reflection of the little mirror nailed above the sink.

I smooth the curve of my eyebrow.

"You don't have to tell me."

"I know I don't. You can probably guess it. Hunters. Wolves. Except, in my case, it was three Shifters and a small pack trapped by the Iron Moon. They had guns. We had teeth. Within a few minutes, my entire birth pack was dead except the pup whose scent was camouflaged in the cesspit."

He lowers his head, hands grasping either side of the sink, one finger beating silently on the porcelain. "Three Shifters then. Three Shifters now."

"My birth pack was tiny compared to the Great North. They had no experience of Shifters. We do." I stretch my head to the side, trying to loosen my stiff shoulder. "I watched the three of you during the Iron Moon: Julia is weak, Cassius is a fool. You are the one Tiberius says is the most dangerous, the one who must be watched. But then why did the most guarded and careful wolf in the Great North tell *you* her name?"

He raises his head, looking at me in the reflection.

"Do you see my problem?"

After squeezing some toothpaste onto a toothbrush, he grimaces through a mouthful of beige foam. Looking at the tube, he spits and rinses. "Peanut butter? I don't suppose you have some other flavor?"

"Answer the question."

He rinses his mouth out twice more, then leans against the doorjamb, facing me. "When she first came to the compound, Varya'd been pumped with enough ketamine and fentanyl to kill a grizzly, and that's not an exaggeration. But she would not give up. She was locked up in the basement, throwing herself against things, forcing herself to move. It was nothing but will, and the sound irritated the hell out of August, so he sent me to get her. He wanted her to make the puppies—"

"Pups."

"Whatever. The point is he wanted to see his grandchildren."

I'm not surprised that August wouldn't accept that the four pups playing Bite the Ear and Chase the Tail could be his descendants. He wanted his grandchildren with fingers and words, playing Parcheesi.

"I've seen death come for a lot of people, but this was the first time that I'd seen someone come for death. Varya knew she was alone, drugged, outnumbered, and outgunned, but she kept coming. If I had let them kill her, I would never have another chance at finding out what was worth dying for."

He smooths the growth bristling on his cheeks with one hand.

"Did she tell you?"

"No. But she told me her name and I feel like that was something."

Chapter 8

Constantine

I WORKED A COMMERCIAL TRAWLER ONCE. WHEN I SAY "worked," I mean "slept," trying to keep dried crackers from fleeing the confines of my otherwise empty stomach, until the Coast Guard showed up with their sweeping powers to board any boat and the captain needed all hands to make it look like we were actually what we pretended to be.

I pinballed around the cabin and up on the waterlogged deck. A rope was thrust into my hands and I was told to pull.

Rain whipped sideways across a deck that pitched and rolled. Visibility was nil. I stood ankle deep in flapping fish while more came flying over the front at head height.

I wake up from that dreamed memory, the deck still pitching and rolling, except there is no rain and Tiberius is standing in front of me.

"What?"

"I said, 'We have a job.' Here." He tosses a towel-wrapped packet toward me. "I brought you some breakfast.

"I don't have a job anymore, remember? Boss developed throat trouble."

I start to peel back the towel. Whatever's inside smells like cinnamon.

"Just get dressed. I've got two bodies that aren't getting any fresher. We need to get them to Allagash before they stink up the car."

Mmm. And butter.

"I graduated from cleanup a long time ago. Let Cassius do it."

I lick the sugar from the top of one.

"Cassius is a conniving little shit who thinks he's smarter than he is. I need someone who knows what he's doing."

"Since I'm currently unemployed, it's good to know I've got something to put on my CV: 'versed in intimidation, extermination, and efficient disposal of remains. For referrals, check with the Great North—'"

"I forgot how much humans talk," he says, heading toward the door. "And take the sweatshirt. You're going to need it."

There is a navy-blue sweatshirt with frayed cuffs in the pile of clothes the Alpha left on the desk. I pick it up, feeling it soft and much washed in my hands.

"Ti, wait… Was this the Alpha's idea? Letting me go to help you."

"No, it was my idea and to be clear"—he pushes the red-and-black-checked wool shirt back, showing the textured handle of his gun—"no one is letting you go."

I don't care about the gun or being let go, but the thought that the Alpha might have seen dead bodies and that she'd told Tiberius to take the Shifter, the one with so much blood on his hands, because this is the kind of thing he'd be good at made a spot under my sternum ache.

"Any coffee to go with this?"

"No, but we'll get water on the way." He taps something hollow in his breast pocket.

"Water" turns out to be a stream. The hollow thing is a flask, which he fills and throws to me before leaning down, the blade of his hand holding back the leaves, and drinking straight from the stream.

I knew Tiberius from the beginning. When he was born and when he was small and when his teeth came in. First two flat little teeth at the bottom, then flat little teeth on the top. Some more flat little teeth to the side, then slightly before he turned two, his canines came in right on schedule only they didn't stop. August had already killed the human nanny who had seen his son turn into a puppy one day and hadn't stopped screaming.

Eventually, August had trained him never to turn into a puppy, which was very hard. After that, training him never to smile came easy.

Now when Tiberius straightens up, his fangs glisten unhidden. Water drops from the tips, disappearing in the trickling stream.

"We better get going," he says, and within seconds, he has turned into a vanishingly small spot of red-and-black plaid. When I catch up to him, he puts his finger to his lip, draws a broad horizontal circle in the air, then flicks his thumb. Following his eyes, I see a striped snake that looks to be five feet long. More if you add on the long, fluffy tail and small gray feet protruding from his mouth.

I circle around behind the snake, looking for something, anything. I pick up a stone.

"What are you doing?"

"You told me to"—I put my finger to my lips—"be quiet"—I repeat his circle in the air—"sneak around"—I slice with my thumb at my neck—"and kill it."

"What I told you was to be quiet"—he put his finger

to his lips—"*avoid*"—he circles his finger in the air again—"and get away." He flicks his thumb over his shoulder. "Finger across the throat means 'kill it.' If you kill something on Homelands, you have to eat it. I don't like snake. And that's a lot of snake."

I watch the snake move awkwardly away, its jaw and neck stretched tight over the squirrel, the tail dragging beside it like a tattered boa.

"You're telling me you gave up that penthouse in Centre-Ville to drink from the ground and eat snakes?"

"No, I'm telling you I gave up a penthouse in Centre-Ville to *not* eat snakes."

Tiberius's expression dulls, then his eyes close and he turns his head slightly as though pinpointing something.

"We need to go."

I keep up as best I can until the bright-green leaves give way to dark-green needles. The ground is cushioned under my feet by more needles and fewer bushes and vines. A wolf lopes past, sniffs the base of a tree, then sneezes delicately and licks its nose.

"There," Tiberius says, pointing to a spot of bright blue. At first, I think it's breathing, but when we get closer, I realize that it's simply the wind slipping under a blue tarp held down by rocks. One corner has come loose and folded itself over part of the body.

"Body" is perhaps an overly generous description of this random collection of pieces: a single arm, two legs. Only one of which has a foot with a gray and black sagging sock. A rib cage with a bit of uniform.

"I take it that's the dogcatcher?"

"Hmm."

"But you're not eating it?"

"*We* didn't kill it. The Bone Wolf did." He swings two fingers from eye to eye, and though he doesn't say any more, I know exactly who he means, because if anyone deserved a name like "Bone Wolf," it was the white one with the mismatched eyes who came out of nowhere looking for Varya.

"We leave bodies here for the coyotes, but now deer are flooding in from the lands up north. They have never had predators and"—he shakes his head like a disappointed Sunday school teacher eyeing a dirty picture—"the coyotes are getting picky."

There is another body here, but it's not the man with the hole right in the middle of his forehead. This one is large, naked, and intact except for a small gouge beneath his sternum and a larger gap where some animal has gnawed away the middle of his face.

"Looks like the coyotes at least started on that one."

"That wasn't coyotes." He sends the body flying off the tarp with a sharp kick, then begins to wrap the remains of the dogcatcher. "That was the Alpha. This is the dog who betrayed us. She ate his nose so that he will be unable to find the *Endemearc*, the Last Lands, and will wander forever without pack or territory. Always hungry and always alone."

Tiberius spits three times at the large, pale body with the dark-purple postmortem lividity on ass, legs, and upper back. The dead werewolf's head is bent awkwardly and his eyes are open, pleading above the gaping hole where his nose had been, like someone who has only just understood what a vast desert loneliness is.

Tiberius slings the dogcatcher over his back, and we walk on until we reach a spot where ferns and grasses have been flattened by repeated three-point turns. Tiberius reaches into his pocket for keys, and with a push of the button, the back of the muddy burgundy Range Rover glides up, releasing the sick, sweet smell of death.

He dumps the blue tarp on top of the guide whose head ran into a bullet, and I clamber into the passenger seat beside Tiberius, while he starts the car and opens the windows.

Before putting on his seat belt, he lifts his gun from the holster and makes sure that I see him putting it into the cup holder in the door.

"You have Magnus. Where is it that you think I want to go, Tiberius?"

"I don't know, but I don't believe in leaving anything up to chance."

Something stabs into my ass: I feel around, retrieving something that looks like a sawed-up piece of driftwood.

"Antler," says Tiberius. Before I can throw it out the window, he snatches it from my hand and starts gnawing on it with his back teeth.

"That's disgusting."

I start searching around the side of the seat, looking for the lever that will allow me to get a little more leg room. There's change on the floor. I pop the three quarters and a dime into the cup holder.

"The Alpha says you helped Varya kill my father."

Buttressing my feet against the floorboard, I plop the last dime in the cup holder while watching Tiberius's hands in case he reaches for his gun. He didn't care for August much, but I don't believe in leaving anything up to chance either.

He does move but only to stretch out his left hand, his

thumb hooked around the steering wheel. His ring finger bends crookedly to the side, and there is a star-like scar in the middle of his hand.

I was there when Tiberius tried to kill his father. I was there two days later when a dog spike was pounded into Tiberius's palm on August's orders.

"All the rest were mercenaries. My father always said Lucian would turn on him if he was less afraid and someone paid him a quarter more. I told the Alpha to keep an eye on you because you were the one most loyal to him."

Finding two more coins, I drop them into the cup holder.

"So what changed, Constantine?"

Under the floor liner are three quarters.

"I asked him for one thing. A promise, but he broke it." One of the quarters turns out to be a Susan B. Anthony dollar.

"What promise?"

The coin falls with a dull metallic clap on top of the change I've accumulated. I can't find anything else.

"I made him promise never to turn Magnus into me."

Tiberius frowns.

It was the only thing I'd ever asked of August. I hated going to him hat in hand, so I remembered every word. "I don't know why," he'd said. "You are so good—so very good—at what you do, but yes, I promise not to turn Magnus into you."

He held to it until we started losing men to his disastrous obsession with the Great North. Then he didn't.

"You promised."

"I promised not to turn Magnus into you," he'd said coolly. "But he was never going to be you; he will, however, learn to do what you do.

"Oh dear. Constantine has that evil look. You will thank me, Constantine of the Evil Look. In time you, will see it as a blessing. You were never going to let him grow up but now he will. Now, he will earn his fucking living."

Tiberius chews thoughtfully on his antler, his elbow on the open window frame.

"Do you remember that time in Hamilton?" he finally says.

"Yes."

"We stopped somewhere. A bakery maybe? I don't remember exactly. All I know is you said you wanted to get something for Magnus."

"Hmm-hmm." I do remember how magnanimous August was in 2014. When he'd destroyed the last of his opposition in the crucial port in Ontario. "Go, go," he'd said when I said I wanted to pick up something for Magnus. "Here," he'd added, peeling off a couple of brown-gold bills with Robert Borden on them as he always did to signal his pleasure. I never took the money. In my tortured imagination, the line between being a warrior and being a thug was drawn in cash.

"As soon as you left the car, Atticus asked why Magnus never had to go with us, even though he was older than I was."

"I noticed you waited until Constantine was out of the car before you asked," August had apparently said. "Does that mean you are more afraid of him than you are of me?"

Tiberius says Atticus tripped over himself trying to assure August that he was not afraid of me at all.

"You should be," August said. Or at least this is according to Tiberius. "I know how to control all of you. Wipe that look off your face, Lucian, before I slice it off.

"See? It's really just a matter of fear, greed, and tits, but not Constantine. I am a dangerous man because I know exactly what I want and have the means to get it. Constantine has nothing. And a man who is empty, who wants nothing, cares about nothing, is so much more dangerous than you can imagine. Magnus is the leash I use to control him. Leave him be."

August's real power was that he knew people too well, knew how to exploit their weaknesses. I made him nervous because he couldn't figure out that my loyalty, my willingness to follow whatever order he gave me, was lethargy. He never did understand the abyssal weight of emptiness. How hard it was to move. Magnus didn't tether me. He just gave me a reason to put one heavy foot in front of the other.

I remember squeezing into the back of the car and snapping at Atticus to move over. He'd responded with a loud "fuck off," which I now realize was playing to August. Everyone laughed until I broke his arm with my elbow, then ate a chocolate walnut brownie while staring out the window, the little white box balanced carefully on my knees.

"And you? That combination of fear, greed, and tits didn't work with you," I tell Tiberius.

"Don't fool yourself. I was exactly the same as all the rest." Tiberius rubs the leather necklace at his throat between his finger and thumb. "Until I wasn't."

"What is that?" I nod toward him with my chin. "Your necklace? I've seen it on other werewolves."

"*Not werewolves.* We are 'wolves' or 'Pack.' And this is not a necklace either. It's a braid, the sign of a mated wolf."

I lean against the window, catching sight of myself

in the rearview mirror. I really do need a shave. "Bit of a cliché, no? Big man tamed by the love of the little woman?"

Tiberius slams on the brakes, sending my head whipping forward. "Call her runt, she is one. Call her bitch, she's that too. But don't ever call her a 'little woman.'"

He signals the driver behind him to go on.

"And she didn't *tame* me," he says, looking in the rearview mirror. "She made me wild."

We head toward the Allagash River for old times' sake. Revisiting the hilarity of our shared heritage, but at the end, when we're handling the detail work, Tiberius becomes uncharacteristically anxious.

"*Be careful of the hammer.*"

"What?"

"You're going to ding it up."

"What am I supposed to do?" I shake some more teeth from the ziplock bag onto the granite rock. "Go into some town and ask if they've got a cutting board? What has gotten into you?" When I hit the teeth with the hammer, they pop like peppercorns.

"Here." I throw him another ziplock bag, this one filled with fingers. "Why don't you go find some crayfish."

Tiberius catches the fingers without comment but cringes again when the hammer hits the stone.

"You going to feed the crayfish?"

"Yeah, I got it." He grabs the bag of fingers. "But you're going to tell Sten about the hammer."

We stop at a coffee shop on the way back. As we enter, a bell rings. It's old, attached to a curved piece of metal that jostles when the door opens.

It was Otho, Julia's father, who taught me to read the room before doing anything else. I check out the two men at the Cup 'n' Cake. One has the jacket sag of someone with a concealed weapon. He leads with his left foot, his coffee in his left hand. Ex-military. He's hanging around, flirting with the girl at the counter who is helping the second man—glassy-eyed, sloop-shouldered, and beyond even the small hope required for flirtation.

There are no cameras, even though the tip jar is filled with change, meaning people pay with cash. There is an open back door. Paths worn into the linoleum lead down to the basement. The music there is loud. No one would hear anything. Not that I intend to do anything. It's just habit.

The girl at the counter is carefully pressing down the plastic lid on a cup of coffee. She hands it to the hopeless man, along with his change. Small coins, judging by the sound they make on the scratched countertop, but he doesn't bother to pretend he can afford a tip and scrapes that little bit back into his hand, turning his back on her and her tip jar.

"What can I get for you?"

"I'll take a coffee and a brownie," I say.

"Two coffees," Tiberius answers. "Forget the brownie."

"I'm going to use the bathroom," I say while the girl scoots away to get coffee. He looks suspiciously toward the back door.

I head into the bathroom to wash my hands and the coins I retrieved from the cup holder. There are no towels, just an asthmatic blower. I toss my coins from hand to hand.

The girl sprays the countertop with glass cleaner, keeping her bright-pink rhinestone-studded nails hyperextended away from the damp cloth. One takeout cup sits on the counter. Tiberius is leaning against the wall, blowing on the other.

I stand at the counter and stare down at the pastry case.

"And I'll take that brownie," I say. "Double chocolate."

Putting away her blue spray, the young woman reaches for a thin sheet of wax paper and snaps open a small, white paper bag. She has a tattoo on her wrist that says *Justin* and a necklace that says *Brandon* and a biddable expression. I smile my usual nonsmile and leave her staring at the big handful of damp change, scraped from the floor of a werewolf's Range Rover.

Back in the car, I prop my feet up on the dashboard and stare out the window. The wheels on smooth concrete sound like a whispered spray.

Tiberius makes a sharp turn onto the narrow dirt road with deep trenches on either side. Here, below a rusty sign that reads PRIVATE DRIVE, she watched us as Lucian stopped to report back to August. She couldn't have seen me through the tinted glass, but still I swear she stared at me, her fire-colored eyes glaring at me. Pitting herself against all of us.

"So, Ti?" I ask, breaking off a piece of brownie, trying to sound casual and disinterested. "Lucian said the Alpha's name once, but I've forgotten and—"

"There is no possible scenario in which *you* could ever need the Alpha's name."

I brush an invisible crumb from the front of my shirt, trying to pretend that the spat-out *you* doesn't matter.

"You want some?" I ask, lifting the bag to him.

His eyes flicker toward me. "Wolves don't eat chocolate."

I break off a big piece and wave it around with a flourish. "Good thing I'm not one, then." Then I pop it into my mouth and bite down so hard I think I've cracked a molar.

My stomach is cramping.

Maybe it really is the chocolate.

Or maybe it's the fact that with every foot up this bumpy dirt road, I get farther and farther from the bright-blue sky and a world that has been sanded down for my convenience. Tiberius makes a sharp turn, and the last ribbon of blue sky dissolves into the sullen overcast green. Through the open windows, I hear a short yip. Silent shadows ripple beside us, dissolving into dark trunks and reappearing later.

Silver opens the gate, because now that it is no longer the days of the full moon, werewolves have fingers.

As soon as Tiberius jumps down from the cab, a flurry of silver hair flies into his arms, making soft growling noises. She sniffs at him, smelling his head, his neck, his chest, then rubs her face against his, like she can't get enough of the feel of his skin.

They drop me off at the main building then disappear into the trees, Silver's legs curled around his hips, her dirt-rimmed feet crossed above his ass.

They call it the Great Hall, but there's nothing truly "Great" about it. Especially not the entry, which is really just a mudroom filled with neatly arrayed boots—muck and work—along one side and children's shoes along the other. There, a boy sits on the floor trying to tie his shoe. He's almost the age I was when I lost my parents and my humanity, too old to have such trouble tying shoes.

He stops for a moment, using ass and heels to shuffle over to my boots. He rocks forward, sticking his nose in the opening.

"You one of the new Shisters?" he says, straining to reach his tongue to his nose.

"Lukani." I squat down beside him. "We call ourselves Lukani."

His tongue still out, he goes back to making two loops.

"Gran Jean sayd that you don' turn into wolfeses during the Iwon Moon?"

"That's right."

He tries to tie them together. "What you turn into?"

"People."

"Peoples?" he says, losing his knot. "How'd you do that?"

"I didn't mean we turn into people. I mean we stay people."

He starts all over again. "An...an...an your pack? What they do?"

"Well, there isn't really a pack, not like you have here. It's just a bunch of people. Do you need help with that?"

"No! 'm Fist Shooos. I gotta do it my*sef*." Taking both loops in one hand, he lifts the other over his head and rubs his ear against his raised shoulder.

"What's fistshoos?"

"Fist." He holds up one finger. "Fist." Then he holds up another finger. "Secon." And one more. "Turd."

"First...?"

"Shooos." He holds up his foot and taps at the shoe.

"Whem we staht weareding skin?" He tries to enunciate but it still takes me a moment to figure out what he means.

When we start wearing skin.

He tucks the now-shod foot under his leg and starts with the other, a pink Croc with a gently gnawed toe that goes on easily. Now he rubs at his ear with his wrist, his foot shaking until he is done. Jumping up, he thunks awkwardly toward the outside door, but then stops short. He fishes for something in his pocket and returns to me, wiping an orange stick against his shirt.

"A presence," he says, holding it out to me.

The orange stick smells salty and rich and vaguely earthy and makes my mouth water and my stomach clench. "A present? What for?"

"Because I god a pack. You only god a buncha peoples."

Then he clumps away again, his uneven footsteps picking up speed as he heads to the door. I hear him thump down the stairs yelling, *"I talged to one! I talged to one! I gave it my sheese shew!"*

Staring down at my pity prize from a prepubescent werewolf, I feel the heat of eyes the color of fire and turn around.

Chapter 9

Evie

I WATCH EDMUND THROUGH THE PANED WINDOWS that give onto the mudroom. Like all wolflings in this first year out of pupdom, he is awkward. I've seen him stretching out his fingers and circling his thumb in the air, trying to make sense of these new digits. I've seen him yawn wide, popping his ears, trying to make them work. I've seen him stick his stubby, thick tongue out, trying to lick his cheek. I've seen him stick his short little nose in the air, sucking in big panicky breaths that tell him not nearly enough.

I don't know why it's called the Year of First Shoes, when it could just as easily be called the Year of First Forks. The Year of First Pants. The Year of First Words. The Year of First Lurching on Two Legs.

The First Year of the End of Innocence.

As soon as I scent steel and carrion, my shoulders tighten and my legs coil in case the pup needs me.

Like all wolves, Edmund is curious about the newcomers and scents the Shifter's boots. Like young, protected wolves, he doesn't know to be afraid of humans and anyone who smells like them.

"You're one of the Shifters?" Edmund says, staring up the long length of him.

"Lukani," the Shifter says, squatting down. "We call ourselves Lukani."

The Shifter folds his hands under his arm. The muscles at his back are loose as he talks softly to Edmund. Once, he extends a hand, but Edmund says no and the Shifter retreats.

When Edmund starts for the door, the Shifter stretches out his long legs, watching him disappear and return holding out his cheese chew. A present, Edmund says, because he has a pack, and the Shifter only has a bunch of people.

The Shifter stares at it for a long time after Edmund leaves, an odd look in his eyes that is both inward and absent. It's a little chewed at one end, the cheese chew. It probably doesn't look like much to someone who is not Pack, but they are objects of constant tussling among our pups and much prized.

I hope he doesn't throw it away.

He slides the dry end into the pocket of the worn flannel shirt, holding it there, his hand to his heart, until something seems to call him and he turns, his eyes catching mine.

He's a Shifter in our midst and I should be watching him, so I don't know why I feel awkward, but I do and I start to busy myself distributing chairs. I hoist an armload of them toward the table farthest away. With a flick of my wrists, I open two at a time, settling them into place with a hollow metallic clang.

I don't like it. It's not like the heavy sound of our old wooden benches.

We copied the old hall as closely as possible: the fireplace, the birch-branch balustrade of the stair leading to the second floor where the pups and juveniles and grans live, the big tables that draw us together when we are in skin. The smell of fire is only slowly subsiding and the new cedar we used is still too strong. It will all gentle over time and eventually be like that other hall, thick with the scent of pine and turkey feathers and sweetgrass and deer musk and wolves.

Then there will be less to remind us of what we lost to the Shifters. Not of the hall—that's just a thing, ultimately—but of the lives: Solveig Kerensdottir, Orion Tyldesson, Paula Carlsdottir, Celia Sorensdottir.

And John Sigeburgsson.

I miss so many things about him. As the two strongest wolves of our echelon, our mating was long assumed, but he was my friend even before and I miss that more. He was so confident in his decisions. In a way, that is what I miss most of all: the certainty born of a long line of Alphas in a pack that had been unchallenged and undisturbed for 350 years. Such certitude is harder as an outsider guiding a pack that finds itself suddenly exposed and vulnerable.

The door closes.

The floor creaks as it settles. I take a deep breath, turning to face the inevitable *Alpha?* that will announce whatever problem or question or need requires my position's attention.

But the Shifter says nothing. He stands silent in front of a window that gives out onto birches charred the night the Great Hall burned. If they had not leafed, we might have cut them down, but they did and now they dapple the room in the pearl-green light of summer.

His gaze feels like a physical weight. He asks for nothing and I feel uncomfortable, like I no longer know how to deal with someone who doesn't have a problem that needs to be signed or read or arbitrated or disciplined. So I go back to setting out the chairs. There are not as many tables out as there are for the Iron Moon Table, the one meal when the whole Pack is together and in skin, but with enough places for the two-hundred-plus Homeland wolves. I open two chairs and another two and—

"Don't you have people to do that?" he finally asks.

"Neither."

"Neither?"

"There are no 'people' here, only wolves, and I do not 'have' them."

A cable tie has popped loose from the chair in my hand. I set it aside. They were never meant to be anything but a temporary solution.

"We took care of the bodies."

"Hmm," I say, heading over to the corner and the ridiculously ornate, glass-front china cabinet, another temporary solution that hails from Sten's storage and before that from an earlier gilded age when the Pack first bought the Great Hall and its surrounding buildings.

"Is that all you're going to say?"

"I get enough questions without answering questions that aren't asked." Fishing around in the back of the leftmost shallow drawer, I extract two cable ties.

He coughs out a broken laugh. "August would've expected a detailed report so that he could be sure everything had gone according to instructions."

I thread the cable ties through the teetering joint and pull them tight. "Yes, well, wolves are not employees; an Alpha is not a boss. Tiberius would have told me if there was a problem."

Then I set the jury-rigged chair down. It will hold a

while longer, but it is time to start on something more permanent. I will tell Sten to start work on—

"Alpha," says Soli, carrying the quarterly tax estimates due June 17.

"Alpha," says Tara, bringing proposals for the renegotiated flight plans from Potsdam Municipal Airport.

"Alpha," says Gran Jean, trailed by Gyta and Adam. Jean crosses her arms in front of her and says nothing because Adam is favoring his hind leg, so I already know.

"It's the second time, Gyta." She is young still, not even fifty moons. Pups that age are not expected to be much in skin, so we don't have clothes that fit her. She plucks at the outsized shirt and pants held up by a bungee cord. "You will be in skin until the next moon."

"Bwedonsaranix, Apa! *Bwedonsaranix.*"

"It doesn't matter what he did," I say, partly because I have no idea what she's saying, partly because it genuinely doesn't matter. We've been through this once before. "Wolves *do not* bite sleeping packmates. Wolves wake wolves up, *then* they bite them. *Ongiet?*" Gyta doesn't reply, and her lower lip trembles.

"*Do you understand?*" I repeat, and this time, she nods.

"Apa?" she says plaintively, cocking her head to the side. I bend over her, touching her face, rubbing first one cheek, then the other, letting her rest in the crook of my shoulder for a moment of wordless comfort.

With a subdued bark and a whimper, the other little wolf calls for my attention too. I bend over, picking Adam up, checking his leg, and letting him bury his muzzle next to mine.

When I turn around, every place at every table has a chair, except for spaces that the Shifter is in the process of filling with the two metal chairs stenciled with *UUFP* on the back, a constant reminder that while these chairs might have been sufficient for Unitarian Universalists in Plattsburgh, they are not sufficient for wolves.

"Alpha?" Leonora's voice echoes from the top of the basement stairs.

I search through my memory, trying to remember why my human behaviors teacher is wearing a long, red gown spangled with glitter like a crow's wet dream.

Then four juveniles reach the top of the stairs behind her, looking wretched in equally outlandish finery and I realize I'd forgotten about the juveniles' formal dinner practice.

"Leonora."

She instructs her charges to move one of the big tables off to the side. My eyes water at the sick, sweet berry scent of the perfume she wears around her more advanced students. It's her way of training us not to rely on scent. Two entirely different people may both smell like baby powder, but to confuse them will make the humans suspicious and that is something we cannot afford.

"Are those the female Shifter's shoes?" I ask, nodding toward Avery, who wobbles miserably on several inches of bright-red sandal.

"She didn't want them anymore," Leonora says.

Avery whimpers as she stumbles by, carrying the heavy table. "They hurt, Alpha."

"It is a flesh wound," Leonora says gently, "and a useful lesson in the discomfort humans undergo in order to propagate the species. Get the tablecloth and don't be smug, Adrian. You're wearing them next."

"But...but I thought only the females had to wear them."

"Female *humans*, but as you are not human, *you* are next. Tablecloth."

The two young wolves extract a length of white cloth from one of the big canvas bags we use to carry firewood and shake it free of bits of bark and dried leaves. Soon, one end of the table is covered with a linen tablecloth damasked with cabbage roses and stained with the faded remains of hunters' blood and hunters' wine. It is set with hunters' crystal and hunters' silver.

"If you're doing candles again," I say with a nod toward the glass holders, "make sure there is a bucket of water nearby."

Soon, the 11th Echelon will be bringing out dinner. I can tell by the sound of clattering plates and the smell of freshly cut bread. Picking up the quarterly estimates, I fit my cold coffee cup between my fingers, then stick the awkward roll with the flight plans under the other arm. Loose pages on the inside of the roll slip out and fall to the floor.

The Shifter slips his hand under the coffee cup still sloshing in my hand.

I hold it tight, and when he bends down to try to retrieve the loose curled pages on the floor, I plant my foot firmly on top of them. The coffee sloshes as I squat down to get to them, but his hand is already there.

"Let me help."

I stare at him for a second until I remind myself that he isn't Pack and doesn't know what it was like to be Alpha. To project strength every minute of every day so that when my wolves are anxious, they can always look to me and be reassured. Even when I was furious and heartsick and my body was racked from my lying-in and the Pack was faced with threats both outside and in, they could look to me and say, "Ah, well, the Alpha is picking up her own damn papers and her own damn coffee so our tiny corner of the world isn't done yet."

"Follow me," I say, pulling the pages away. He lets go with a confused look.

In my office, I put everything down: cup on my desk and the flight plans next to the larger roll of schematics I set on one of the chairs earlier.

"My Gamma will help you get settled." I spread my hand on top of the worn manila folders I need to look through.

"Alpha?" he asks.

"Hmm." I open the shallow pencil drawer in my desk and pull out pencil, pen, eraser, and bright-pink stickies.

"I heard your name once, but I've forgotten."

I jot down a quick note, scribble Sten's name on the other side, then hand it to the Shifter.

"That wolf no longer exists. Now there is only the Alpha," I say, leaving that name a hole in his memory.

Chapter 10

Constantine

She handed me a note written on a bright-pink sticky at the door. "Give this," she said, "to my grandma." I moved toward her just as she reached out her hand, but because we both moved at the same time, what had been perfectly judged becomes misjudged and her fingers scrape across my chest. She pulls her hand away, looking surprised at her fingertips fisted tight against her palm. It lasts only a second then is gone, her expression becoming closed and guarded again.

"Alpha?"

As soon as the door closes behind her, I lower myself to retrieve the pink square. It says *STEN* on one side. On the other, *BENCHES* and then words I can't understand. I sound them out as best I can, but I know none of them are her name.

"Hey, get out of the way."

Dazed, I look up from where I am kneeling on the floor, a pink Post-it pressed to my nose, as a werewolf comes out of the kitchen with a huge earthenware bowl that smells of garlic and lemon and thyme. Other werewolves stand impatiently behind him bearing more plates and bowls. I jump up to let the line of werewolf caterers through.

The Pack is already filling up the Main Hall. They clot around the table, a greedy crowd grabbing serving spoons and spilling food and snarling at each other. The Alpha's office door slams open and she strides down the hall. The werewolves look at one another but they're crowded too close together to get away.

"*He, He, Wulfas!*" she says, banging the hilt of her dagger against the huge table three times—*thoom, thoom, thoom.* Before she even fits the knife back in her sheath, a line has formed and the wolves shuffle forward, their heads bowed sheepishly.

I see Julia near the front of the line. She's clean at least. Dressed in running pants and a long-sleeved blue T-shirt that says *I BELIEVE IN BUFFALO*, even though I would lay long odds on her ability to find Buffalo on the map. When she gets to the head of the line, she stops. A woman beside her pushes a plate into her hand and points her toward the food. She hesitates again, threading the plate through her fingers, looking hesitantly over her back. The woman says something to her, and Julia starts to fill up her plate.

"Get in line or get to your table," says a voice. Turning around, I see a woman with a whole mob of werewolves crowded behind her, waiting to get in line.

"I'm looking for the Alpha's grandma."

She blinks a couple of times until a man next to her elbows her with a snort. Finally, she turns around. "Hey, Sigegeat," she says. "Shifter here says he's looking for the Alpha's grandma."

Werewolves who are human start to laugh. Those who are not skitter out from under the tables, tails tucked in away from the stomping feet.

A man with rusty hair stands at another table, thumping heads as he moves between rows of laughing men and women. It isn't until he reaches the head of the table where all the platters of food are that I get a good look at his face. He is a squat, broad man with a brownish-red beard and wild unkempt hair that obscures much of his face. Much but not enough to hide the several star-shaped scars along the top of his cheek.

"It's Gamma, Shifter, not Grandma. I am Sigegeat Guthlacsson, *Gamma* of the 7th Echelon of the Great North."

"It's Constantine, *Ziggy*, not 'Shifter.'"

One by one, the voices stop until the room goes silent and wolves run to sit down like children caught out at the end of a game of musical chairs.

"Come," Ziggy says, pulling at my arm. He points to the table where he had been and where the Alpha quickly takes a seat, soup sloshing up the side of her bowl.

"What is—?"

"*Now.*" He pushes me down and lowers his head over the empty plate in front of him, his hands nervously plucking at the edges of his napkin.

Other wolves bow their heads over their plates, and even the Alpha sits, bent over, prodding at the contents.

I hear something now, a faint wheezing on the stairs outside, labored and slow. Eyes flicker to the Alpha. She manages to squeeze a spoonful through her jaws before they clamp shut again.

I watch her long throat move as she forces herself to swallow.

Whatever is outside takes another step and stumbles.

The Alpha stares at the spoon in her bowl, seemingly unable to take another bite.

My body tenses, preparing for whatever thing is coming that has the power to silence the entire Pack.

A huge wolf emerges from under the table and

whimpers, burrowing its head into the Alpha's arm. She scratches it behind the ears.

The door begins to open, first a sliver, then a narrow gap, then a space just wide enough to admit Arthur, the man who should by all rights be dead. No one else seems to notice him. Instead, they all continue to look bleakly at their plates while he struggles toward the front table, his fists tight at his sides, his shoulders back, his chest hunched in an awkward S-shaped contortion of pride and pain. His eyes are dark and deep in his bloodless skin. His breathing is shallow.

The only person who looks at him is Tiberius's wife, the silver-haired werewolf who ripped him open. Then she lowers her chin slightly and he responds in kind.

At the main table, Arthur grabs the edge for support. When he does, his elbow hits a heavy bowl with a narrow base that wobbles against the thick wood, emitting a hollow, careening sound that makes the silence so much louder.

The plate in his hand shakes, so he sets it down on the table while he begins to serve himself. Dark lines of blood seep through his T-shirt.

A chair hits the floor with a metallic bang and Julia walks toward him, oblivious of everything else: of the fallen chair, of the sudden surge of noise, of Cassius's shouts.

I barely know Cassius and never liked what little I knew. He insisted that being Julia's fiancé made him part of the inner circle and, with Tiberius gone, August's heir. He said little about Julia herself except to say that "she could've been a model." That he said so often and so inevitably that it has colored the way I'd seen her. There she is. Julia CouldaBeenAModel.

As she pushes her way through the werewolves, her diffident expression, constrained demeanor, and cramped posture melt away like ice cream on summer asphalt, and for the first time, I see something beyond Otho's daughter and August's niece and Cassius's CouldaBeenAModel.

I see a woman who no one else here knows. A woman with the shoulders, jaw, furious gray eyes, and deadly determination of August's estranged wife. Otho's homicidal sister. Julia's aunt.

Drusilla.

The Alpha doesn't bang her knife again. Instead, she looks pointedly at the man with the little blond ponytail sitting at the head of Julia's table. As soon as he catches her eye, he rushes forward like an actor who had gotten so swept up in watching a play that he forgot he had a part in it.

Wiping his mouth on a faded dish towel, he points Julia back to the table. She ignores him. He takes both her shoulders and turns her around, once again directing her to sit down. Then Julia hurls herself at him.

She is not a fighter, that much is clear, but raw, desperate fury in a strong body should never be discounted and Ponytail is caught off guard. He stumbles backward and Julia moves next to Arthur, holding out her hand for his plate.

The man turns toward her, flinching as his shoulders shift. Shaking his head with a sad look on his face, he whispers something to her, and just like that, the Bitch of Vancouver is replaced by the woman with the apologetic expression who lets herself be led back to her seat by the man with the blond ponytail. She looks worriedly toward Cassius, who glares at her.

Someone claps hands and barks out a forceful "Eyes here," and every werewolf looks toward the single table off to the side that was not set with mismatched Corelle and industrial ceramics but with white linen and candles and porcelain. A woman—Leonora—outfitted in a bedazzled red dress, her shoulders bulging broad and strong from under the tiny rhinestone straps, looms over a small group of teenaged werewolves, all tugging on uncomfortable formal wear.

"Gently," she says.

"They're not going to make it," Ziggy whispers to the woman next to him.

"There's always a first time," she says.

It takes me a moment to realize that the teenagers are lifting champagne flutes in a kind of slow-motion toast, while Leonora keeps up a steady patter.

"Slowly…slowly. Now, you're not banging them together, not clinking, not tapping. Just the tiniest touch—"

The glasses meet in the middle and shatter.

"*Wes hæl*!" shout the laughing adults, toasting with their sturdy earthenware and pewter mugs.

Only the Alpha is not laughing. Her head is bent close to the doctor's. When her eyes catch mine, she looks tired.

Chapter 11

Evie

He knows. He's already pushed away the chair, shoving his way shoulder first through laughing Pack distracted by the juveniles.

Tristan stands abruptly. "I'm going to get something to eat, Alpha. I have a feeling it's going to take a while."

"Tell Eudemos and Tiberius to be ready as soon as I call."

Tristan lowers his eyes and heads to the table where the 14th Echelon, Magnus's echelon, are sitting.

"Is it Magnus?" the Shifter asks, threading through the tables.

I push vegetables and rice onto my fork with coconut-curry-soaked bread.

"Tiberius says you were August's right-hand man." I say, taking a bite.

"Is that a question?"

"No. But this is: If you were his right-hand man, why were you not the one to bring the hunters here?"

"I never went on hunts with him. He preferred to use my talents elsewhere."

"It had nothing to do with Magnus being sick?"

He doesn't answer and I swallow, trying to remember the last time I had hot food. In skin.

"And when the Great Hall burned down? Was Magnus sick then?"

He takes a seeded rye roll from a bowl of them. "There were enough men going. Besides, August needed someone to stay with him."

"You're not answering. Was Magnus sick? Was he often sick during the Iron Moon?"

He tears apart the roll with a puff of steam and caraway and pops it, soft and warm, into his mouth.

"I'm not a werewolf. I don't pay attention to lunar phases."

"You may not be a *wolf*, but Magnus is, and he can't help but pay attention. The moon has always called to his wild but now the smell of fur, the smell of blood, the sound of the hunt, Evening Song. Everything in Homelands calls to him, and resisting it is tearing him apart."

"So let me take him out of here. I—"

"*That is not what he needs.*" I wipe the last bit of curry with a piece of bread. "Taking him away may slow his decline, but it's not enough. He refuses to change and that is what he needs to stop dying."

He takes off down the hallway and I disentangle myself from the chair and run after him. I didn't have a chance to warn him that Magnus looks worse. I push past Constantine. Tristan and I had just changed the bed liner, but it's bloodstained again.

Because Magnus is not drinking anything, his body has shrunk, his joints are even more distended, his skin hangs from his bones, stiff, dry, and crinkled like parchment. I pour out a glass of water from the sweating earthenware pitcher. Leonora has contributed a straw from her collection of human artifacts.

Magnus screws up his eyes.

"Try, wolf. Try."

He does manage to open his mouth, not to drink but to grind out one withered sound.

"Con?"

The Shifter pulls himself together and moves toward Magnus. "I'm here," he says, setting his hand gently on the sick wolf's hair, but even that is enough to make Magnus whimper.

When the Shifter looks at his palm, it is covered with dark hair.

"You've looked better, Mags," he says. It's meant to be humorous, but the crack in his voice is not. I roll Tristan's stool toward him and slide the water closer so the Shifter will remember to try to make Magnus drink.

A shiver runs up Magnus's back and across his shoulders. "Is there another blanket?" Constantine asks.

"We tried. The weight is too much for his skin."

Rolling Tristan's stool closer, Constantine sits with his hands tucked under his arms. "Oh god, Mags. What have I done?"

When Magnus gives Constantine a labored smile, his chapped lips split and bleed.

"I should have talked to you after...well, you know. After what happened. But you didn't want to and I thought it was probably best to leave it like that. Leave you afraid of changing. I mean, you saw what August was capable of and I'd been with him forever. He actually *needed* me."

Magnus manages a weak smile, just enough to show the bloody ridge of his teeth.

"So now I do have to talk to you and I don't really know how. I don't have the words for it, but they do. Varya did. She had words for what it felt like to be human and to not be human. But I've forgotten them."

He raises his eyes to mine.

"*Anfeald*. That's one. It's how we describe being in skin." I do not chide him for thinking we are ever human. This is not the time for it. "It means alone, singular, the feeling of being cut off from the world. But when we are wild, we are not alone. We are ourselves, but we are also one with the land and the Pack. Then we say we are *manigfeald*, manifold and complex."

A wren flies by, a silvery twig in its beak.

"That's what it feels like, Mags. I was not a monster, whatever August said. I was myself but more. I was the seaweed moving in the rock pond, the salt air, the hearts of birds hiding in beach grass. I was part of something bigger. Maybe that's why August couldn't bear it, having us change. It's so much easier to control something small."

Slowly and painfully, Magnus pulls a hand up and points to his chest with a rickety finger.

"No, it was not your fault. You were worried and who else could you turn to? But everything that happened... that was all on August."

Constantine crosses one leg over his knee, rubbing the mutilated skin of his ankle.

Magnus's eyes wander in their orbit until they finally focus on me. He blinks once, his eyes so dry I can almost hear the lids scraping against his cornea.

"Should I get Tristan?" I don't say it in my usual clipped Alpha way. It was just a blink after all. He swallows once, though there's nothing to swallow, and opens his mouth. I wait for him to say something, but he can't and nods instead.

I head out to find our doctor.

"Tristan!" I call as soon as the door is closed behind me.

"Hew, Affa!" Tristan answers from the kitchen, a dusting of cheese popcorn on his chin.

"It's time."

He takes one more handful of cheese popcorn.

"Have you ever considered that if you hunted something bigger than bunnies, you might not be hungry all the time?"

He wipes his hands together, then holds them up. "What do you see?"

"Cheese dust?"

"*Under* the cheese dust, though, you see a surgeon's hands. No hoof-crushed proximal phalange, no fang-torn abductor pollicis. And that, my Alpha, is why I am—and will always be—a bunny hunter."

I rub the bent ring finger of my right hand against the scarred base of my thumb.

"It's time, lads," Tristan calls into the library. "Bring that with you. This may take a while."

He holds the library door wide while Tiberius backs out carefully, carrying one side of a half-played Scrabble board with Eudemos on the other side, a shallow, often-taped box tucked under his arm.

"Hold it while I get a cart," Eudemos says as soon as we arrive in Medical. A moment later, he returns with a cart that rolls easily across the polished cement, jostling only once as it hits the drain recessed into the middle of the floor.

"So," says Tristan, tying on a rubber work apron over his clothes. "Where's the patient?"

"There's the patient," says Eudemos, setting the Scrabble board on the stainless-steel dressing trolley. "He's the one on the bed."

Tristan sighs and fishes around in a pocket. "May the moon save me from the literalness of wolves. Yes, Eudemos, I was aware. Anyone else want a Tic Tac?"

Only the Shifter holds out his hand to take the two pale-green pills of wintergreen that for every wolf is a shameful signal that one has visited Medical for a flesh wound.

As soon as Tristan has finished scrubbing his hands, he tells Magnus to "hop" down. The Shifter slides his arms under Magnus's body, and when he lifts, he almost sends Magnus flying, overcompensating for weight that simply isn't there.

Tristan retrieves a plastic sheet from a drawer and shakes it out. I take the other side.

"Support his head," Tristan says, his voice uncharacteristically gentle. The Shifter says nothing; I'm not sure he could. His mouth is so tightly clamped shut I can hear the grinding of his molars. He lifts Magnus's shoulders so his head falls against his own broad chest.

Once the plastic sheet is tucked in, the Shifter sets him down. He disentangles the light blanket, settling it once again over Magnus's laddered ribs, his chest rising fast and shallow, his skin mottled with bruises like a windfall apple.

What have I done? his eyes seem to say as though he knows I've asked this same question over and over.

What his voice says is "It's going to be all right. It's going to be all right now." It is the first of several lies he tells Magnus, though "No one is going to hurt you" is the most egregious of them.

"Oh, I wouldn't say that if I were you," says Tristan, drying his hands and taking out a pair of rubber gloves. "Because this is most definitely going to hurt."

"*Tristan.*"

"Ah, yes," Tristan says. "I forgot I was supposed to be upbeat and solicitous. Well, young man, if we are lucky, they will all be flesh wounds and that will have to be solace enough."

I stand at the foot of the bed, arms crossed, staring at my doctor and wondering if Torquemada was still alive and teaching bedside behavior at Massachusetts General. Tristan sketches out the procedure, adding a cheerful coda. "I believe," he says at the end, "that your bones are still flexible enough to bend and not shatter. I hope."

There isn't enough honey in Homelands to make what needs to be done palatable.

"Now let's see," Tristan says, pulling his gloves on with a snap. "Where do you think you put your wild?"

Magnus looks confused.

"Have you ever had a twinge somewhere on your body and thought, *That felt nice or different or like I could really suck down a blood pudding?*"

Magnus shakes his head once.

"Mine," Tristan continues, "is right behind my knees. I have to be very careful picking up pens. You know once," and he prattles on with that story about when he dropped a fork during Evening Meat, hyperextended his knee, and flopped muzzle first in a huge Crock-Pot of black beans.

He leaves out the part where John and I plucked him from the casserole, salvaging our costly doctor, if not the frijoles.

The entire time, he pokes and prods Magnus, looking for a reaction.

For a while, the only sounds are Tristan's whispered suggestions and the comments about the viability of words coming from the Scrabble players.

"Wait, 'benison'?" Eudemos cranes his head to look around. "That's not a word. 'Venison,' that's a word."

"It is so a word. More of a word than 'Rhos.'"

"Of course 'Rhos' is a word. Like Kari and Per are both Rhos."

"I won't fight you over 'Rhos' but I will not yield on 'benison.'"

"If I'm right, it's the same as last time?"

"Why does it always have to be beaver liver? I don't even *like* beaver liver."

"But we both know who does."

"Just look it up," Tiberius says. "I'm not wrong. You can deliver it to her yourself."

Eudemos takes out his phone and begins with thick clumsy fingers the long process of jabbing and erasing the tiny buttons.

The Shifter and I turn Magnus on his side so that Tristan can continue to poke and prod and Magnus can continue to suffer. The Shifter settles his hand on mine, and when I catch his eyes, I see a mirror of my anxiety, both of us anxious about the promises we made to Magnus that neither of us can keep.

Wolves live in a world of touch: we bop noses to say *Chase me,* bite ears to say *Listen to me,* put teeth to throat to say *Trust me.* Set muzzle to neck to say *Want me.* Drape paws across shoulders to say *Comfort me.*

I don't remember the last time someone tried to comfort me.

"Hunh. 'Benison: a blessing, a benediction.' Who knew?"

"*I* knew. And that's 3, 1, 1...9 with a double-word score...18. You writing it down?"

Tristan's stool shoots across the floor. "*Alpha!*" he cries, clinging to Magnus's flailing body. Tiberius and Eudemos jump up, spilling Scrabble tiles across the floor.

The Shifter and I are already shoulder to shoulder, holding on to Magnus until the jerking stops and his body curls in on itself like a fern.

"It's here," Tristan says, pointing to an innocuous spot two inches below Magnus's right shoulder blade.

"I'll take his feet. You two take his shoulders and arms. Shifter, you're at the top."

In his last act as he loses all agency to the change, Magnus's frightened eyes seek out the familiar face above him. The Shifter opens his mouth, straining to say something. Finally, he gives up, resting his hand gently on Magnus's cheek instead.

Magnus chokes on a scream.

"All right, folks," Tristan says. "It's going to be a rough ride."

I plant my feet and hold on to his ankles, making sure that Tiberius and Eudemos have a grip on his arms and shoulders.

"Hold firm," I remind them, "but don't break him."

Blood starts to stream from Magnus's mouth. His eyes are beginning to change. He's blind now and deaf, too, unable to hear anything but the reverberations of the screams inside his skull.

"Shifter," Tristan says. "You need to hold his head."

He doesn't respond to Tristan's demands that he hold Magnus's head. Instead he stares frozen at the bone, muscle, and organs as they slither under Magnus's skin like snakes in a balloon.

"*Constantine,*" I say. It's not loud or forceful or

commanding like the Alpha voice. It's quiet and wholly my own, but his head snaps up, instantly intent. "Hold his head."

He exhales like a swimmer surfacing and takes hold of Magnus's head. Tristan squeezes a metal clamp to keep his jaws open, then hooks a suction tube over that as well. He feels around with the fingers of one hand, followed by metal pliers in the other. Metal scrapes against bone, followed by a jerk, and something drops onto the metal tray. A bloody tooth, a dulled canine with perverted roots. Within seconds, something strong and sharp begins to push its way through.

Blood slurps through the suction tube.

Tristan yells something over Magnus's choked howls and tosses scalpels to Tiberius and Eudemos and me. I hadn't heard, but Tiberius must have. He holds Magnus's shoulder down with his elbow, then bends his contorted arm and cuts deep into the tip of a mangled fingertip. As he moves on to the next finger, a slick claw pushes its way out from the blood and flesh.

What have I done?

I see something twisting under the skin of Magnus's toes. Moving as quickly as I can, I slice along the line marked by his scars. At first, the cut is too shallow and the claw of one toe starts to twist and turn under the skin before I slice deeper, setting it free.

What have I done?

With each tooth, more blood streams into his mouth, too much for the suction tube to handle. To keep him from choking, Tristan gives Constantine a long length of rubbery pipe. "Like a straw," Tristan yells. Constantine holds the pipe between his teeth, sucking out blood whenever Tristan dumps another deformed tooth on the tray.

All of us are slick with sweat and blood by the time Magnus has stopped struggling. The metal tray is littered with little semihuman teeth: half flat and enameled, half bone with monstrous curlicued roots.

"Alpha?" Tara stands at the door, signaling to me.

I roll my shoulders back to unleash the tension of what feels like hours spent hunched and straining, but in the end, all that effort was worth it because there is one more wolf. He is thin and weak and exhausted, but he is another wolf. I put my cheek to his bloodstained fur and whisper in his pointed ear.

"*Wilcumeþ, wulf.*"

Welcome, wolf.

Chapter 12

Constantine

Tristan says that Magnus must remain in this form for a while. How long, he can't say, but his body is too weak to go through another change. It will take time spent wild to recover from all those years spent dying.

Nobody much feels like talking. Eudemos and I lift Magnus while Tiberius pulls out the blood-covered sheet and balls it up with Tristan's discarded apron. He hands it off to two waiting werewolves to take to the laundry while Tristan helps slide a fresh sheet under him. Eudemos and Tiberius scrub the floor until only thin wisps of blood flow into the drain. Tristan washes the equipment.

I take a blue paper towel from a pile of them next to the sink and dampen it. Then I try to wipe away the blood and gore around his mouth and muzzle, but he whimpers and I stop, having gotten nothing but a few brown flecks.

"I'm leaving this for you." Tristan holds up a big syringe, making sure that I am watching when he puts it next to the pitcher. "He needs water but be careful. He won't know how to use his tongue."

He heads for the door, his hand over the light switch. "Off or on?"

"Off."

It seemed like hours ago that I first came to Medical, but the early summer sun has a few more degrees yet before it sets. The low light makes the room shimmer with the shadow play of leaves. Finally, one pale-blue eye, the color of thick ice, opens. "Sorry, Mags." I don't know what I'm sorry for. For his pain. For the lost years. For not having understood.

His tongue flaps loose, feeling for the points of his teeth. He breathes in through his open mouth and his nose wrinkles. Using the syringe, I drip water into his mouth. Most of it dribbles into his fur or onto the pillow, but he gets a little and closes his eyes again.

I open the window on the off chance that he will hear the heartbeat of birds, or the scent of the wind will make him feel like he's part of something bigger and make it all seem worthwhile. Then I settle back onto Tristan's rolling chair, my hand perched on Magnus's foreleg, moving in time with the labored rise and exhausted collapse of this wolf's chest.

There is a "B" tile on the floor. Two points.

Benison. Blessing. Benediction.

"You will thank me, Constantine of the Evil Look. In time, you will see it as a blessing." August might be right, but not in the way he thought. If it weren't for his broken promise, I wouldn't have hesitated to kill Varya. I would not have warned the Great North. I would not have brought Magnus here. "In time," I will discover whether this was a blessing or if I've simply condemned Magnus to die harder.

As soon as the sun goes down, the Alpha howls, like she does every evening. I've never seen her do it, but I've heard it. The low resonance that just as it starts to rise is joined by other wolves right across Homelands. It rolls down the mountains and settles into the valleys, pulling the howls of wolves with it.

Constantine.

I play it over and over in my mind, the way it sounded on her lips, the way it lay down a path through the maze of guilt and anger. The way it shimmered like a silver string.

The way it led me out.

Magnus whines, stretching his nose toward the open window. His breathing seems a little stronger, and with each rise of his lungs, a claw scrapes against the plastic-covered mattress. This is not where he should be, not surrounded by the smell of antiseptic and the touch of plastic and the sound of metal and cement.

"I'll be right back." Taking two of the doctor's blue paper towels, I fold them up, using one to prop open the door to Medical, the other to hold the screen door leading outside. For a moment, I stand in the cool air, my face up.

He is too easy to lift. I felt it before when I picked him up so the sheet could be changed. I move carefully so that I don't jostle his carved-up paws or anything else. With a quick kick to the screen door, I dislodge the makeshift wedge and it closes behind us with a *thunk*. I left my boots, but at least I can feel the dips and hollows of the ground, the dampness and dryness, the changing density of the ground cover as I move deeper into the trees until I find a little space in front of a big trunk and slowly lower myself and Magnus to the ground. There's a star-filled hole up above and a smattering of sucklings down below.

Magnus pats at my hand with his front paw, leaving blood on the cuff of my sweatshirt.

Once when he was very young, I told him to wait in the car while I ran an errand. Then we'd go to White Castle. I will never forget Magnus's eyes when he stared at the cuff of my shirt, which had gotten not so much bloodstained as blood-soaked. There was no more talk of White Castle.

I was always careful after that to clean up, no matter what. Showered, clean clothes, because I needed to be sure that I'd gotten rid of every trace. But this is his blood, and I lay my hand on his thin shoulder and sit with him. Soon when the wind blows over his fur, it releases a raw fragrance that is both green and bitter.

He sleeps again.

I'm sorry, Magnus, for that. I'm sorry for everything. I'm sorry we sliced into your fingers and toes to make way for claws. I'm sorry we pulled your teeth out of your skull to make way for fangs. Most of all, I'm sorry for telling you that what was best for you, what you needed, was to be human.

Magnus's eyes are closed but his ears start moving: one way during an outburst of song (*whip, whip, whip, whippp*), another way as bats flit across the oculus onto the stars, this way again toward the distant wheezing of frogs.

The next time they rotate, he lifts his head, staring expectantly over his shoulder until a burly gray-and-beige wolf emerges from the woods.

I know—as surely as I do that a .22 LR with a suppressor is the best choice for a silent kill at intermediate distances—that this is Eudemos. His eyes on Magnus, he moves, crouched close to the ground, his shoulders rolling. I watch him carefully as he sniffs at Magnus's feet, his paws, and then he starts to lick. Magnus kicks at him with short jerky blows, but Eudemos growls and keeps licking. I can feel Magnus stiffen, until with each stroke at his tortured paws, the tension eases. His eyes close and his head sways until he collapses back against me. Eudemos moves on to the next paw and the next and the next, and each time, the tension and resistance at the beginning is shorter and the relief more pronounced.

After, Eudemos moves closer, holding his muzzle next to Magnus's. He does nothing, but I can feel the tension until Magnus lowers his eyes and his head, and with his tongue, Eudemos cleans away the blood that I with my blue paper towel could not.

Benison. A blessing, a benediction. 3, 1, 1...9 with a double-word score...18.

When he is done, Eudemos pushes his head under Magnus's chin resting on my thigh, thumping him once, twice, three times until Magnus starts to hobble up, awkward and stumbling. He turns to look at me but underestimates the length of his muzzle and bops me in the eye.

The forest twinkles with the green lights of wolves' eyes gathering closer as Magnus struggles toward them. As he swings his head back toward me, his eyes are a little closer than the rest but in all other ways the same. Glowing green in the dark.

Trusting neither the steadiness of my voice or my smile, I lift my hand. Then all the green lights turn and the wolves close around him.

I stare at the matted boughs for a long time.

Chapter 13

Evie

I watch Constantine, sitting against the beech tree, his knees bent, one hand raised as though waiting for the wolf to return. He never will, or rather he will, but he won't be anything like the Magnus he knew.

"Have you had dinner?"

"No," he says, still looking in the direction where Magnus and Eudemos and the 14th disappeared. "Not really." He gets up and brushes off his pants, trying to seem casual.

"Neither have I. Come."

He hadn't gone far from the Great Hall, just far enough to carry his wolf into the wild. It's pitch-black now and he relies too much on his eyes. I can tell by the way his hesitant pace picks up as soon as he catches a glimpse of the soft glow spilling from the kitchen window.

The dishes have been washed and put away, and the counters are cleaned except for big bowls of bread dutifully rising under towels made from flour sacks.

"You okay with cereal?" I ask, setting my coffee cup down on the table. It's a big one with a blood-spattered moon, howling-wolf silhouette, and the words *Lone Wolf* in clawed bloodred letters.

"Anything."

I reach for a yellow box on a high shelf. My shirt rides

up, I know because I feel the summer cool through the window rolling across the groove of my spine and the softness of my belly, and when I turn back, Constantine looks stricken or caught out or something. He drops his eyes to his hands splayed out on the table.

"Bowls are in the cabinet nearest the door. Spoons are in the drawers to the left of the sink." He opens the door to the cabinet and peers in for far longer than is needed to get two bowls from the random hundreds of them we have.

I get out the milk and close the refrigerator door with a flick of my hip. Constantine busies himself gathering the spoons, then putting them on the table along with the two mismatched bowls.

As I open the box, he switches the bowls, taking away the one that is a scratched remnant of a huge cache of beige industrial porcelain and pushing toward me another one with gold-green interior like the striations of an iris.

I wait for an explanation, but he doesn't give one.

"Weetabix are for wolves," I say, surprising myself.

"What?"

"Something a friend used to say." John. John was the friend who used to say it, but I still find it hard to say his name. "It always made him laugh. I have no idea why."

"It's kind of funny," he says.

"Is it? Wolves find humor difficult to understand."

"I don't want to mislead you. It's not really funny, but it is odd."

I put two ovals of what looks like particleboard into each bowl. "I only ever take two. They get soggy otherwise."

Then I pour the milk. He seems to be watching my

arm, where the muscles overlap, rather than the milk over the particleboard in his beige industrial bowl. "Say when."

"When," he says.

I stop and screw the lid back on.

He breaks the biscuits up with the side of his spoon and looks through the window.

"When I was sitting with him," he says, "Eudemos came and cleaned Magnus's feet. The thing is I've only ever seen Eudemos human—"

"*In skin.*"

"In skin. Yes. I'd only ever seen him in skin. I'd never seen him as a wolf. But I knew who he was."

"And you're wondering how."

"Yes. I guess."

"Humans think that what is *seen* is all that is. That what is spoken is all that is said. But wolves know that life happens in the very crowded spaces between what is seen and what is spoken." My spoon scrapes against the side of the bowl. "Ælfrida, the first Alpha, almost lost a wolf to the witch trials in Boston because he knew things that couldn't be seen. She taught the Pack to be much more careful after that."

I hold up the yellow box. He shakes his head. "I'm good," he says.

"You recognized Eudemos the same way you recognized Magnus. Just because you don't see something doesn't mean it's not real."

Sealing up the box, I put it back on a shelf of them.

"I think you are wilder than you like to admit, than you feel is right for a Shifter."

"Lukani. We don't use Shifter. It's like 'werewolf' for us."

I scrape up the few last flakes in the bottom of my bowl. "What does it mean?"

"Lukani? Nothing. Not that I know of anyway. It's just the name of a tribe in southern Italy that we're theoretically descended from."

"So that's why you all have Roman names."

"*We* don't have Roman names. *Romans* had Lukani names. Romulus and Remus were Lukani; the wolf was their mother." He drinks down the last of the milk. "Rhea Silvia, they called her: Villainess of the Woods."

"Villainess?"

"Because she was a wolf, of course."

I don't exactly laugh, but I chortle, which is more than I've done since John died and I became Alpha and wolves no longer saw me but the Symbol of Pack Endurance.

Symbols of Pack Endurance do not chortle.

Constantine looks at me, smiling like a wolf settling in, waiting to coax something from its burrow, but I know exactly what happens to things coaxed out of burrows by wolves.

"You wash, I'll dry," I say, picking up the bowls and spoons.

He picks up my coffee cup.

"Leave it there," I say. "I'm still working on it."

"It's pretty cold."

"My coffee is always cold." I take a sip before setting it beside the sink.

Pushing his sleeves above his elbows, he squeezes soap on a brush hanging from a hook on the wall. I shake out a towel. The window in front of us gives out onto the trees. Like all the windows of the Great Hall, it is open and the lungs of the forest pull air out, then breathe it back filled with cool and damp and balsam and fern and the murmurs and shuffles and yelps. He moves slowly, each circle coming close to my arm, not touching but heating the air between us long enough for me to miss it when it's gone and anticipate its return like a breath, a breeze, the beat of a heart.

I pull my arm away.

"Do you think Magnus will be happier?" He hands me the bowl with no change of expression.

Staring out the window, I rub it dry.

"Do you think he'll be—" He starts again.

"I heard you. I was thinking."

When I finish, I hang the towel over the bar of the upper oven.

"Happiness seems like a luxury when you are trying to survive. But Magnus will belong and that is something. And that will not change."

Staring out the window above the sink, the Shifter raps his knuckles absently against his chest with a slow and hollow beat.

Tock.

Tock.

Tock.

I pick up the big novelty coffee mug, tilt it back, and finish the icy dregs inside. I look at it for a while, at its blood-spattered moon, at its lone wolf.

"This"—I turn the thing upside down—"is empty."

He looks at me, his brow drawn. He holds out his hand to wash it.

I slam it against the edge of the sink and it explodes into fragments.

"It's not empty now."

He stares at the black handle in my hand. I set it on the counter, brushing a few bits from my arm, then retrieve the wooden brush and dinged black dustpan from under the sink and begin sweeping the black and red and white pieces into the dustpan.

I dump the shards in the trash.

“Always hated that cup,” I say, sliding brush and dustpan back under the sink.

Chapter 14

Constantine

I HATE THAT SHE HAD TO WALK ME BACK TO THE dormitory like one more thing she has to take care of.

"Someone will pick you up in the morning," she says, and when she turns away, I almost call after her. I would except I can't bear to hear another querying "Alpha?" even if it's in my own voice.

She walks off without hesitating through the dark and the trees, and I wonder how she can possibly see where she's going.

"Humans think that what is *seen* is all that is. That what is spoken is all that is said. But wolves know that life happens in the crowded spaces between what is seen and what is spoken."

I turn on the lights and then turn them off again. Without the lights, the shadow of a moon-framed tree still seeps through and sways back and forth across the floor. I walk across the dark room, trying to feel the way the floor settles, listen to the echoes of wind against the walls, smell the rhythm of slightly musty bedding interrupted by the scent of slightly musty pine needles on the forest floor.

Taste the new toothpaste the Alpha promised.

Ah. Liver.

I rinse my mouth and brush again with water, then look at the dark silhouette of my head in the mirror.

Someone will pick you up in the morning.

That was what Drusilla said to her brother the day she left. She'd stood in the doorway, everything about her stiff and perfect as she held her compact and outlined her mouth in dark red. Her hand shook, and her lower lip sprouted a bloodred barb. She didn't bother wiping it away.

Behind her, the driver waited with her suitcases. She was leaving but she gave Otho one day to choose. His sister or August.

The next morning, Drusilla's driver came to fetch him, but Otho stayed with August. It was his only choice. Still, he had seen something in his sister's face that made him afraid. Over the years, Otho had made himself a master of situational awareness, though he died in the end by his sister's hand.

People who don't know think situational awareness means being aware of everything, which is just bullshit. It's a total focus on things that matter—cover points, ambush positions, escape routes, weapons of opportunity, the stress tolerance of men—and a complete filtering out of things that don't.

The problem is, Homelands is nothing *but* the things that don't matter. Rocks and trees and birds and mud and bushes and weeds and things that slither between the bushes and weeds.

Wolves know that life happens in the crowded spaces between what is seen.

Closing the door behind me, I step out into the forest stark and grim and all the things I cannot see.

"I was supposed to pick you up from the dormitory."

"As you can see, I found my way here."

I don't tell Ziggy how much time I spent wandering around completely and utterly lost before finding my way back to the cabin or that I woke up to the sound of a bird that sounded like a rusty swing—*Whe-heee. Whe-heee. Whe-heee*—and spent the next hour finding my way to the Great Hall, a walk that has taken ten minutes when accompanied by the Alpha.

"So," he says, sitting next to me, dropping a plate piled high with green eggs. "I got to ask you: Do you know Leo Fafard?"

Ziggy turns out to be very talkative for a wolf. He is also desperately curious and desperately clueless about Offlands, which includes every place that is not the Great North's territory. In Ziggy's impaired imaginings, Offlands is about the size of Delaware, populated entirely by a quirky subsection of celebrity.

"Should I?"

"He was the star of *WolfCop*," he says.

"So you're saying he's an actor."

"I'm saying he was the *star* of *WolfCop*," he repeats with an excess of emphasis.

"I met Idris Elba in the bathroom at Citizen in Toronto."

"Unh-unh," he says and continues to push his green eggs onto a fork with a piece of dark bread.

"And Meryl Streep in Croatia."

He looks thoughtfully into the distance. One eye has a deformed iris and a cloudy pupil and I'm guessing is blind.

"Who are they?"

"Actual actors."

"Never heard of them. What have they been in?"

I spread apple butter on the thick buttered pancakes.

This meal, I discover from the chatty starstruck werewolf, is called Day Meat. There is one other meal called Evening Meat. In between, there are beavers, muskrats, voles (woodland and red-backed), lemmings, woodchucks.

In other words, breakfast, dinner, and rodents.

"So you're telling me that neither Evening Meat nor Day Meat have any meat at all?"

"You mean carrion?" Ziggy says.

"Not carrion. Meat. Like bacon. I'd kill for some bacon." I break open a hot biscuit and slather it with blueberry jam. "You do see the irony here."

"No, I don't. You may call old flesh you haven't hunted 'meat' but *we* call it carrion."

The Alpha's voice precedes her down the hall. She is accompanied by two men. One in a suit walks beside her with a tablet. She listens for a moment before signing the tablet with her finger. Another man—tall, with a stringy, dark-blond beard that he combs repeatedly with his fingers—leans into the back of her neck, his nose under her hair.

As I turn away, feeling suddenly irritable, Ziggy rustles the paper, positioning it in front of his whole eye.

"What happened to your face?" I ask, circling one finger around my own eye and cheekbone. "Looks like you were hit with a 12 gauge."

"It wasn't a 12 gauge; it was a 12 pointer. And it really—"

"Oh, by the moon, Sigegeat," a woman groans from the table behind us.

"He *asked*," Ziggy snaps. "As I was saying, that deer"—he hesitates again like a carnival barker sizing up the crowd—"really bucked up my eye."

A combination of groans and growls circulates around the room, and I find myself laughing at Ziggy's high hopes for such a low joke.

"See, he likes it," Ziggy says, "and he knows Idris Alba and somebody else famous." He raises his chin dismissively at the rest of the room before turning to me and muttering that "Wolves have no sense of humor."

"Sigegeat," says the Alpha.

Every eye and ear turns toward her, standing at the coffee urn. It's bad enough that a hundred wolves watch everything she does and everything she says, but now she has Stringy Beard sniffing her personal space like a dog at a fire hydrant.

She makes a motion with her hand like a hammer striking a nail, though when she pulls back her fist with the imaginary hammer, she punches Stringy Beard in the cheek.

Then she turns to pour herself coffee with the trace of a grim smile.

Something about the hammer made Ziggy take off, and for a man with one eye and no depth perception, he is fucking fast. No matter how often I tell him to slow down, he doesn't until my heel slides down a moss-covered rock and I twist my ankle in the stones gathered at the base of a meandering stream.

"Who was that with the Alpha?" I ask when he comes back to get me.

"I don't know. There's always someone with the Alpha."

"It was a big guy with curly, dark-blond hair and a stringy beard."

"I don't know. What does he smell like?"

"How the hell should I know what he smells like? He's

got curly, dark-blond hair and a stringy beard and he had his nose stuck in the Alpha's neck the entire morning."

"S'gotta be Poul, Alpha of the 10th Echelon. Can't you move any faster?"

"No, I can't. And *why* did Poul, Alpha of the 10th Echelon, have his nose stuck in her neck the entire morning?"

"He does it all the time," he says, motioning to me to get moving. "He's checking to see if she's receptive."

"What do you mean 'receptive'?"

"For *cunnan*. Fucking."

I'd watched Poul follow her to the coffee urn, so close that he stepped on her heel. She'd done nothing, just leaned against a table and pulled up the sock bunched at her ankle. Still, her mouth was tight and her eyes hard, and she looked nothing like last night when I saw something, an openness, even a hint of recklessness.

"And does she want him?"

"'Want' has nothing to do with it. It'll be many moons before she'll be fertile again, but whenever it happens"—he waits for me to clear a toppled tree—"she will take him because strong wolves mate with strong wolves to make stronger wolves. Almost there," he says, pointing to a gap in the trees.

"What's the point of being Alpha if you don't get to do what you want?"

"The *point*, Shifter, is that when the Alpha speaks, the Pack follow immediately, not just because she's strong but because she has the willingness to sacrifice. Wolves have to know that their Alphas won't go letting what they *want* get in the way of what the Great North *needs*."

The clearing opens onto a long, low hall with a patchwork peaked roof of gray and beige shingles.

"I hope Sten hasn't locked the door," Ziggy says, and I try to remember where I heard that name.

This place is less like a workshop than a cathedral to wood. Light streams in from clerestory windows tucked high under the eaves and at either gabled end. Instead of pews, there are workbenches with massive vises. Instead of featuring stained glass and ex-votos, the walls are decorated with collections of wood and metal tools, carefully curated into things that cut, things that bang, things that carve, and things that smooth. The altar wall is built-in pigeonhole storage filled with rolled papers.

And officiating over it is Sten.

I have never seen Sten—never heard any description of him. All I know is the fear in Tiberius's voice and that is enough. The Great North are enormous, but the man who thumps toward us is a giant even among them. He wears what I can only imagine is an XXXXL and TALL that still strains across his chest. Carhartts that had been golden brown but are faded to beige and splotched with wood stain and teak oil. His hair is powdered with sawdust, and he smells like creosote and linseed.

He is carrying two hammers. One is a mallet that looks like a mailbox atop a flagpole but is made out of wood and bears the scars of many banged things.

The other is the cross peen hammer I'd used to crush teeth. This he holds in front of him like a crosier.

But you're going to tell Sten about the hammer.

The other wolves move back while Sten stalks toward me, twirling the mailbox around like an ancient wrathful god of mead and/or smiting.

"*Swines tord,*" says Ziggy and steps away.

With a sigh, I stand back, watching Sten come.

Dominant leg. Patterns. The range of his swing and the drop at the end of it. Wasted energy. The catch in his left shoulder. Then I remember the little piece of pink paper that, in all the confusion, I'd forgotten to give to Ziggy. I pat at my jeans before finding it in my breast pocket.

Sten stops in front of me, bending his head to look at the pink note sticking to my finger. His mallet drops to the floor with a thud; it stands by itself, handle upright. Sten takes the note from me, caressing it tenderly with his thumb, then he turns the paper and reads it. Ziggy looks over his arm, angling his head so he can see it with his one whole eye.

Sten's anger deflates like air from a slashed inner tube. He sniffs the note, then slides it into his chest pocket, patting it reverently.

"Door," he says, in his first word of the day.

A wolf hurries over to slide a thick bolt into steel brackets, a blunt and impassable blockage.

Sten heads back, putting the offending cross peen hammer in its place on the wall and swinging his cudgel. He rummages through the pigeonholes.

"What did it say?" I ask Ziggy.

"You didn't read it?"

"I did, but except for the word 'benches,' I didn't understand anything."

"Henh," he says with a curious nod that could have meant anything. "She wrote '*Genog med bitli,*'" he says with a chuckle. "Means 'Enough with the hammer.'"

Sten returns with a roll of paper and sets it on a huge pile of two-by-fours at the front. He swings his mallet in a fast arc that ends in a dainty tap on the paper, then says what I discover will be his last word of the day: "Bench."

Within seconds, the wolves are gathered around the two-by-fours, rolling out the piece of paper. One runs to get pencils from a container; another levels and tape measures. I watch them, heads together, drawing calculations and angles on the wood.

I keep looking toward Sten, waiting for… I'm not sure what I'm waiting for, but more. I'm used to August, who gave very long and very detailed directions toward an outcome only he knew. Take this duffel to this place at this time. Do not talk to anyone. An iced-mocha metallic Lincoln Continental will be parked on the southwest corner. A man with the tattoo of a raven's claw on his cheek and a black Tom Selleck mustache will be at the northeast corner. If he is not there already, do not wait. If he is there with anyone else, kill the other person or people but keep the duffel bag.

Sten is like Bizarro August. He wants an outcome that is "bench." The materials and blueprint and tools are there; the rest is up to us.

Ziggy points me to the bucksaw across from another wolf who introduces herself as Kristin, the Delta mate. I have never used a saw, not on wood at least, but how hard can it be?

As soon as the two-by-four slides into place, I notice the blood spatter. Now that is firmly within my field of expertise. I can tell the difference between arterial spray, expirated spatter, transfer patterns. How blood that's been loosed by a pool cue looks as opposed to blood from a knife wound.

"You do know what that is?" I point out the various browned smudges and drops.

Ziggy jots something down on the wood's edge. "What I know is that it is good sturdy wood—" He uses his pencil to tap a two-by-four with each word. Good [*tap*] sturdy [*tap*] wood [*tap*]. "And that with enough time, the asses of wolves will erase the blood of their hunters."

As soon as he tightens the clamp keeping the wood in place, Kristin pulls the bucksaw and I stumble forward, stirring up a light sprinkling of sawdust. She waits, her eyebrow raised, for me to regain my footing, and I pull back hard.

The saw sticks until Kristin unsticks it. I'm doing something wrong because whenever I pull, it sticks. Eventually, the piece doesn't so much fall off as gives up, tearing at an awkward angle.

Kristin calls for another wolf.

With a sigh and a pitying look, Ziggy hands me some already-cut pieces and tells me to hammer them together like so.

The nail bends with the first blow.

"Not so hard," says the wolf at the next bench.

I yank it back out with the claw and start again. I was good at my job. I manipulated markets, altered outcomes of elections, imported large quantities of goods without interference, took lives that no one imagined could be taken. *I fucking made the world safer for cabba—*

I did it! I look around to see if anyone notices how smooth and even and secure this nail is, but no one else is paying attention. I'll show them that I can make bench. Not just bench, but a bench that is sturdy enough and strong enough to support even the lead weight of the Great North.

Time seems to speed by, though without my phone, I can't be sure. Then Sten heads to the door, puts his cudgel head down on the floor, and proceeds to strip down to his unabashed hairy nakedness, hanging his clothes from the top of the handle.

Within seconds, the rest of the wolves have followed him outside, leaving me alone except for clothes hanging haphazardly from hooks or dropped to the floor. When they come back, they are as naked as when they left except for the odd bits of fur or sap. One of them snaps at another, and blood flows from the cartilage of his ear. Kristin interrupts her discussion of the mouth feel of summer mink to lick it clean, then rubs her face against him.

Dressed and back at the worktable next to me, Ziggy burps. "Goose," he says, punching his chest.

Days pass this way, marked by benches and belches. Each day, they get better—the benches, that is; the belches have already reached their pinnacle—until one day when they are all out at lunch. I have been working on this particular bench slowly for two days, making sure that it is sturdy and steady. I hand plane the grain ends, then burnish them with 320 grit sandpaper until the whole thing is smooth. Into its underside, I burn a fish with an open caudal fin that is supposed to be an *α*.

At the end of each day, we march our benches back to the Great Hall, ready for wolfish asses to scour bloodstains away, until like cockroaches and tardigrades, the benches outlive us all.

Today nobody notices that I put mine at the head of the 7th's table like a throne for the Alpha on the odd occasion when she does finally sit.

Chapter 15

Evie

So far I haven't heard the sound the perimeter wolves warned me about. The machines came for two days, they said, then disappeared again. We hoped they were gone for good, but when they showed up last night, Leonora theorized that they had been celebrating the weekend, the two days out of every seven that humans put aside for mischief.

If that is true, she says, then they should return tonight as well.

The lawyers are not optimistic. It's not our land, they say, and since *our* land is "unimproved," nothing that lives here has any legal right to complain.

Not the frogs at Clear Pond, or the beavers or the deer or the coyotes or the big horned owl or the little saw-whet. Not the rabbits loudly warning one another about the presence of wolflings.

"Pups these days." I lean back against the birch trees. "Did we ever *not* know how to hunt bunnies?"

In the distance, a door slams. Something large and fast begins moving this way. The pups go silent, hiding until Gran Jean signals the all clear.

There's nothing to worry about except the clumsiness of their bunny hunting.

The Shifter stands at the tree line to the south. He

turns his head like he's searching for a noise. I wait, silent, my hand protecting the smooth bone beside me.

"Alpha?" he says, jogging barefoot over the long grass. He gestures toward Clear Pond and the windblown roots and lumpy hillocks that are home to a thriving rabbit colony. "Didn't you hear it?"

"Didn't I hear what?"

"It sounded like a pup screaming."

"It wasn't a pup. The pup was hunting. A rabbit was screaming."

"A rabbit? Rabbits don't... Rabbits scream?"

"Hmm. Watch where you're stepping."

He freezes, looking down to where my hand lies protectively over the skull that has been stripped of fur and skin by the passage of time and beetles. Bleached bright and white as a mushroom, John's razored teeth and hollow eyes stand out in sharp relief against the dark ground and the shadow of my fingers. Grass has grown up between his jaws.

The Shifter steps back.

"Is that..."

"John. My mate."

Constantine hadn't been here. I know because every Shifter who came that night is dead, killed by wolves or by Tiberius. A single human escaped, though he left half his face in Silver's mouth.

"Your mate," he repeats distractedly.

"Yes. He was killed here. Then the coyotes ate him."

The Shifter begins to slide down against the smooth, speckled bark of an alder, then stops at an awkward halfway point.

"Do you mind?"

I shake my head and he slides the rest of the way down.

"I am," he says and hesitates, pulling his knees up and away from the damp ground, "sorry."

I pluck a blade of sweetgrass from between John's jaws, hoping that I do not disturb his running through the *Endemearc*, the wolves' last hunting ground.

"I've never understood the word 'sorry.' It seems to mean both regret for something you have done and sympathy for something over which you have no control. Regret and pity. To us, it seems either you have power over your actions, in which case 'sorry' is a poor excuse, or you have no power, in which case 'sorry' is unnecessary."

"What is this?" he says, twirling a blade of grass between his fingers.

"That is cottongrass. It's nothing. This"—I hand him the fragrant stems—"is sweetgrass. Wolves like it. Settles the stomach."

He takes it from me and bites down tentatively.

"Do you have a mate?" I ask, and he barks out a sharp laugh.

"No."

Another piece of sweetgrass between my teeth, I try to remember my human behaviors classes. I was still a juvenile when it became clear that John and I would be an Alpha pair—and eventually *the* Alpha pair—and would never need more than the most rudimentary understanding of human courtship rituals.

"Is it because you are not decorative enough?"

When he coughs, his breath is the heady green of summer.

"I'm plenty decorative," he says as soon as the coughing stops. "It's handsome, by the way. Pillows are decorative, men are—I am—handsome." He straightens his spine, rolls his shoulders back, then stretches out one leg, bending his foot so his thigh tenses. His eyes shoot to mine to see if I notice.

Of course I've noticed that his shoulders are broader, his thighs stronger, his ass tauter. The hollows under his eyes and between his hip bones have filled out. His skin is gold, his hair is longer, tousled after his run through the woods and peppered with leaves and twigs, making him look like the Grenemann, the Green Man, the dangerous protector of forests.

I rub my hand against the smooth bone. John never felt dangerous. My earliest memories of my time with the Great North are intertwined with memories of him. We were inevitable: the two strongest wolves doing what was expected of the strongest wolves since Pack first left the Ironwood.

The thing I miss most of all is the utter lack of doubt that was his inheritance. John was descended from wolves who'd spent 350 years coddled by Homelands' sanctuary. I am not. I have known doubt and I have known fear. The fear of making a decision, the fear of being wrong, the fear of others paying the price, the fear of being the last Alpha of the last pack of the last wolves.

Wait… Is that it? Sitting upright, I focus my attention on the gap between the High Pines and Westdæl and the sound coming up a distant road, like the whine of giant mosquitoes.

"What is it?"

I've forgotten the name of the machine.

"It's, umm…" I rotate both fists forward in the air.

"ATVs?"

"Yes, ATVs. They like to drive them in the mud of the land up north. They come now and ride around at night, but they are very loud and they worry V...the Gray. The forever wolves." My voice hitches. "I want them gone."

He looks toward Westdæl, running his fingers through his hair. Strand by strand, he plucks away a stick, a seed, a leaf, a needle, a burr, until all the traces of the Grenemann are gone.

Don't.

But I don't stop him, because I know *he* was the one who tore the north lands apart, and all the sticks and stems and seeds and samaras in the world will not turn him into a fierce protector of the forest.

"Alpha," he starts, pauses, then starts again. "That land was muddy before we cleared the trees, but afterward, it became almost impassable. We had to put in culverts and drains or we wouldn't have been able to get in. I know where they are—the culverts—and if we took them out, used them to block the access roads, I would bet it'd become impassable again."

Somewhere high in the icy ether, an invisible airplane leaves contrails across the starlit sky.

"You're not going to escape."

He shrugs. "What's the point of escaping if I don't have some place to escape to? I've crossed hundreds of borders working for August so I know it takes more than crossing borders to make a man free."

It's hard for me to even imagine what it's like crossing hundreds of borders. *This* is my place. Wolves don't travel more than a day's drive from pack territory, but it makes the Pack nervous if the Alpha is away too long, which means I've rarely been farther than Plattsburgh.

"Do you miss her?" he suddenly asks.

"Who?"

"Varya."

"Of course not. She is still here." I brush my hands against my jeans; Francesca and Lorin are probably waiting for me already. "And still as much a member of the Great North as she was when I could talk to her."

Constantine pushes himself off the ground, his back scraping up against the tree. He holds out his hand to me, but I don't need his help. Coiling the muscles in my thighs, I raise myself with no help from ground or tree or Shifter.

He stays with his hand extended when a light breeze rolls down from Westdæl, blowing his hair across his cheekbone. A scent that I would have caught easily if I'd been wild is hard to make out with this nose. It is faint and muddied by the fading carrion and steel and burned-over ash. Without thinking, I move closer and breathe in deeply and remember the winter we ate too many deer and the spring when the undergrowth grew unchecked and the dry summer when the hiker made a fire with cottonwood that sparked and snapped.

We didn't tell him "Stop" because we couldn't. We just ran for our lives, followed by everything that was fast enough and the cries of everything that wasn't.

Eventually, the fire ended and the rains started, and not long after, tiny mounds of bright green sprouted tender and tentative on the puddled gray earth, the smell of water and green life and resilience and hope.

He doesn't move as I breathe it in again and again until that sound like a giant mosquito whines louder and reverberates through the gap between the High Pines and Westdæl. Even Constantine hears it. I know because I feel his stubbled jaw brush against my cheek as he turns to listen.

"Let me help," he whispers next to my ear. "If not for you, for Varya."

In the night, the bright-green streaks of his eyes fade into the pine dark. He moves closer. I look down at his mouth, feeling his breath against my cheek.

"Alpha?" calls a voice from across the Clearing.

I jerk back and only just manage to sidestep John's skull before I break into a run toward Francesca. Tiberius was right. Constantine is dangerous, and if I'm not careful, I will forget who I am.

Using calculations based on blackfly and moon phases and bank holidays, we finally settle on a date for Francesca and Lorin's braiding. After they go, I take advantage of the night quiet to make myself a cup of tea and finish up a few things tucked in a battered manila folder on my desk before heading outside.

Why is the 14th so close to the Great Hall? Prey is sparse here. Eudemos sits alert and watching on the bench carved from a fallen tree trunk decades ago. His Epsilon, Geir, drops down with his legs splayed out in front, hindquarters shivering in anticipation. As soon as Eawynn races up to him, he leaps into the air and comes down on top of her, playfully nipping her muzzle.

Then he flops onto his back, shimmying back and forth. Eventually, he stills, his head angled back, looking up to the star-strewn sky; his bedfellow takes his throat between her sharp teeth and strong jaws for a wolf's kiss that means *I know how vulnerable you are and I would never hurt you.*

As soon as the door closes behind me, wolves who are drinking from Home Pond look up, silvery drops clinging to their muzzles. Eudemos doesn't look, but his ear pivots, following me as I head to the bench. When I fold my legs under me, the 14th's Alpha lowers his head and scuttles forward just enough to squeeze his nose under my crossed thigh.

We sit watching our wolves, including the dark-gray one with the pale-blue eyes sitting next to the man with the broad back at the end of the dock. Even from here, I can see that Magnus is doing better. His body has filled out, his fur gleams, and he moves without faltering. For the first time, I can see presenting him to my wolves and asking them to decide whether he brings strength to the Pack.

Constantine stirs the water with his feet, rippling the moonlit surface of Home Pond and making the tall grasses at the shoreline whisper—*shwuh, shwuh, shwuh*—while he scratches at Magnus's withers. I sip at my cold tea until Eudemos stretches out his forelegs and jumps down, announcing that it is time to go.

Slowly, he lopes toward the forest, drawing the 14th away from tree line, water, and dock to join him.

I am content to sit in silence, embraced by the sound of summer water and summer leaves and the scent and feel of damp wood until it is time to exchange my skin for fur and run to Westdæl for my nightly check on the Gray. I stand up, shaking my jeans loose from where they are caught on my calf.

Then I hear something. Two syllables I haven't heard for a long time, at least not said with such tenderness.

"I remembered," he says. "I finally remembered your name."

As I stumble up, my legs heavy and bloodless, he says it again in a whisper across the water.

"Evie."

Chapter 16

Constantine

Do you have a mate?

Why did I laugh when she asked me that? It's a perfectly rational question. Is there someone who is going to come looking for you? Is there someone you dream of escaping to?

There were some who tried to convince me: The one who glanced coyly at advertisements for engagement rings. And the one who cooed endlessly at babies. Then there was that blond with the grating habit of sharing real estate listings for little houses on little squares of grass on little cul-de-sacs inhabited by little women growing littler each day, staring blankly through the delft-pattern curtains.

Gnawing on raw tongue as they dreamed of a forest stark and grim.

Each time, my throat grew tight at the sight of them. I couldn't bear to hear their voices; even their texts made my skin crawl. Sometimes they would come to the compound inquiring after my health, and August told them women were not allowed here, slammed the door, and looked at me with a sly smile. One player to another.

August thought he understood everything, but one thing I knew that he never did, was be afraid of women made small.

I no longer walk to Carpentry. Instead, I run, chased by a ravenous black cloud that cuts away skin and teethes on blood. Every morning, Inga waits by the door, ready for the last of the echelon to run in. By the time Sten shouts "Door!" Inga has already slammed the bolt into place against wolves from other echelons who pound on the stout door. Through the window, I see blood streaming down their pleading faces.

"Sten!" they scream, leaving scarlet handprints on the glass.

Sten walks slowly toward the door, picking at his teeth with a splinter, and pulls down the sun-bleached green shade.

Blackfly season is here.

No amount of blood or screaming convinces Sten, but a few days later, Sten himself runs to the front, flicking the thick plank to the floor like a twig. He stands looking eagerly through the trees, one foot tapping excitedly on the floor. I crane my neck, seeing her moving fast and unhurried like a hand through water.

"Shifter?" Järv says, waiting for me to pull at the bucksaw that had defeated me when I first came to Homelands. Now, I work at holding my back so my spine doesn't seize up. I know how to pull and stretch out, taking from Järv on the other side and relaxing when he takes from me.

The Alpha steps in, peels off the deep hoodie, and shakes out her hair. She motions Ziggy and Sten to the side, whispering something to them. Ziggy answers, looking at me. Then Sten tilts his head to the side, a wide-eyed, expectant look on his face. The Alpha lightly taps the mallet he holds in front of him. Sten puts it down quickly and bends low toward his Alpha. He shivers, but when the Alpha leans in, her hand to his skull, and rubs her cheek gently against one side then the other, Sten—gruff, monosyllabic, hammer-smiting Sten—sighs contentedly. The Alpha lets him stay, snuggling and snuffling into her touch, until he is done and heads back to his table. He does it with a smile, his mallet swinging jauntily at his side.

Taking the stretch of elastic wrapped twice around her wrist, the Alpha smooths back her hair, first one side, then the other, securing it with the band so that it spreads out like a halo around her face.

The fucking blackfly got her. They're not bloodsuckers like mosquitos; they are flesh tearers, opening up the skin to get at the blood underneath. Blood runs down from the side of her forehead to her jaw.

She stands behind Järv, who relinquishes his spot, his eyes lowered. Taking a deep breath, the Alpha rolls out her shoulders, stretches her neck, curls her hands securely around the wooden grip, and lifts her eyebrows toward me.

Are you ready?

My fingers loosen and curl tighter around the smooth wooden handle. I pull.

She pulls back hard. I don't know why she is here and no one else is asking. Maybe she does this sometimes, takes a little break to be just one of the Pack. After a few more furious drags, I wonder if it's something else. Some visceral need to do something physical. To pull and tear and smell the scent of sawdust warmed by the friction.

Wordlessly, Järv slides wood into place for us. Equally wordlessly, Ziggy picks up the pieces as they fall.

As we pull at each other, it's like a conversation without words. *Are you strong enough? Yes. Yes I am. I don't know for what. But yes.*

She pulls and I give. She gives and I pull. A slight cramping builds along the inside of my shoulder blade. I drag her arms toward me, she drags my arms back. I watch her body move, coiling and uncoiling, muscle and sinew tracing graceful arabesques along her arm and her shoulder.

Wood drops to the floor with a hollow *thunk* until the slight cramping is a solid agony, but I refuse to stop. If what she needs is to take her anger and turn it into work, I will keep going until something burns.

Yes, I am strong enough for anything.

A gilding of sawdust picks out the damp between her breasts and mingles with the blood that drains along her jawbone and down the side of her neck to her collarbone. Black scars peek out from the narrow strap at her shoulder.

I've seen other bite marks on other wolves in the Bathhouse. I've seen males bend over females in the woods. Her scars are old, given to her by John when he was a man. Each tug on the bucksaw makes my body respond to hers. What kind of shit am I to look at the faded marks left by her dead mate and think about the feel of her skin against mine, licking the marks at her neck like I could erase them with my tongue.

Suddenly, she stops. Taking a thin, clean rag from one of the small piles of them used to wipe sweat or stain or excess wood glue, she wipes off the sawdust, still looking at me quizzically. She drags the sweatshirt back on, pulling the hood up high, the sleeves down low. Then she thrusts her hands deep into the front pockets. Järv opens the door and she exits quickly, heading in the direction of the Great Hall and her office and whatever thing waiting for her there that is more maddening than the swarms of blackfly.

Unwrapping my blistered hands from the grip, I head to the window. She's already gone, leaving nothing behind but a rippling of leaves and branches in her path.

That and half a dozen idiot wolves banging one another's backs while they bend over, howling with laughter.

"*What's so funny?*"

Ziggy rubs his hands on his pants, then rubs his tearing eyes and taps his nose.

"You smell," he says, tapping his nose, "like a juvenile."

Shit. I bend my head to my armpit, inhaling a deep breath.

"Not there, Connie. *Here.*" And Ziggy cups both hands over the fly of his pants.

I look down at the heavy salute straining against my zipper.

Then a terrible thing occurs to me about the Alpha's cocked head and questioning gaze.

"Do you think she…*knows*?" I whisper to Ziggy.

"You don't get to be Alpha if you don't know wolves."

"*But I'm not a wolf.*"

"If I smelled that smell on a turtle"—he slams the table with another hiccupped chuckle—"I would still know what was going on in his turtle brain and his turtle cock."

Oh god. I rub at my eyebrow and then my eye and then my mouth, staring out the window at the wall of green where she disappeared, her enigmatic smile now humiliatingly clear.

"Nothing to be embarrassed by. Every unmated male would cover the Alpha if he had the chance. But since only dominant males have that chance, most of us don't go all"—he makes a dismissive *tchck,* flipping his index finger high in the air—"all *oop-richte.* That's when"—he points to the bulge in my pants—"your penis is—"

"*I got it.*"

I'm grateful when Sten thumps his hammer on the floor. He doesn't do it hard, but the sheer weight of it vibrates through the floor and up into the table. Everyone stops and turns expectantly toward him. The problem is Sten is very good at getting everyone's attention but has no idea what to do with it once he has it.

He grunts at Ziggy.

"Rupf," says Ziggy, foundering around for where to start. "So we have to… I mean, the Alpha… Wait, no. So humans have these things up in the north," Ziggy starts.

"Humans have lots of things up north," Inga says.

"These things have wheels and are very loud on *weekends.*" He says *weekends* with a special preening emphasis like a child with a new word that none of his friends know.

"What's a weekend?" Järv asks, dubious.

I edge slowly away toward the far back corner of the room where there is a huge worktable with two big bench vises holding a massive plank.

And that is where I am, fly unzipped, rearranging my bent and aching penis, when Ziggy turns to me and asks me to explain weekends to a batch of curious werewolves.

They are all in my dormitory. Every single one of the 7th Echelon has come into the place I have come to think of as my own. They pick up everything—library books, clothes, toothbrush—and sniff at it.

Because of blackfly, we won't start work until after Evening Song, so the Alpha wanted us to get some sleep. Here. Which is why the entire echelon is sniffing and stripping.

Ziggy holds the tube of toothpaste to his good eye.

"I don't like the liver flavor," he says with a frown. "Tastes like—"

"Out. I'm taking a shower."

It doesn't matter that there is a passel of wolves separated by the thin door; I fist my cock as soon as I get into the shower. Leaning my forehead against the tile, I remember the amber fire of her eyes, the sawdust gathered in the curve leading down to her—

Evie.

I turn off the water, waiting for my breathing to slow as I watch the evidence of my release swirl away down the drain.

Stumbling out of the shower, I dry off while chewing on a Teeny Greeny Breath Fresh Teeth Treat. Dressed, my hair finger combed, I come back out to the wolves wild and gathered in a furry puddle on the floor.

Ziggy is chewing on the strip of birch bark I'd been using to mark my place in a thick tome about the Salem witch trials that I'd gotten from the lupine library. I lift my mattress, sending him scrabbling frantically to the floor along with my piled blankets, then I lie down, open the book, trying to remember where I'd left off reading the night before. Trying to ignore the shuffling and contented sighs of the wolves beside me.

I can't find my place.

Grabbing my pillow, I leave my book and lie down on the piled blankets on the floor. Beside me, jaws pop in a yawning whimper. Paws scrabble in hunting dreams against the wooden floor. The musty, musky smells of fur and wheezed wolf breath mix with the breezes and the rustling of leaves and calling of birds and the humming of crickets and all the lulling sounds of life being lived in summer.

After Evening Song, we load the trucks with shovels and picks and chains and start the long drive to undo what I spent so long doing.

I wasn't there when August bought this huge tract of land, but I was certainly there when Daniel Leary, August's human consigliere, passed a manila envelope to a state administrator. I stood silently behind Leary, my hand on the back of the commercial-grade chair, looking at a rust stain on the threadbare carpet. After Leary explained the need to speed along permissions and reports, the man hesitated.

They all do, the first time. My job was to raise my eyes when he hesitated. As soon as he saw the crumpled steel chair back, he slid the envelope into his desk drawer.

Then he began talking nonstop about area jobs and progress and improvements to the land. Like they all do.

The first time.

Ostensibly, everything was done to prepare for a pipeline from shale plays in Nova Scotia to points south. In reality, August wanted to tear a path into Homelands. He put me in charge of the human work crew, and when two of them had to be decommissioned, I drove the excavator that tore through the land at the edge of Homelands myself.

This was the last stretch we cleared. August didn't want the Great North knowing what was going on until it was too late to start the slow remedies of law and lobbying.

At the top of the access road, Ziggy pulls the truck to a stop. Wolf after wolf jumps down from the truck, hitting the ground with a heavy squelch. Since I was riding the hump, I am the last one out, landing next to a circle of dumbfounded Pack. Their backs are silvery in the headlights of the truck, long shadows stretching out across a field of mud, exposed stones, and wood chips. There is a deep, silty pond near the middle, left by the stump of a particularly big tree. A few more stubborn stumps remain: those we cut low, drilling in holes filled with potassium nitrate. A dead bird lies moldering near the roots of one.

I stare at the ruined desolation of muck and sawdust, all brown and gray except for that same muddied yellow excavator. The wind smells like rust and iron and diesel, like blood in a wound that will never clot.

Ziggy squats next to a sapling bent into the mud. When he tries to lift it, it snaps off in his big hand. He stares at it, distraught, then he strides toward the gap between the mountain to the west and the range to the north. It had been filled with loose rock until the very end. When the hunters were celebrating their upcoming trophies and the Great North lay helpless as the Iron Moon took hold, the excavator ripped open access to Homelands. The bearded devastation of Ziggy's face does nothing to disguise his heartbreak. I stand next to him, looking over the dark profile of Homelands like I had on that first night when it reminded me of my mother's warning about forests stark and grim.

"The Alpha said to wait for her," Ziggy says without looking at me. "She doesn't want us to start until she is here to watch over the forever wolves."

"I've never understood the purpose of the word 'sorry.'"

I feel just how small a word *sorry* is and I don't say it. Instead, I push up my sleeves and dig my fingers deep under the rough edge of a huge stone, ripping it from the dirt. Then I stumble toward the gap and drop it. That's all the 7th needed to wake them up from the shock, and soon they are all carrying small boulders, looking like the grainy school video of ants moving things many times their weight that I had watched back in the days when I assumed I was human.

As I drop another stone, I catch the Alpha watching us, her eyes glowing between the trees.

Sorry, sorry. Regrets and pity.

Then she turns away. I strain, listening vainly for any sound of her.

"Time to get started," Ziggy says, clapping the dirt from his hands. He starts barking out orders, making clear that he didn't become Gamma of the 7th based solely on his expertise in obscure werewolf movies.

We start with the pickaxes, digging a groove around the culvert so the claws of the excavator's bucket will be able to get a grip. I'd forgotten that we'd run out of the corrugated galvanized steel and been forced to use the much thicker steel gas pipes. I clamber into the excavator.

The cab has been sealed tight for weeks now and stinks of stale corn chips. In the storage box is a handful of beef sticks, grease seeping to the bottoms of their packages. A bottle in the door drink holder says Sprite but smells of cheap vodka. The key is under the safety beacon.

Turning it on, I dig around until the teeth of the bucket hit the culvert and the cab shimmies. Something bangs against the side window. At first I think it's a tree limb, but then it happens again, and when I stop, Ziggy opens the door and pulls himself up.

"They're coming."

"Who?"

"Listen," he says, hunched over. "Where's the passenger seat on this thing?"

"It's an excavator, Ziggy, not an Uber."

He folds his big body, filling up whatever airspace is in the cab, his ass jammed halfway out the window.

"*Go. Go. Go!*" he yells, gesturing down the access road.

I'm about to ask *Who?* again but then I hear it, the unmistakable roar of ATVs in the night. Not just one either. I twirl the seat around, lock it in, and bounce down the dirt road.

Three sets of lights bounce around wildly, the beams painfully bright in my eyes. Only when I see how fast they're coming do I turn on the forgotten twenty-inch light bar stretched along the top of the cab. How is it that I'd been working all this time in the dark and hadn't noticed?

With the light bar on, they see me. One ATV blasts on a custom horn that sounds like a fake siren. "I'll deal with this," Ziggy says.

"You?"

"I'm the Gamma. It's my responsibility," he says and he throws himself against the door. Something pops, metal clangs against metal, and his body falls to the ground, the door swinging drunkenly on its one remaining hinge.

"*Turn around!*" Ziggy shouts, waving his arms over

his head while jogging toward the lights. "There are no humans allowed."

Ah, shit, Ziggy. I kill the engine.

"What do you mean 'humans'?" says a man in a red-and-black pleather jacket and a helmet with an ogre's face that says *Gremlin*.

I reach for the beef stick and jump down.

"I mean no *other* humans." I can almost hear a stack of mimeographed printouts from some ancient human behaviors class blowing off the desk of Ziggy's brain.

"What my brother is trying to convey in his own inimitable way"—I start to peel the greasy plastic wrap from the shriveled brown rod—"is get the *fuck* off our property."

"This is your property?"

I take a bite from the stick, chewing slowly. I've eaten these before. Have they always tasted like aluminum? "I represent the owner."

"The owner's dead," says Gremlin, taking off his helmet. He pushes his hand through thinning blond hair stuck to his scalp.

"And Canadian," says a younger, watery-eyed version of Gremlin, as though being Canadian made August even less of a threat than death.

The third man takes off his helmet with red devil horns painted along the sides. He's about Gremlin's age but stockier. His face is a mask of broken blood vessels and there's a bruise across his cheekbone. All signs of the kind of man who indulges in macho posturing at bars in the minutes before last call.

Yips and soft barks come from the direction of the Great North's territory. The sound is so clear to me, but none of these men seem to be able to hear and suddenly all I want is to have them gone. I will not have them near Homelands.

I pop the tail end of the beef stick into my mouth, crumple up the empty plastic wrapper, and toss it into the Red Devil's ATV.

"*What the fuck?*" he yells, looking for the trash I threw onto his muck-covered floor.

He can't find it in the shadows. He turns around, tossing his jacket over the seat, and rolling up his sleeves. There is a tattoo of a skull with a tongue of fire.

The other two remove their jackets with the usual knee bouncing, pointless stretching, and air boxing of men who haven't spent their lives fighting and have no idea how tedious it is.

Ziggy moves beside me. I know he's fought—I've learned enough to know that's the way wolves move up in their echelons—but his fists are clenched around his thumb like a child, and I realize for all his size and power, he's probably never fought in skin.

"Hold back. You come if you see I need help," I say, knowing full well that I won't.

"What the hell happened to your face, freak?" the Red Devil shouts, pointing at Ziggy.

Ziggy steps back into the shadows, his hand to his cheek, and something inside snaps like a dry twig and kindles something I haven't felt for a long time. I feel it take root and burn, and then I lean into the fire of being angry.

Red Devil swings at me with his helmet, but helmets are bulky and Red Devil hadn't counted on air resistance, allowing me to hit him hard in the armpit. When his arm goes limp, I hit him in the temple with my elbow. There is a soft crack and he goes down.

"*Get the fuck up.*" I drag the unconscious man up from the ground, shaking him. Trying to force him to fight me because it was over too fast. I am only barely aware of the two other men coming behind me. I throw the Red Devil's prone body at them and, as they stumble back, crack the two Gremlins' heads together. I stride back over to the Red Devil, but Ziggy steps in front of me.

"That's enough," he says, grabbing my arm. "The Alpha will not have it. Killing humans just brings more humans. Help me toss them in the truck."

I help him toss them in the truck and drive them to the edge of the road. I soak them in cheap vodka as a finishing touch.

"What is a brother?" Ziggy asks on the way back.

"What?"

"A brother. You told them I was your brother. I don't know what it means."

"It means having the same mother and father."

"But we don't have the same mother and father."

"No, neither do Magnus and I. It was really just a way of warning them, in a way that humans would understand, that I would fight for you."

"Like Pack, then," he says.

Chapter 17

Evie

What does the Gray remember? It's not that I expect her to remember the Pack with its laws and hierarchies and histories. All I'm hoping for is some familiarity with my scent, some vague recollection of trust.

I can't afford to take any chances with our fragile understanding. Most every night since the Iron Moon, I have changed and run the perimeter of her territory, making sure the Bone Wolf's injury is healing. Those first few days, the Gray was preoccupied with her mate, so I herded a deer with a broken ankle toward Westdæl, a kind of wolfish Meals on Wheels.

Varya could have killed it with a sneeze, but I didn't know about the Gray until I heard her explode from the trees and take it down with a single jump. The smell of blood, the growl in the back of her throat as she started the laborious process of pulling it higher up into her territory where her mate was recovering.

The first two nights, I split my time between watching the Shifters and making sure the Pack understood these new boundaries. Now when I go up, I lie down somewhere nearby and sleep. I feel her watching me. It's not aggressive and not frightened, more curious, like she feels she knows me from somewhere but can't quite remember from where.

Tonight I hope she remembers enough to let me protect her.

As soon as the blackfly are gone, I head to the spot I have marked near the Great Hall, where the pine needles are soft and fragrant. There are trees that protect my naked body from the coldest breezes but also serve as a sounding board for Evening Song.

When the change is done, I wake to dream of the wild. Shaking out my fur, I throw back my head and call to my Pack, listening so that I can be sure that wolves who have positions are in them. Then I start my run for Westdæl, letting Homelands flood my mind: NighthawkWheekWheekWheek, AspenGossip, OldDenDryCold, WarmDampDenSkunk!, Fireflies, RattlerJump!, HayFernThickUnderPawsSlllooooow, BeaverSlapSplash.

The 7th is already there when I reach the Gin. For whatever reason, my eyes search out Constantine first. He is carrying a boulder the size of a juvenile bear. He drops it so suddenly that I smell blood mixed with earth and stone. He pulls down his sleeves.

The wolves of the 7th have arranged huge stones and small boulders into a low wall across the break between Westdæl and the High Pines, as though they are trying to make sure that nothing will leak out or, even more importantly, nothing will leak in.

As soon as Sigegeat lowers his eyes in recognition, I run, deliberately crossing into the Gray's territory. Then I slow, waiting for her to come. Eventually, I smell her. She's from cold lands and has a cold scent that could easily be missed if I didn't already know it. When I feel her nearby, I lean into my hips, my front paws on the ground before me, my tail wagging slowly. Come, my old, cold friend, let me entertain you. Let me keep you safe from a wolf's most dangerous, most fatal instinct.

Curiosity.

The Gray, as wary now as she was before, simply watches my invitation to play. Time is running out and I need to get her toward the south side of the mountain, away from the Gin. I start bounding toward her, then cutting away well before I reach her, just so she would know there is no aggression to it. Finally, the Bone Wolf joins in, jumping toward me, chest out, tail whipping back and forth. I run away, circling back. His leg is better but not perfect. I make him work to keep up with me.

The Gray has been moving silently behind us at a distance, at the ready in case play should turn into something else and her mate needed her. I am very careful not to touch him: Varya had always been a fierce fighter, and I don't want there to be any confusion about my intent. I would never hurt her, which would put me at a disadvantage if she felt threatened and attacked.

She comes closer and I squat back into my haunches again, tail wagging, my forelegs low to the ground, watching her consider me.

I yelp, flick my ears, ask her without words to remember me.

Remember me. Just a little.

She cocks her head to the side. I watch her eyes move to her mate, a silent signal to him. Then she finally comes forward, slowly, slowly and stands in front of me, chest high, tasting the air around me.

Only the tip of her tail twitches.

I stay low and wait.

Varya had always been so controlled, but I really need the Gray to let go, so with a quick and gentle twitch of my paw, I bop her nose. She looks startled. I wag my tail, just about to reach out again when she leaps.

Zigzagging across Westdæl, I lead them to the southernmost area of her territory where it was ringed by the embrace of Homelands, though all the wolves of the Great North have been told in no uncertain terms to keep their distance downwind.

As soon as I slow down, she throws herself at me, her foreleg across my shoulders, her jaws on either side of mine. If we had hands and tongues instead of fangs and claws, maybe we would hit each other and say "Tag, you're it," but we don't.

For us, even play involves risk and I didn't know how much the forever wolves know or remember, but aside from the scrape of her fang across my muzzle, the Gray doesn't hurt me.

Until that loud alarm goes off and all hell breaks loose. The Gray and the Bone Wolf are instantly on alert, racing north to find out what they need to fight. They have a head start and I need not to catch up with them but to get in front of them, head them off. That's why when I came to the steep gully formed by years of winter runoff, I leapt straight across rather than heading up where it is narrower.

I made it to the other side, but not before jamming my ribs into a shattered root sticking out from the far wall.

But I keep going.

I have no choice but to keep going.

Chapter 18

Constantine

It's early morning by the time we are on the quiet country highway heading back to Homelands. Luckily, there's no one around to notice the naked werewolves twitching nervously in the truck bed.

As we turn into Homelands, they leap away, the cab bobbing with each jump. As soon we reach the parking lot, Ziggy follows, leaving nothing behind but a pile of clothes slowly deflating on the driver's seat.

Filthy and exhausted, I slam the door shut and start for the Bathhouse.

The Bathhouse is a large and mostly windowless building buttressed on one side by a woodshed and on two sides by a screened-in porch festooned with sprays of leafy branches hanging from the rafters. When I've been here before, long empty chairs have been occupied by naked werewolves, their sauna-heated skin steaming in the cool evening air.

Inside smells clean and damp and woody with overtones of eucalyptus and a smell I can only identify as damp feather pillows. I collect a towel and a brush and, on a whim, a bouquet of branches. In the shower, I scrub myself raw with the determinedly neutral shampoo they use.

There is a large mirror built into the tile of the shower

room and spotted with black spots where water has condensed underneath. While I've caught sight of myself in it from time to time, I don't do any real "gazing": something to do with the dozen or so naked werewolves sniffing around my crevices and saying, "What is that smell, Egbert?"

The man in the mirror pulls his hair back same as I do. He stretches his lips over gritted teeth same as I do. I still can't quite believe he's me. All the emptinesses have been filled in. Even the gaunt hollows under my eyes and my cheekbones are gone.

I stroke the beard over skin that looks more golden than before. Or maybe that's a trick of the gold trickling from the fogged window of the sauna.

Someone needs to turn the light off.

Among Lukani at the compound, menial labor was left to the humans. It was a point of pride.

"Someone needs to take out the trash." "Someone needs to fill the ice-cube tray." "Someone needs to turn off the light of the sauna and bank the stove."

If there'd been a poll at the compound, I'd probably have been voted least likely to be "someone." Exhausted as I am, I head to the sauna to turn off the light and bank the stove... Except when I open the door, water explodes into steam on hot rocks. The Alpha drops the ladle back in the bucket of water and sits down on the lowest of the ranged benches, a towel wrapped tightly around her. It's unusually modest for pack.

"Close the door."

I only then realize that I've been standing here a while, letting all the heat out.

"They're wild," she says, half question, half statement.

"Yes."

"Glad." She stares unseeing at the stove. "Will it work?"

"I think so. We'll know better after a decent rain."

"Hmm."

"Alpha..." I pat my shoulders with the branches. "There was a little trouble with men who came. I—"

"Crushed their MTVs. I saw."

"ATVs actually, but yes. The men too. A little." I take down the branches so that I will have something to look at that isn't her.

"I'll tell the lawyers."

"I doubt they'll be any trouble. I don't think there was any lasting damage, and men like that...three against one. They won't report it. Point of pride."

She starts to laugh, then draws up short, her face tight. "Still," she says. "Lawyers."

Feeling suddenly awkward, I continue my futile swatting with the dry branches.

"Here." The Alpha holds out her hand, taking them from me. "I'll show you. Turn around."

She submerges the branches in the bucket filled with water next to the stove. The first thing I feel is the cool lash of water against my overheated skin, followed by the beat of stems. The caress of leaves. The green embrace of birch.

I drape my arm between my legs, hoping the friction from the rough towel will tame the bulge my exhausted mind could not have imagined a few minutes ago. It doesn't, though, because she's touching me. Maybe it's not skin to skin, but her body is just there. A short branch-length away. My breath is pained and ragged as if I were actually being beaten, not lightly slapped around with birch leaves. My mind knows I should tell her to stop, but I'm spinning and my body won't allow it. My skin is torn between the two, stretched to splitting like a thumb against an overripe plum.

"No...no more." I twist around, taking her wrist. "Please." I hear her breath, the thrumming of her pulse, the slight movement of her arm as she tries to stop the towel that is slipping down. The word echoing around my skull:

Please.

Please.

The towel had nothing to do with modesty. Nothing to do with hiding the soft weight of her breast above the curve of her waist. Not the sinewed muscle of her back ending in the perfect curve of her ass, but a ragged gouge that connects the two.

"I needed to stop her, the Gray," she says, as much to herself as to me. "The jump went wrong."

She doesn't bother to cover herself now. With her free hand, she curls her arm around the back of her head and smooths her hair back from her cheek. She is so close to me that I can see tiny beads of sweat sparkle in the filigree curls at her hairline and another rip through the deep-brown satin of her cheek. Her tired eyes don't leave mine, daring me to notice that she is not invulnerable.

All I want to do is gather her to me in this hot and silent place, where no one is calling to her, and touch my lips to those tiny sparkles at her brow and to the cut on her cheek and tell her it's okay to be vulnerable, but I know that for her, it really isn't.

"Long night," I say, trying to make it light. "I'm not sure I'll be able to make it out the door."

"Sleep on the porch. Wolves do it all the time. Not so much when the..."

She wiggles her fingers in the air near her ear.

"Blackfly?"

"Hmm. Not so much when the blackfly are out. The chairs," she says, "recline."

"Would you show me? I mean when you're done."

"I'm done. I was sitting here because I was..."

Because she was tired but won't admit it. I open the damper and sit beside her silently while the fire burns hotter and then dies. We close it down and turn out the light.

She stumbles on the way to the porch while I pretend not to notice. I forget the whole point of my flimsy excuse and lower my chair before she does. She gives me a wan smile.

I sit down.

Something barks out a loud, trilling yell.

"What is that?" I ask, stretching out.

After a moment's hesitation, she lies down on her undamaged side, her head cushioned on her crooked arm.

"Raccoon," she says.

There are no walls, only screens, and the wind kisses the still-damp hairs at the base of my neck. Wings flap suddenly from above. There is a growl and a scrabble and the soft sound of her breathing that eventually becomes deeper, lulled by the forest stark and grim that breathes in the flutter of wings and breathes out the death of prey, that breathes in the rot of old trees and breathes out the roots of seedlings.

Finally, the bow between her lips opens. Silently, I get up, returning to cover her with two clean towels.

Her mouth contracts to a tiny moue, a leg kicks free.

I reach across and pull a single tight zigzag of hair free from where it has stuck to her lower lip. Then I let my hand stretch across the narrow divide between us, my hand under hers.

Chapter 19

Evie

I DREAMED.

It started out normally enough, with anticipation, waiting. Keeping low and silent, listening, scenting, looking. I don't know what we're herding or where we are herding it, only that someone I trust has the far flank.

I must be upwind, but why? No hunter waits upwind. Suddenly, all my wolves turn, surging around me. I see the terror in their eyes as they pass, smell it on their fur, but have no idea what they are running from. I run around snarling and biting and trying to get them to follow. I don't know what's ahead, but whatever it is, I can't do it alone.

No wolf stays, and soon, the pack is nothing but the whisper of hundreds of quiet pads fading into the forest.

A figure on two legs emerges from the mist. He is dressed in leaves and carries a sprouting stem. In my relief, I call to my wolves to tell them to come back. It is the Grenemann, the Green Man come to protect his forest, to protect us, wolves, the protectors of the woods.

I bound toward him, toward the figure dressed in green and brown, carrying a stick. Toward the man in camouflage with a gun.

His eyes are pine dark, streaked with the green of bright-summer leaves.

My eyes snap open, my heart beating. It takes me a

moment to recognize the scent of dried birch and cold water, to hear the small breezes sweeping through the aspens. To see Constantine across from me, one hand warm and sleep-slack under mine.

He has put towels over me.

I slide my hand free. He twitches but doesn't wake. I begin the painful process of sitting up. The rib isn't broken so it's pointless to go to Tristan only to hear him say "It's a flesh wound" and offer me a Tic Tac. Not that I think he'd be so brazen, but one never knows.

The walk back to my cabin is slow. I step cautiously around obstacles I would have leapt over and walk terrain I would normally run. I keep the towel wrapped tight around me so that wolves drawn by their curiosity to the smell of blood don't see the extent of their Alpha's injury.

In my cabin, I peel away the towel and the wound opens again. I look for a black T-shirt and start the slow process of getting dressed. *One Salty Bitch*, it says, though I really don't feel like it.

I contemplate my hair band, but I would really need both hands for that. Instead, I finger comb with my left hand, loosening the sleep-crushed hair and double-checking for burrs. I feel the fang mark on my cheek.

When I walk, I am careful not to favor my right side.

The Pack quiets as soon as I climb stiffly up the stairs. There's no disguising that I've been hurt, but as long as I pretend the injury doesn't matter, my wolves will too.

In the mudroom, I lean against the wall. Bending is excruciatingly painful and there's no point to it, so I scrape off each shoe with the toe of the other. When I open the heavy main door, the muscles around my torso contract and my ribs ache.

We are all playing our roles. The Pack bends over their bowls of buckwheat and plates of eggs while I walk on. Head up, back straight. Jaw tight. My right hand trembles as I reach for the coffee cup. My left is steadier. Best to use the left.

"Sit down," Sigegeat whispers to someone behind me. I know who it is without looking, and sure enough, Constantine says, "She's hurt."

More wolves start wrestling at the table, meaning it's time for me to take charge.

When I turn, picking up an oatcake so it will look casual and unconcerned, I catch his green eyes staring at me, like I knew I would. He is still standing despite the combined efforts of Sigegeat, Inge, and Järv trying to force him to sit down. My lids flutter down for a moment and I shake my head, hoping that he isn't so human that I have to put everything into words.

I rub the back of my hand, trying to wipe away the trace warmth of his palm supporting it. Finally, Constantine sits down, angrily yanking his arms away, and I manage a controlled descent without showing how much it hurts. I reach for the butter and the remnants of last summer's mulberry jam.

A wolf snarls.

Skirmishes are a common enough occurrence, but I have to be careful. It may be the usual posturing over hierarchy or fucking rights, but wolves will act out if they fear the Alpha is weak. They need to feel I am in control and can't help but test the issue if they are unsure.

I watch the Pack carefully. Luckily, it's nothing but a minor tussle over dominance between the Gamma mate and the Delta of the 13th. Esme, their Alpha, jumps in quickly, banging them around until they come back to the table looking sheepish, their heads cocked to the side. Waiting for Esme to mark them so that they know, whatever their pettinesses, they belong to something bigger.

Had I not been watching so carefully, though, I might not have noticed Cassius take advantage of the chaos to knock into Constantine. I wouldn't have seen tiny Theo picking up the folded piece of paper in his teeth because anything that falls to the floor belongs to the pups.

I would, however, have noticed Cassius pinioning Theo's little tail with his big fucking foot. No way I would have missed that because Theo yelps loudly and tries to skitter away. Leaping over the table, I grab Cassius and throw him bodily toward Elijah, my shredded skin screaming at me to stop until Elijah takes hold of Cassius by the collar and drags him away, the Shifter's feet churning desperately against the floor, trying to keep upright so he won't choke on the fabric tight around his trachea.

Constantine sits on the floor holding the whimpering Theo, but the piece of paper that had been in Theo's spitty mouth is gone.

You see, my furious heart says. You let yourself be deluded. There is no one to hold your hand while you hold the Great North together. This is on you alone.

I am so tired and my body hurts and I don't know how to save the forever wolves and I have let Shifters into Homelands and one of them was dangerous enough to make me lose track of who I am.

The Alpha of the Great North Pack.

I drop to my knees, pulling the tiny pup from the Shifter's hands. A sweet cheese dumpling bounces onto the floor and Theo jumps away, his little tail high and straight as a flag.

Then I turn back to the Shifter, my jaw trembling as—

He holds out the tightly folded piece of paper.

"Alpha?" he says as the wave of my anger recedes, leaving my heart flopping on the shore, panting and breathless.

My left hand stinks of Cassius. My right hand is still holding that now-crumbled oatcake slathered with butter and last summer's mulberries.

"Should I read it?" he asks and I nod, licking at the butter and mulberries while he unfolds it carefully because it's been stapled together by pup teeth.

"It's for Julia." He points to the name on the outside. "He tells her to get away from...Logan?...and meet him in the basement the day after tomorrow. At breakfast."

He holds it out to me and I almost laugh with relief. It's a mash note. Constantine was only a messenger boy.

"Lorcan," I finally say. "It's Lorcan. Cassius thinks the 12th's Alpha wants Julia, though if he took a single whiff of him, he'd know it wasn't true."

He stares at the little piece of paper.

"That *man,* the one who's always sniffing around you..." he starts.

The door opens and closes on Rieka, naked and gnawing on a hoof. She scans the room, looking for me. She'll find me soon enough, but I haven't finished looking over the USDA prelicense application package (Class C), so I really have nothing to say to her. I crouch down lower, hiding behind the backs around me. She'll find me soon enough.

"You mean Poul?"

"Yes."

Constantine folds the page carefully, lining up the holes made by Theo's sharp teeth.

"Does he find what he's looking for?"

"Alpha?" says Rieka, standing at the end of the row made by benches and wolf backs.

Letting out a pained breath, I push myself up again.

"No," I say quietly.

Chapter 20

Constantine

There is a bit of dark jam and butter on her lower lip, but she sucks it clean, then darts her tongue out to check her mouth for stains of summer fruit.

Oh god, I am not okay.

She starts down the hall because of course someone needs something done. She's got these jeans, they must be old favorites, worn and soft with holes at the left thigh just big enough for a flicker of brown skin as she walks away.

She stops to listen to someone in the library.

Turn around.

At the threshold of her office, a wolf stretches up his head and she leans over to mark him.

Look at me.

She responds with a terse wave of her hand to someone in the kitchen.

See me.

She disappears into her office.

Evie.

The door closes.

When a wet nose touches my ear, a broken breath hisses from my throat. Magnus brushes his chin on my shoulder. Everything about him looks so much stronger now. The small, sunken wolf with the dusty lackluster fur and rheumy eyes is now large and strong with fur that is light gray on top and dark gray underneath. His eyes are the same, though: true blue, the color of cloud.

Magnus was ripped up by the transition to wolf, so Tristan wants to wait until his bones are strong, his body is fully recovered before letting him become human again, though honestly I know by the way he cocks his head to the side and scratches under his chin that whatever he becomes *when*ever he becomes, it will not be human.

He turns over on his back and bends his hips back and forth, his paws high in the air, his mouth open on white teeth. His tortured paws have healed, and the claws are not as sharp as they were when they first emerged. Sanded down, I suppose by running across granite. He stays on his back but stops wiggling, looking at me from his upside-down eyes. His forehead touching my leg. We were never very demonstrative. Partly because so many things hurt him. Partly because that wasn't who I am, though it feels less strained to pat him on the belly or scratch behind his ears.

One of the pups runs up and starts to clamber over Magnus's face. Aside from a gentle snap at the pup's leg scraping his jaw, he does nothing while the pup sits on his muzzle and tries to catch Magnus's ear flickering teasingly out of reach.

"Is there an oatcake with jam?" I say to Järv.

"Peach or mulberry?"

"Mulberry."

Järv passes one down to me on the floor, then he and Ziggy launch into a discussion of mulberry trees somewhere on Homelands. How ripe they are, how abundant. Who is still small enough to climb high into the branches and jump up and down while wolves below hold out sheets and blankets waiting for the berries to rain from heaven and be turned into another batch of summer jam.

Magnus's ear pricks up, and a second later, he flips over, trotting toward the door. Without a backward look, he puts his paw on the lever of the door, pushes his nose through, his body slithering after.

"That note," says a voice above me. "It's for Julia, isn't it?"

My eyes travel upward toward the messy blond ponytail towering above me. I jump up. Don't like being towered over.

"Yes."

He holds out his hand for it, and as I have no skin in this game, I give it to him.

As soon as he reads it over, he hands it back. "What are you going to do with it?"

"What do you mean?"

"Are you going to give it to her?"

I start to wonder if the Alpha was wrong about him. It would make sense after all: a girl like Julia always needs a protector—Otho, August, Cassius, and now this man, the latest in a long line.

"Why? Do you have a thing for her?"

"Me?" He says it with his lip curled back like I'd just accused him of kissing a tapeworm. "I'm the Alpha of the 12th Echelon of the Great North. Why would *I* have a thing for *her*?"

"What do I know? She's very…decorative?"

"*Decorative?*" He scratches an eyebrow with his pinkie finger. "You knew Varya?"

"We talked a little. I watched her rip orifices in body parts that don't usually have them. But I wouldn't say I *knew* her."

"She was my Shielder. I asked her to be my mate. You know Varya well enough to understand I have no use for the merely decorative."

His fingers go to the rubber band holding back a ponytail. When he pulls it out, his blond hair brushes his shoulders.

"I miss her," he says. "But she was so strong that I didn't have to be. Now I do. I'm not saying that Cassius is anything like Varya, but I do see a little of myself in Julia. Letting someone else bear the responsibility for decisions that should be hers."

Behind him, Julia talks animatedly to Arthur, who listens closely before answering. As soon as she sees me heading toward her, she drops her eyes to the table, pushes her plate away, and sits on her hands so she won't have to look at or take the paper with "JULIA" written clearly on the top. Maybe she hopes that it and I will go away, that I will take responsibility for the decision, so that she can say to Cassius that I never gave it to her and technically it will be true.

But I'm not her indulgent uncle or her indulgent father, and I can stand here forever with the stupid piece of paper. When she looks to Arthur, he says only, "It's for you."

Her lips quiver and grow tight, and when she grabs the note from my hand, she keeps the steel-gray birthright of her eyes hard on mine while she rips it to shreds and throws it on the floor.

"And yes," she says to Arthur, "I know I have to sweep that up."

He chortles and she smiles a big smile with lots of teeth that makes her cheeks look fat like Cassius always warned her it would, and I know that Cassius has misread the signs and doesn't understand that the man he should be worried about is not the Viking with the ponytail, but the slim man with the brown hair who splayed himself naked on the damp ground, his jaws clamped shut, his eyes wide open, waiting to be ripped apart by wolves.

Chapter 21

Evie

My first Offland meeting as Alpha had taken so much preparation. For days, Tara had prepped me on questions of engineering; Josi, on questions of the law; Leonora, on how to handle humans. I needed to be able to answer every petty, pointless question so they did not have any excuse to inspect Homelands.

I've gotten better at it, better at lining up my facts, better at identifying what Leonora calls bullshit. But in the end, to protect my Pack, I have to know four times as much as all the humans in the room.

I unroll another map, holding it open with skunk skull from the shelf of First Kills, rehearsing my responses for the Community Wildfire Protection Plan meeting.

The chart with water pressures riffles and floats slowly to the floor in the suddenly bright air. At the window, I taste the coolness of the breeze and the warmth of the ground and the scuttling lacy clouds against blue.

I'm not the only one who feels it: Pack emerge blinking into the sunlight. They are ill-tempered and ill at ease. Days spent inside hiding from blackfly do that. Soon, they begin circling me, bodies shivering with need.

"Go! Go!" I say loudly. "Before it's too late."

And they go.

"*Rinnaþ, wulfas,*" I whisper to myself.

Run, wolves.

The wild bursts out of them, and in their excitement, things are left undone. The stove is still on. The milk is out. A screen in the library is wide open. Clothes are strewn everywhere.

"Alpha," says Leonora.

"Aren't you going out running?"

"I thought we'd take this opportunity to go swimming, but"—the children are already pulling off shirts, whooping around, their arms waving in a premature celebration of nakedness—"we will need some adults."

"I'll arrange it."

Arne runs back in, his back covered in pine needles.

"Forgot to turn off the stove," he says.

"I did it, but, Arne, as soon as the 8th is changed, send them to Home Pond. Leonora is taking the class swimming."

I squat down to pick up an armload of clothes.

"What's happened?" says Constantine. "We were working and then everyone disappeared."

"Blackfly don't like strong winds and bright sun. It gives the Pack a chance to run."

"Why'd humans hafta wear clowes t'go simming?" complains Edmund, coming up the stairs. "And why is the shit and pans so liddow?"

"Because humans think that by hiding evidence of their fucking, they can pretend they are more than animals," she says. "The quicker you get dressed, the quicker we get to the water. Now, let's see how well you've done."

Edmund emerges from the stairs, pulling on a clearly uncomfortable blue-and-white-gingham bikini. Aella is wearing a pair of long shorts with skulls and a daisy-print tank top. Leofric has on a pink one-piece that covers the back but leaves the nipples exposed, which as I recall is acceptable because he's male.

"Alpha? Would you like to comment on how the class has done?"

I wave her off. Those lessons were long ago, and I've forgotten everything save for that single arbitrary fact that while male nipples may be exposed, female nipples must never be.

She turns around. "Shifter, you will know," she says.

"It's Constantine, Leonora," I say. Leonora pauses for a moment then her eyes flicker down, acquiescing. She starts again. "Well, Constantine, how has the class done?"

He had been watching me, a curious expression on his face, but now he reluctantly turns to the children. I know they're not right. Their legs twitch, their dirty feet shivering in anticipation. They are unsure what to do with arms that until recently were used for running. And Margaret is really too old to be licking Oliver's ear.

They hold their heads cocked to the side in hopeful angles.

He turns back to me. "Beautiful," he whispers, a low hitch in his voice.

Then with a steadier voice, he tells Leonora that her charges are perfect.

Leonora's eyebrows rise and her lips tighten in disapproval, but she shepherds them to the door, unwilling to keep them confined a minute more.

"*No one on the dock until the adults come,*" she yells.

"You know they aren't," she says without turning to look at Constantine.

"Aren't what?"

"Perfect."

"They're only children," he says.

"*That* they definitely are not." One of our "children" has found a vertebra that has been picked clean; she puts it to her hind teeth, gnawing happily. "They are wolves. They have a hard enough time fitting in already. They don't say what they don't mean. They don't ask things simply to make conversation. They sense things no one else does. They don't understand things that everyone understands. Rainy!" she yells at a First Shoes who has reverted to running on her toes and fists. "*Two* legs!"

Rainy looks back, then pushes herself upright. It's the angle of the slope that's giving her trouble, but it can't be helped. She must learn.

"You know what humans are like with anyone who is strange," Leonora says, "and these *children* are as strange as they come."

Something splashes, followed by excited yips and yells made by children who aren't used to the form until one of the older ones calls out: "Tasha felled!"

Leonora starts to run, hampered by sandals. I run, too, hampered by the jostling of injured ribs, but Constantine races past me, wolf-fast on two legs. The children huddle to the side of the dock as his feet pound down the dock and he launches himself far out into the water, cutting through it like an otter.

At the edge of the dock, I lie down, my arms in the water where she should be, searching. Tasha isn't even First Shoes and doesn't know how to swim in skin.

The sun catches something bright in the churned water and I grab for it, pulling. My ribs scream even though she is being pushed up from below.

Constantine emerges as I gather her, tiny and coughing and terrified, into my arms, marking her over and over again until the shaking subsides.

His fingers grab hold of the edge of the dock, just below my bent leg.

"Coodn beethe," she sobs.

"It's not the same in skin. That's why you have to learn. That's why I told you to wait."

I let my leg fall, feeling his fingers, cold and damp even through my jeans.

"I don' wann be in thin. Don' lig it."

"It doesn't matter what you like or want, you will do what you must. Like every Pack."

Leonora is next to me now, in her bright-orange bathing suit, her handbag shaped like an oversize plum made of shining purple stones, bristling with antlers and cheese chews.

"Tasha, what do we say to the Sh—Constantine?"

I feel her tighten in my arms, her head raised to me for help, but honestly, I have no idea what Leonora wants from her.

"He saved your life. What do you say?"

"*I don' know,*" she wails.

"'Thank you,' Tasha. You say 'thank you.' Wolflings, I have said this over and over, but I can't emphasize how important it is. Humans are not Pack. There is no assumption of mutual support. A human may help another human or they may not. Because of this, there is *always* the expectation of gratitude. They will look very poorly on you if you do not say 'thank you' every time they perform any service, no matter how small or obvious."

Licking away the last of the water dripping into Tasha's

eyes, I set her upright as the 8th emerges from behind the Great Hall, racing toward the water.

I lift my leg from Constantine's hand, but one finger catches on the loose threads at the hole of my jeans. I lean back down, letting him free himself, and immediately regret his absence. Water beads on his hair and on his face, dripping down to collect in the notch of his collarbone, and I am suddenly, unaccountably thirsty.

"They're coming." He opens his mouth to say something to me, but whatever it is, there is no time to say it before Arne and other wolves of the 8th charge the length of the dock. At the end, they leap, paws extended, noses to the sky, before dropping with an unceremonious splat against the water.

Other wolves walk more daintily into the water's edge.

Constantine's sopping flannel shirt lands on the side of the deck with a damp splat, followed quickly by his pants. His hair swirls against his broad shoulders. He leans back, his throat long and exposed, the striations of the muscles of his chest glistening in the water. Upright once more, his hair smoothed back, he watches the children jump or wade in, all of them paddling around. It's the littlest ones, the ones who aren't used to the tiny squat noses, so unlike the longer muzzles, who have so much difficulty keeping themselves above water. There is a lot of coughing and flailing, but only for the moments it takes for an adult to swim closer. Then little fists curl around the long guard hairs and they lean their heads into the fur, their unfamiliar bodies swaying to the rhythm of their protector's strokes.

Constantine swims around them, sleek and muscular, strong and fast, making ever-widening loops. He's not guarding them anymore, not watching. He's just a shining hint of gold and dark heading out into the middle of Home Pond.

With a ferret-quick twist, he turns his body, spreads out his arms, and floats, far removed from everything.

"Should I send Arne?" Leonora says. "Before he gets too far."

I raise my hand. Wait.

I stare after him.

Come back. Stay there. Show me how. Help me.

Where is this coming from? He's an interloper, an outsider. He has no purpose in the Pack. I must choose someone like Poul. Or maybe Lorcan. Let them fight it out for *cunnan-riht*. For fucking rights. Between the two of them, it's a rock and a hard place. A pot and a kettle.

John was my friend. We knew each other. I trusted him, and when he died, my heart shriveled and dried. Why is it when this, this...this *Shifter* looks at me, touches me, I feel just how parched I have become?

Lifting his head from the water, he combs his hair out of eyes with long fingers. He looks around like he's only now realizing how far he's gone. Catching my eyes, he starts back with a slow and exaggerated stroke, coming for me.

Chapter 22

Constantine

Fuck, it's glorious. Spring fed and cold, but nothing like the frigid rough seas off the coast of Nova Scotia. After the numbing shock comes an almost blissful thaw.

Water flows through my hair and over my skin. Stroke by stroke, it covers me, coddles me. The liquid thickness buoying me, making it easier to forget, to get away, to go loose to my very bones. Everything is erased except the pleated shadows of summer sun rippling across my closed eyes and the wash of water as my arms slice through the surface.

I flip over, my chest to the sun, my back to the deep. Warm on top, cold underneath. The splashing near the dock has subsided to a gentle slosh that licks my body and whispers against my ears.

Eventually, I lift my head, realizing just how far I've gone from the distant yips and voices at the dock. Combing my hair from my face and the water from my eyes, I see the Alpha at the distant dock, her eyes fixed on me.

Next to her, Leonora watches tensely.

With a slow and exaggerated backstroke, I start back so she will understand that I am not making a break for it. At the compound, I dreaded the moment when some asshole would shatter the sky with a .460 Magnum, so there would be doubt that I was being summoned from the water that took me in and made me part of something bigger. I hated each stroke back to the rocky beaches and whatever smug Lukani had been sent to fetch me. I hated feeling myself growing smaller.

Now I don't.

By the time I reach the edge of the dock, the children are gone, tumbling in the grass surrounding a crumpled blanket that is empty except for a few plates of food.

The Alpha is alone, sitting with her arms wrapped around one knee, the other foot tracing patterns in the water. I grab at the corner of the dock, pretending that I don't feel the tiny waves lapping against my nipples. That water isn't tracing paths down the muscled curve of her calf. That if my mouth forms the word *Alpha*, her name won't emerge instead.

Evie.

"Are you getting out?" she says.

No, I'm not getting out. I've got an erection the size of a two-by-four stuffed into 80 percent cotton and 20 percent Spandex.

It'd frighten the children.

"I think I'll swim a little more," I say. "Not far. Just near the dock."

Someone calls to her and she pulls her foot out of the water. I reach for it, unthinking, but stop before I touch her.

"Would you teach me?" she says, looking over the broad expanse of water. "Teach me how to swim like that? Away?"

Oh, Evie.

"Yes," I say, hoping my voice is neutral but knowing it's not.

"Alpha!"

Why can't they leave her be? Just for a moment?

"Tomorrow night," she says quickly and quietly. "When the moon is in the Endeberg Notch."

She leans forward, cupping her hand into the lake, then scrubs her neck and face with handful after handful of cold water. "The juveniles have made a picnic," she says, louder this time. "If you wait too long, there will be nothing left but avocado-and-jelly sandwiches."

The water drips down her skin and onto her shirt. Her nipples are tight underneath. I smile my unthinking smile while using my thumb to slide the crown of my immoderate cock down beneath my waistband.

Mustn't frighten the children.

Poul is almost at the dock. The Alpha puts both hands on the worn wood, then pushes up with a sigh. I've never said a word to him, but that does not stop me from hating him. Hidden by the water still murky from churning feet and paws, I slip under the dock, creaking beneath Poul's weight.

"Alpha," Poul says. Through the slit between the planks, I see her stand utterly still while he leans in to sniff at her neck.

"Alpha," he says again, more urgently. "You smell like—?"

"I *smell* like pond water." She slaps irritably at the air near his nose, like she's swatting away blackfly. "I'm getting something to eat."

A little water drips from her body onto the dock, through the planks, and onto my upturned face. Through the scent of wood and wolves and forest and fur is one I haven't smelled before. I suck it in one breath after another, trying to figure out what it is, like a word that remains just beyond my grasp, until suddenly, I know. It is granite covered by the delicate stems of bright-green moss. A forest in miniature, a fragile world growing on bedrock.

The scent of Evie imprints itself on my brain.

On the grass, the children pluck at the uncomfortable bright fabrics confining their skin. Others, in their barely contained wildness, tussle and wrestle and lick and bite. I wish I could say that there is forgiveness enough for the strange and the unworldly, but I'd be lying.

Heading back out into the water, I wait until everyone is gone and nothing is left but the peculiar avocado-and-jelly sandwiches made by these strange and beautiful children.

They are delicious.

The sandwiches, I mean.

The next morning, I take a newspaper on a long wooden rod from the bracket along the library wall that's filled with them and settle into the sofa in front of the cold fireplace, coffee and cranberry-and-pumpkin-seed scone slathered with butter at hand.

I tap the scone on the plate so I won't have to sweep up the loose crumbs.

There's a serendipity to reading these physical objects and the news that is not filtered for my taste by predictive algorithms. Wolves have already marked things that they think are of use to the Pack, like the business article about tech stocks or a vulnerable state senator or a potentially worrying invasion of feral pigs into Upstate New York. At least three wolves have circled the article, adding a superfluous *SWINE!!!*

Before long, I hear the endlessly irritating monotone bellyaching. I brush the crumbs from my hands, put my plate in the bin, and hang up the newspaper. In the basement, I lean against the metal cage of dry storage and wait.

"What are you doing here?" Cassius whispers as soon as he sees me.

"She's not coming." I keep my voice neutral.

"It's that shit Lorcan, isn't it?" He doesn't wait for an answer, just balls up his fist and circles around, looking for something to hit that isn't going to hurt him back, but this is not a place of soft surfaces so he then stops again in front of me.

"That fucker won't let me near her." He picks at a callus on his hand. "Look at this." He shows me his roughened palm. "You know what I'm doing? Laundry. I've got a fucking degree from U of T, and I'm doing laundry."

"Elijah is a lawyer. He's got to have at least two degrees."

"Elijah's a *dog*. He doesn't know any better except to fetch and sit and lie down." He finally peels the yellowed skin off. "I hear they got you banging out chairs."

I can almost feel the crunch of bone against the heel of my palm. Feel the soft pop of eyeballs beneath my thumbs. Hear the gagging. Smell the blood. *Benches, asshole. I make fucking fine benches.*

"Hunh," I say, though even that noncommittal grunt takes effort.

"I'm sick and tired of being told what to do," he says.

"What? Like August didn't tell us what to do?"

"That's not the same thing at all. He *paid* us. Good

money, plus people knew I was somebody when I worked for him."

Somebody making the world safe for cabbages.

"What's so funny?"

"Nothing. Something August said about cabbages."

"What the fuck are you talking about? We are trapped here in the middle of a jungle, no way out, nobody knows where we are, and you're talking about cabbages?"

"More to the point, nobody cares." I reach my elbow around to stretch the cramping in my back. "Besides, what would you do if you did?"

"Did what?"

"Get out, Cassius. Our skills are not readily transferrable, and August isn't going to be writing any letters of recommendation."

He looks at me with the sly expression of an idiot discovering a thing that everyone else has already learned and discounted.

Don't say it, idiot. Don't say it.

"August wasn't the only Leveraux out there."

I told you not to, but you said it anyway.

"Cassius, we never spent much time together, but I'm going to do you a favor anyway. You don't know her."

"I met her once. With my parents. She was pretty and made me cookies. Oatmeal and raisin."

"Just because she bakes cookies doesn't make her a good person. She killed her brother. Cut him into tiny pieces, and he was a better fighter than you will ever be." I rub the ball of my thumb. "You are August's man. Never underestimate the power of her hatred."

"That's exactly what I'm counting on because I can give her the one thing that she hates more than August."

The cold creeps up my back, and when he says it—when he says, "I can give her this Pack"—it takes my heart like frostbite.

Otho was the only person I talked to about my mother. "She was a powerful wolf," he said, like every Lukani who'd known Maxima. "A little like Drusilla in some ways." I waited for him to say something else, but he just went back to cleaning guns. He was fanatical about making sure every gun was cleaned, zeroed, and loaded, so we did that a lot.

He wasn't a big talker and wouldn't say more than he felt like at the moment he felt like it.

Finally, when it was all done and he'd slid his .44 in his shoulder holster, he said, "Never try to make a powerful woman small." He cupped his hands together into a ball and made as though he was pressing the air inside. "There's only so small you can make them before they"—he shot his fingers apart into the air—"explode."

I looked at the prominent scar at the base of his thumb.

"Kind of like stars that way."

And that was all he said.

When I found him in the steam room of his health club in Toronto, that was the only part that was intact, the fleshy muscle of his thumb, with the scarred-over bite. The distinctive marker left by Mala, the wolf who had made Drusilla feel small.

Chapter 23

Evie

"HOW LONG HAVE YOU BEEN HERE?"

The dock creaks, the swallow song melds together into a dull murmur, while the water rustles through the grasses at water's edge.

"Since Evening Song," he says from the Adirondack chair at the end of the dock. "I wasn't sure whether you meant on the dot of Moon in the Endeberg Notch or Moon in the Endeberg Notch-ish."

"You have no idea where the Endeberg Notch is, do you?"

He shakes his head.

Resting my elbow on the arm of the chair, I lean down, pointing to the last mountain of the northern range and the notch between it and the pile of rock that was too small for our ancestors to bother giving even one of the unimaginative names they specialized in. Westdæl, the West Place. Norþdæl, the North Place. Endeberg, the End Mountain.

"The moon's coming up now. Right there." I pluck at something sticking to my lashes. "You won't see it if you don't look."

"You have..." He touches his own eyelashes, then reaches his hand toward my cheek. "Should I try?"

I close my eyes, feeling the edge of his hand anchored

cool on my cheek, his thumb and forefinger gentle as though I were something precious that needed care. He is close enough for me to feel his warm breath eddy against my skin. When I open my eyes, he is holding a black straight hair on his thumb.

"Do you want it?"

"Why would I?"

"To make a wish."

"A wish?"

Now it's his turn to close his eyes. He takes a deep breath and blows. "It's a human thing, making a wish on an eyelash."

"Does it work if you make a wish on a guard hair?" I free my hair, sliding the wide band into my pocket. "Because that was a guard hair."

Then I reach for the hem of my shirt, pulling it over my head. It's still covering my eyes when I hear Constantine suck in a deep breath and stumble. When the shirt is off, he is squatting behind the Adirondack chair, his back to me.

I lower myself naked into the water and paddle around, my nose high in the air like wolves do, until I hear the splash of a body on the other side of the dock.

I look toward the Great Hall, making sure that the Pack is safely dispersed through the more distant parts of Homelands where prey is more plentiful.

Constantine emerges from the water, his head back, hair streaming, water cupped and glistening in the valleys and indentations made by bone and muscle. I reach for the dock, pulling myself farther away.

He swims in a broad, lazy loop around me. I watch what he's doing and how he's doing it. It looks easy enough but when I push off from the dock, I founder and return to the steady churning with four limbs, running through water like wolves always do.

"That's called the dog paddle," he says and twists away when I snarl at him for using the d-word. "You need to stretch your legs out like one of those birds."

"Geese?"

"No, not geese. I know geese. They shit on August's old compound. I'm talking about the ones that have long beaks and long legs, and when they fly, you can see their legs stretched out behind them."

"Heron?"

"Maybe that's it."

I imagine a heron, legs and beak almost a straight line, my arms spread out, flapping above it all until I sink and I churn my way back to the surface, Constantine's voice echoing in my head.

"You have to keep your legs up," he says when I reemerge. He holds his arms stretched toward me. "Here. Take my hands."

I turn away and try again, but as soon as I stretch out my legs, my back arches and my legs sink down. This time when I come back up, he is at the dock, his back to me, staring toward the fireflies flittering around the honey locust.

"Is it because I'm not Pack?"

"I don't know what you're talking about."

"I'm asking why you won't ever let me help you. Not now, not yesterday when you were hurt, not before when all I was trying to do was pick up some stupid papers—"

"It's not because of who *you* are." I grab hold of the edge of the dock. "It's because of who *I* am. You don't understand wolves. The Pack is so strained, so skittish; they get combative if they think there isn't a firm hand at the top directing them." Pups chase something through the blueberry bushes behind the Boathouse. "My Beta is an engineer. She once said the Pack is like an arch and the Alpha's the keystone, making sure that pressure is directed. But if the keystone fails, the arch crumbles."

They skitter to a stop as a squirrel scrambles up into the birch tree.

"I am not a wolf."

"No."

"And you are not a stone."

I say nothing.

"So is there any way that I could pick up some fallen papers or hold your hand without it signaling the end of the world?"

A bat zigzags low over the water in a flash of leathery wings and he holds his hands out for me with a slow, lost, asking smile that doesn't make sense on his hard face, but still I let go of the dock and take his hands and...

The world doesn't end.

It is easier to stretch my legs out like a heron. I start to kick slowly. I feel the currents stirred by his legs as he pulls me along until I start kicking faster and bump into him. Hair in my eyes, I hold on to his shoulders, thick and broad and hard under my hands, while my legs float forward and my thigh brushes his knee.

A shudder runs through me that has nothing to do with the cold, and he pushes my wet hair away from one eye, his palm rough from working with wood on my cheek, his mouth open, but with no breath, there are no words, just the unspoken question.

Would the world end?

The moon rises above the mountains to the east and shines on both the water and on my fingers silhouetted on his shoulders.

I push away from him across the surface of the water. He's hovering not far away. I feel it in the way the water ripples against my skin. I don't want to be watched. I need a little time when no one is looking to me for anything so that I can think.

Pulling my legs and arms in tight, I let my body descend into the dark and silent deep where there is no Great North, no forever wolves, no humans, no Shifters, no Constantine, no nothing.

Then it is really and truly just me.

Chapter 24

Constantine

Where is she?

I tried to give her space because it's what she needs. It's what I need too. Get away from her. From everything: the twist of the attenuated muscle that leads to the graceful fillip of her collarbone. The way the water clings to her hair like diamantine on velvet. The way she arches her back, trying to push her legs higher, and her perfect ass comes above water dotted with tiny goose bumps.

Every word I said to her—*kick, breathe, straighten, bend*—was a broken substitute for the words I wanted to say.

Lick, breathe, suck, open, come.

So I put distance between us, checking on her with each pass as I spiral outward. Then at one turn, I look for her and see neither her nor a trace of her on the water's smooth surface. I watch for seconds and minutes. Don't be an idiot, I tell myself.

She's strong. Nothing could happen to her.

The Great North cannot bear the loss of another Alpha.

She'll be back up soon, I tell myself.

The lake remains huge and dark and smooth, and it makes me panic in a way that no riptide or undertow ever could and I dive deeper and deeper until my lungs are about to burst, not because I give a fuck about the Great North, but because Constantine can't bear the loss of Evie.

Finally, I see her above me. A silhouette picked out in the moon, legs crooked, arms tight. Only her hair spreading around her in a rough crown. I rush up, dragging her with me to the surface. Twice, I've seen people being rescued from rough seas off the Maritimes, and in both cases, they coughed and struggled. Evie doesn't do either, and I suppose that should have given me a clue. Instead, she leans back, breathing steadily, her hands floating loose on the water, her head against my shoulder, her eyes shining as she watches the sky drift past.

I swim for the shore opposite the dock, both because it is nearest and because it is farthest from any Pack. If they can't accept the idea that someone might carry her coffee cup, who knows what they would think if they saw her being rescued.

Except she's not being rescued. As soon as we reach the other side of the lake and her feet touch the bottom, she grabs for a slim tree that bends precipitously over the water, pulling herself onto the shore with a hop. Her arms bent, muscles beside the wings of her shoulder blades form a V angled toward the runnel of her spine that leads to two shadowy dips, one on either side above the perfect curve of her ass. The tear along her ribs.

I turn away. "You're all right."

"Of course," she says, squeezing at one side of her hair. "Wolves run for miles. Our lungs are strong." Before she can say more, a wolf calls in the faraway forest and Evie is instantly rigid, leaning into the sound, until she hears a clipped response followed by a *rah-wup*.

She squeezes out more water and shakes her head, her hair coming alive like sea foam.

My legs start to shake and I lower myself to the base of a nearby tree so nobody needs to see. She sits at a tree opposite.

"Do you know why this is called Home Pond?"

"You mean when it's really a lake?" I sit with my knees up, my arms draped between them, my eyes trained on the water, because she is so naked and I am not wolf and while I've gotten used to the nakedness of other wolves, I don't think I could ever "get used" to seeing her.

"I mean the 'Home' part, not the 'Pond.'"

"I guess I assumed it was because of the Great Hall?"

"It was *Holm* Pond. With an L. A holm is a little island. *This* is the little island. We still call it the Holm, even though the name of the pond was changed a long time ago. That is not our home." She points with her chin in the direction of the Great Hall, now almost entirely dark except for the moth-spangled light leaking from one window. "*That* is just a stage set where we learn to play our parts and say our lines."

She lifts her eyes to the sheltering forest and the distant mountains beyond. "Our *home* is there."

I look out toward the woods that when I first came here seemed monolithic, undifferentiated. Menacing. Viewing it now under the star-strewn obsidian sky, I know better. I've seen the countless tiny accommodations life makes with life under its graceful living arches, stained with moonlight and green leaf-light and echoing with a thousand prayerful sounds. Now it seems like the sanctuary of a church whose tenets and rituals I am only just beginning to understand.

"Before, when I thought I was human, I lived on a cul-de-sac. There was a mountain that we could see from the rear window of our little house. We always kept the window covered because whenever my mother looked out to it, something snapped inside her. She would stand there, frozen, until my father led her away. Then late at night, she would tell me stories about someone who went into the forest and got lost. Not just lost their way, but lost something else. Their souls, I guess. I couldn't tell whether she was trying to explain herself or warn me."

I scrape my hair back from my forehead.

"They always started out the same way: 'In the forest stark and grim live unspeakable things.'"

She bends her head to the side, no longer looking across to these mountains and these forests.

"Was your mother a wolf?"

"She was a housewife."

The Alpha rubs her thumb over the arch ofher eyebrow. A tiny drop of water curves around her cheekbone.

"I ask because we have stories about the Eisenwald—the Ironwood—where Pack come from, and those stories always start the same way: '*On ðære wald stearc and grim, alifde ðæt ðæt unasecgende sceolon.*' But '*stearc and grim*' doesn't mean 'stark and grim.' It means 'strong and fierce.' Protective." She looks back to the distant trees. "And it's not 'live unspeakable things.' It's..." She hesitates, her mouth open, her jaw moving slightly while she looks for the exact translation. "'Are lives that must be unspoken,'" she finally says. "That must always be secret."

She rocks to the side, finding a stone under her thigh.

"It meant us. Wolves. Our lives are the secrets protected in the forest strong and fierce."

She tosses the rock far into the water. It jostles the moon's path along the surface.

"How can you be mated to a house?" she asks after the rings have faded back into the lake.

"Mated to…? You mean housewife?" She nods. "She wasn't married to the house. It only meant…" I stumble trying to come up with something that will explain Maxine Brody, recording secretary for the bake sale committee of the Rainy River Elementary PTA in terms that the Alpha of the Great North Pack will understand. "It only meant that the house was her territory." She turns her head toward me again, her cheek resting on her arms crossed above her knees, silent, one eyebrow raised. "That's a very small territory."

I manage a half smile.

"Everyone I talked to after she…" I was going to say "passed away" but I refuse to insult the Alpha with something so hackneyed and I refuse to pretend that Maxima, who was shot and immolated, went gently.

"After she died, everyone said that she'd been a very strong wolf. Her name was Maxima." I don't know why I tell her, but it seems important. "She wanted to hide us, my father and me, from August. She did such a good job of hiding everything that I assumed we were human until the day she burned the brownies and turned into a wolf."

I have resin on the pads of my fingers. "There's nothing like a rumor of wolves to find out how many of your neighbors have guns."

Every year, my mother bought Thin Mints from Mr. Gallantin's daughter, though she didn't like our neighbor. She never said so, but I could tell by the hard look in her eyes whenever he came to the door. He smelled like formaldehyde and the fat of the dead animals he mounted in the workshop in his basement.

His excitement as he ran past our window was palpable. He unzipped his rifle case and dropped it on my mother's patio furniture as he went. My father, though, was already hunting and got her first. They got into an accident off the gully bridge near the old mill far from home.

I explode my fingers with a whispered *poom,* then sit lost in thought, looking at my fingertips.

"You know what I wished for on your eyelash?"

"My guard hair," she reminds me. "No, you didn't say."

I take a deep breath and launch myself into the void. "I wanted to understand how wolves flirt."

"Flirt?"

"It's the things you say and do to show that you're interested but want to pretend you aren't in case the other person isn't and you don't want to be embarrassed."

She scratches the tip of her nose with her thumb. "That's why it's one of the eight primary forms of human misrepresentation."

"Misrepresentation? I wouldn't call it misrepresentation. And there aren't eight."

"Yes there are," she says and starts counting off on her fingers. "JAFFEWIP. It stands for Jokes. Advertisement. Falsehood. Flirtation. Exaggeration. White lies. Irony. Politics." And as the last long finger rises in the air, I find myself unable to argue with a single one.

"Flirtation is only taught in Advanced Human Behaviors so that wolves heading Offland will understand how to interpret obscure signals."

"What's it like? The class."

"I was never going to be an Offlander, so I have no idea."

A squirrel runs through the branches overhead, loosing a sprinkling of duff. She picks up a branch of long, brown pine needles and twirls it between her fingers.

"Will you tell me?" she asks quietly.

Oh god.

The single light in the Great Hall goes off and I try to collect my thoughts.

"If you were human, Alpha, I would accidentally stand closer than strictly necessary with my back straight so you could see how tall I was. With my shoulders back so you could see how broad they are. I would smile at you, but not a friendly smile, more a smile verging on disdain, so that if you weren't interested in my height or my shoulders, I would seem like I had never really cared in the first place.

"If you were interested, you wouldn't say that straight out. Instead, you might ask me for help that you didn't actually need, like opening a jam jar or working an app on your phone. I would help you with the thing you didn't need with more flair and exertion than was required. Then with the jam jar opened or the app conquered, you might put your hand on my arm and say something about my strength or intelligence. I would then ask you where the nearest coffee shop is and you would say, 'It's easier if I just show you.' When you'd shown me, I would insist on buying you a coffee. If you consented, we would have conducted a successful flirtation."

She shakes her head, a small smile playing across her lips.

"But it's all a lie."

"Not a lie, a misrepresentation. As you said yourself."

She waves her pine fan in front of her.

"When I asked for your help to swim like that, swim like you, did you think I was flirting?"

I know what she wanted. She wanted to find a place that was a little apart. Not run away, just float in the dark for the space of one breath, until some idiot thought it had gone on too long and rescued her, though she didn't need it.

I shake my head.

"So how *do* wolves flirt?"

"It's not all that different. At least until the hierarchy is settled, there are lots of feats of strength. Who drags the biggest windfall from the forest. Who kills the biggest bear. Who lifts the most bales of laundry. The usual. But then…" She leans toward me and I feel the warmth of her body behind me and stop breathing. The air moves behind my jaw, and when I suck in that breath again, the tight tip of her breast scrapes across my arm.

"That's it," she says quietly. "One wolf will smell another wolf to see if they are willing. That is how wolves flirt."

When I turn my head, my cheek lines up to hers, and I suck in a deep breath. My brain is immediately awash with the almost indecipherable complexity of the Pack—black earth, fur, the blood of prey, the fast-running sap of summer trees. But then it settles on that something else underlying it all, the granite and moss, hard stone covered with fragile life, that is Evie.

"And am I?" I choke out.

"Yes," she says, pulling away, her eyes shielded, voice suddenly distant. "But then every unattached male wants to cover the Alpha."

A frog squawks into the night as I take her chin in my

hand, kiss her between the eyebrows, and stride away fast, looking for a tree as big and thick as I am. Leaning against it, I strip off the damp boxers, then take my overfull cock with the other. It feels impossibly heavy even to the companion of lone nights in sterile hotels. I begin the stroke, so primed and tightly wound that my back arches and my eyes close before I reach the root.

"And what kind of wolf would rather masturbate than fuck the Alpha?"

Her arms are crossed in front of her, her expression hard. In the low light, her eyes burn like embers. There's a rawness to the word *fuck*. I suppose that's why it is the most popular expletive, but in her voice, it scrapes like a match on my combustible skin.

"I am not a wolf. And I do not want to *fuck the Alpha*."

"It certainly seems like it." She looks pointedly at my erection.

"Words may not be everything, but they are something," I show her my fingers wrapped around my cock. "I don't want to *fuck* the Alpha." I squeeze tighter. "I want to taste your mouth." I slide down. "I want to tongue your breasts." I reach the border between pain and pleasure. "I want to touch you until you think your skin is going to split from feeling it." I slide my hand up again. "Then I want you to come saying my name." I slide my hand down one last time.

"Like I do."

—

"Evie."

I was teetering so close that all it took was groaning her name. I lean my forehead against the rough bark and in long, throbbing bursts find my release.

"I don't want to fuck the Alpha." I stare at the pale stripes against the dark wood. "I want to make love to Evie."

She silently repeats her name, her lower lip sliding under her front teeth at that seductive "vee."

After an endless moment, she takes a deep breath.

"Constantine?" she says, exhaling the whole unwieldy length of it.

Pack are constantly stripping but when Evie stands here, arms outstretched, she is bare beyond naked. For this moment, she has put aside not only her clothes, which mean nothing, but also her responsibilities, duties, customs as Alpha, and that means everything.

Straightening myself, I brush my forehead in case there are still any little bits of bark left there. I want to touch her, but I move slowly, giving her time with every step to move away. To change her mind. To remember that she is Alpha and I am an old enemy and not worth the risk.

She doesn't move and her eyes never waver from mine except for a brief sweep downward. When she smiles, I close the last few feet, not touching but stopping close enough so that when I put out my hand, I can feel the heat from hers. Then I slowly close the space between our palms until there is no separation anymore. Her breath recoils sharply like she's touched something hotter than she was expecting.

"The question is what do *you* want. What does Evie want." I exhale her name and listen until the last syllable has turned into mist, then I kiss the touching points of our fingers and feel the tremor of my hand.

We are well matched so when Evie leans her head against mine, her shoulders are parallel to mine. I begin to rock her loose in my arms, just a tiny swinging from side to side, to coddle her for a moment and buy myself some time.

"I am not supposed to *want*. I am the Alpha of the Great North Pack. There shouldn't even be an Evie."

She tilts her pelvis, brings her hip bone closer to my growing erection. I curve in to her, touching her, feeling the pressure of her body as it draws the weight of need back into my cock and her face broadens in a smile against my face. I pull back to look at her, at that half-tweaked corner of her mouth, that slight softening of her cheek.

"But there still is an Evie and she, no, *I* want this."

I bend my head to the side. She follows my lead, her nose touching mine like wolves do when they acknowledge one another. *Bop*. She frowns and tilts her head back until our chins touch.

"Have you never kissed before?"

"No. I've seen it in movies," she says. "But getting everything lined up is more complicated than I expected."

This, at least, I can do and I slide my fingers through the cool, damp denseness of her hair, curving my hand at the base of her skull, holding her in place so that this time when I angle my head, my mouth finds hers. There is a slight flutter of the intimate skin of her lips against mine. I slide my lower lip, imagining burrowing into the silk solace, and bang my teeth against hers. I feel like the inexperienced teenager I never really was, because while I had too much experience in things no child should know, I had none whatsoever of first love. None of the feeling of the awkward touching of lips, of inhaling her breath only to feel it turn to drops of mercury in my blood by the alchemy of a kiss.

I pull her lips back to mine and try them gently, then harder, opening her mouth with teeth and tongue. I drink from her. Her shallow breaths, her lips, her tongue. We taste, touch, and try awkward things as though we were awkward, vulnerable people, though neither of us has ever been allowed to be.

Without moving away, she slides her hand between us.

"I've never touched one before," she murmurs, her little finger pressing against the damp crown of my cock.

"But I don't understand. Aren't Nils and Nyala your—"

She waves her hand dismissively. "Of course we fuck, but this"—she spreads her fingers wide across my torso—"is not something wolves do. Touching. I want to know what it feels like. What you feel like."

I lean my forehead against hers and pull my hips back to give her hand space to roam. She is alternately soft and firm, her hand sketching my collarbone to the notch, then following it down my sternum, her little finger brushing my nipple.

"Does that hurt?" she asks when I jump.

I brush my thumb under the curve of her breast up to the hard, dark tip and make her shiver.

"Does that?" I whisper and feel her smile under my lips as she continues tracing the deep line dividing my chest down to the path of curls at my pelvis, skirting my erection. I have never craved anything as much as I crave the skin at the back of her hand. When I say her name, it is with the voice of a man who is only just not breaking.

I think she likes it, having this power that doesn't come with all the terrifying responsibilities of being Alpha. Simply the intimate power that Evie has to make me ache. To slake me.

I don't tell her that I want her to wrap her fingers around my erection. I don't tell her that I need her to scrape her nails along the seam between cock and balls. Because everything she does to my body channels through the levees I have built around me and I feel her rushing in, an ocean of power and beauty filling me in wave after wave.

"Careful, Evie."

She laughs and I can feel the tremor of it race down her arm to her hand reaching around my sac. "I've never touched them, but I've bitten enough to know how vulnerable they are."

Which coming from her is strangely comforting.

Finally, finally, finally, just when I don't think I can take anymore, she traces her hand along the length of my cock, feeling the give at the crown, the flared ridge, the hardness of the shaft. She pulls down the skin.

"It's soft," she whispers. "Like velvet on antlers." Now she wraps her fingers around me as though she's feeling for the bone underneath until I manage to choke out.

"Stop."

She loosens her hand, taking a step back. I can tell by the expression on her face that she thinks I don't like it.

"*Evie.*" I take her hand tight in mine. "It's not about you. No, that's wrong: it's all about you. I want your touch more than anything, but not like this. I want you needing me."

She looks into my eyes, lines between her brows, her lips pursed. "But you know I am receptive."

"I don't want you to be willing. I need you to want me"—I slide my hand around her cheek, my thumb on her chin—"the way I want you."

The stillness is broken when an animal runs overhead

and twigs and bark and needles are loosed from the canopy, falling down around us like snow.

Under my hand, I feel her head turn toward the Great Hall and the High Pines beyond as though weighing her responsibilities to her wolves against what she wants.

When she turns back, she doesn't say anything, but she buries her lips in my hand, and suddenly, I am afraid.

I have always been selfish, fulfilling my own body's needs. I didn't bother to be good, because being good implied the desire for a repeat performance, of a relationship with its discussion of rings, the cuteness of baby cheeks, and the capital appreciation of real estate.

Now with a woman who could never be small, I wish I'd practiced more. All I have is a lifetime of reading people so that I could efficiently snuff out life, and I will use it to make sure this woman burns with it.

I put my hand to her breast. Cupping the soft weight underneath, I rub my thumb slowly across her skin, catching the tip. She sucks in a breath. I spread out my fingers, then I close them gently around her nipple, opening and closing until I feel the tremor through her body.

Then I bend down, tasting her, currant dark, currant hard, and currant sweet. Her body begins to move, swaying, unthinking, trying to get more skin to skin. Her knees buckle and she slides down against me and she lies against the pine-padded forest floor, releasing the scent of pine and rain as I stretch out against her, feeling her, reading her, listening to her, finding all those spots in the vast continuum between what is spoken and what is seen, where life happens.

Her eyes are closed, but I feel the tension of her body, her jaw tight, her back curved, forcing her torso toward me. The air between us thrums like cicadas in midsummer and she opens her thighs.

She puts her hand on my chest and I feel her calling all the wildness that I've kept in check, except for that one disastrous time.

I want every inch of my skin to touch her: chest, hips, thighs all pressed tight against her until I push my leg between hers to open her up and she pushes at me. My overloaded brain just barely manages to register the rejection of her hand and I twist away.

"I wasn't stopping you," she says. "I couldn't see. I *want* to see."

This time when I stretch my legs on either side of hers, I hold myself a little away on trembling arms. Head bent against mine, she watches as I slowly move back into place, nudging her open. Her mouth slack, the tip of her tongue touching the line of her teeth, she watches intently until I am poised trembling at her entrance. I move as slowly as my strung-out body will allow me, watching her want. I stop and withdraw, feeling her clench around me. Then I enter her again, a little farther this time. Each time, deeper until I slide all the way in and I am surrounded by heat and granite and moss and I am so deep that all we can see is the line where my hip touches hers.

She closes her eyes and we leave behind what is seen and what is spoken and enter that part of the continuum that is only felt. I push into her, changing the angle of my hips to find what makes her tighten around me. How deep she needs me to go until she groans my name and arches her back and I empty myself into her, only I am not emptied, because I am shattered.

And like that cup, I will never be empty again.

Chapter 25

Evie

"He's a fool, Alpha. I can handle him."

I can't tell Elijah why, but I will not have any more argument. "Your Alpha," I say, my voice resonating through my chest and skull, "would have Cassius watched. At. All. Times."

Now Elijah lowers his eyes.

"You can't trust Cassius," Constantine told me last night. It was quiet, but I felt the vibration of it at the point where the top of my head fit under his chin and my ear pressed against his chest.

"I don't."

"If he were to escape, it would be—"

"Unfortunate?"

"Much worse than that."

He stays quiet for a while, his lips pressed to the top of my head, his thumb caressing my shoulder. "I know you can't kill him, so let me. Then you won't have to—"

"We do not betray the spirit of our laws by circumventing the letter of them. He has not threatened the Pack, and we do not need him for food. But he will be watched and that will have to do."

When I caught Constantine watching me at Evening Meat, I pressed my palms together, lips to fingers. He responded by drawing a thumb across his lower lip.

Then Tara asked why I was smiling.

The Pack cannot suspect that their Alpha is giving in to her most selfish instincts and fucking a Shifter, so I told her that I'd been remembering Sigegeat's joke about how the 12 pointer bucked up his face.

It was a lie. Tara nodded. Sigegeat preened—the Alpha has recognized his comic genius, after all. Constantine walked stiffly toward the door and I tried hard not to watch him go.

When I get back to my cabin, he's ready, tall and broad and naked.

"You have to stop looking at me like that."

"Like what?" he asks.

"Like you are now."

As the Alpha, I pretend that I don't see him, the hunger on his face, his eyes following me, his mouth opening like he needs to close the space between us with words or his tongue.

As Evie, I am already half-naked by the time the door closes. We struggle awkwardly, our bodies pressed against each other as he slides his hands under my waistband and slides my pants down, not letting them fall but guiding them with his rough carpenter's hands, tracing a path down my ass and my thighs until he is on his knees in front of me.

"Open for me," he says, fingers opening up my thighs. It is a shock that leaves me speechless and breathless, the feeling of his tongue cool and broad and firm against my seam.

He says I taste like salt and earth and sweetgrass.

And after I come, my legs trembling like aspen leaves in summer, he lifts me and settles me down on the mattress in the middle of the floor that I put there because the pups like to jump down from the sleeping loft and I knew I would not be fucking anyone again for a long time.

I thought.

He enters me, my Green Man, smelling of life and water. I taste myself on his mouth while he moves slowly, each thrust a spark against tinder until I start to squirm again, my legs tight around his hips. His back curves and he slams in deeper, then he groans my name, quietly so that no wolves will hear.

Evie.

In the bathroom, I scrub hard, removing every last trace of him. Then I help him, removing the last trace of myself. He doesn't like it, but what can I do? Humans see power as a license for self-indulgence. For wolves, power means responsibility. I am expected to do what the Pack needs me to do, and sadly, the Pack does not need me to be fucked limp by Constantine.

He scrubs his hair dry with the towel, then he stares bleakly into the mirror, feeling the stubble at his chin.

"You should let it grow out." I curl my arms over his shoulders, looking at him in the reflection. "For winter."

For whatever reason—beard, snow, or future—he smiles and turns to me, his lips to my cheek. "Tomorrow?" he whispers.

"Tomorrow is the Iron Moon. Tomorrow if I do this"—I bite lightly on his lip—"it will hurt. Tomorrow if I do this"—I run the tips of my fingers across his upright cock—"you will bleed."

He cranes his head out of the bathroom, looking toward the path of light on Home Pond. His smile burns away, leaving nothing but the bitter scent of anger.

"What happened when you changed?"

He shakes his head, his jaw clamped shut. With the toe of one foot, he scratches absently at the ankle of the other. I've kissed those old ligature marks that ring the gold of his skin in dark and mangled mauve.

"Whatever August did to you, Constantine, it will not be like last time."

Chapter 26

Constantine

It will not be like last time.

Even in broad daylight, I knew the Iron Moon was coming, I felt it in Evie, a kind of dangerous edge. In the Pack's increasing industry as they sealed everything up and turned it off. Mostly it was in a kind of electric anticipation. The inability to sit still, constantly checking the sky, scratching at necks and arms and backs as though if they scratched hard enough, they would tear through that imprisoning skin.

The evening comes like one of those dreams where you're sitting in class or a meeting, but then someone calls on you and you stand up only to discover that you're naked from the waist down. The only difference is I *am* naked from the waist down and from the waist up, and everyone else is naked too. Flagrantly, unashamedly naked.

There is way too much touching going on.

Where is she?

"Connie? Were you even paying attention?"

"Fine, fine," I say, distractedly folding my clothes.

Ziggy chuffs a dry raspberry of exasperation. "So it's fine, fine, if Tiberius shoots you?"

"What?" My T-shirt and boxer briefs go on top.

"I knew you weren't paying attention. If you don't

change when we do, Tiberius. Will. Shoot. You. Won't be the first time we've had to sand bloodstains out of the floor."

A pup wobbles across the back of the sofa, pausing for a moment before launching herself onto a pile of adults.

"Ooof," says the pile.

"Why aren't the pups changing?"

"They don't have to," Ziggy says with a shrug. "The Moon takes us as she finds us and makes us wilder. The pups are already as wild as they can be, so she leaves them alone."

I put my folded shirt on top of the pile of denim, sweats, sleeveless flannel, as well as the occasional Offlander linen shirts and summer-weight wools that belong to the 7th.

I smooth the stack, feeling the absence at its heart.

Where is she?

Then a subtle tension runs through the Pack. It's not that they look to the door, though some do. It's just they know she's coming. I do too. I no longer have to see her to know as surely as if her head was leaning against my neck, as if her hand was on my heart, as if I was gathering her to me in the cold of an Adirondack summer night.

There are a few words exchanged with returning Offlanders, but not many. The 7th's two Offlanders have been pacing anxiously back and forth for an hour, their pent-up wild scraping at the walls of their skin.

"*Wes þu hal*, Erika," Ziggy says to one of them, a woman with red-brown hair standing at the window, staring at the sun. She whips her head around, teeth bared, before turning back to press her hands to the glass, her feet jittering on the floor.

All around us, men and women pace nervously, shaking

out their legs and arms, bending low so they can check the sun's progress through the window. It's not setting quickly enough for them, but to me it seems to plummet from the sky.

The 14th Echelon crowds into one of the few remaining spots.

And for the first time since that horrible moment in Medical, I see Magnus in skin. I know it's him, even though he looks nothing like he did. Before, he'd been a scrawny teenager among giants. A marionette with flopping distended joints and wooden gestures. It's as though his body had stopped growing at the age of his last change, and now in the past weeks, it has raced ahead, making up for lost time. He has a fucking beard. Chest hair.

If I ever wanted proof that he doesn't need me, here it is.

He looks around the room, and when he catches sight of me, he smiles, his teeth bright with only one slightly snaggled canine. He curls his arm around his front, his fingers reaching for that spot at his back, and begins to roll his shoulder blade.

If the Iron Moon finds us wild…

I hit Magnus fast and bring him down hard, pressing his back flat to the floor, my hand cradling the back of his head. Eudemos, though, who has bones made of lead, is not careful and hits me like he wants to hurt me. The scaffolding of my body cracks and groans. My left arm trapped against the floor pops loose from its place at my shoulder and I scream.

"*Stop!*" Evie yells, jumping for Eudemos before she remembers who she is and where.

"Stop," the Alpha commands.

Someone's got their teeth in my upper thigh. I can't see who but if it was painful going in, it's even more painful coming out. Eudemos lifts his body from mine, and when my lungs can inflate again, the agony in my shoulder joins up with the torment in my fingertips.

"What's going on here?" the Alpha demands, looking at me, but pain has locked my jaw and it's going to take me a minute before I can find the key.

"He attacked Magnus," Eudemos says, helping Magnus up, suddenly his great protector. Magnus looks at me, his mouth open, a look of confused betrayal in his eyes, and now I have no choice but to unlock my jaw and explain to him that I'm not trying to deprive him of this new self. I am not jealous of what he has become without me.

"No forever wolf," I exhale raggedly. "Not like Varya. He was..." Without thinking, I begin to roll my shoulder, not even the one that's disconnected, but it's enough and I grunt from the pain.

Evie purses her lips and squats down in front of me. "Tristan? A hand?" She helps me sit up, looking almost apologetic. I want to tell her that it doesn't suit her at all, looking apologetic. Tristan's hands find my elbow and wrist. A blindingly painful twist later, I understand the apologetic look. As my shoulder pops back into its socket, my eyes are blurred and my breathing shredded.

My ass hurts, too, and sticks to the floor.

"Is that true, Magnus?" Eudemos looks at him. "Tell me that's not what you were doing?"

"But..." He looks around at his echelon for an explanation. "Isn't that what we're here for?"

The Alpha raises her eyebrows at the 14th's Alpha.

"I...I...forgot?" Eudemos says with a sigh and begins to unbutton his shirt.

"Just so there is no misunderstanding," the Alpha says, looking pointedly at Julia and Magnus, "the Iron Moon takes us as she finds us and makes us wilder. If we are in skin, she makes us wild. If we are wild, she makes us real wolves. Forever wolves."

"But you don't know if that would happen to us," Cassius says. I notice him for the first time, standing silent and largely hidden in the corner behind the staircase. He is still dressed.

"I don't know. If you'd like to find out, no one will stop you from changing now," she says, making it clear that Cassius as a real wolf would be less objectionable or perhaps dead and either way a better outcome for the Pack.

Using my good arm, I push myself up from the floor. I start back for the 7th, but Eudemos blocks my way with his broad and frankly inhumanly furry chest. My fingers are tingling and my arm definitely weak. If he comes at me again, I'm going to have one chance to knock him out. I can't raise my left arm high enough to protect against a return blow.

He doesn't hit me. He just stands looking at me expectantly, then spreads his arms out at his sides. Evie is watching. So is Silver, sitting on the floor next to Tiberius, pups crawling over her naked skin. "If you're going to bite him," Silver says, bending down to look at the sun's progress, "you need to do it now."

"Bite him? I don't want to bite him. Why would I bite him?"

"He attacked you without provocation. By law, you

may bite him and he cannot retaliate. Although the law places no strictures as to where, by custom, we avoid the cock and nose."

Eudemos's neck and shoulders are surrounded by thick fields of hair. His cheeks too. Whorls of it surround his nipples and belly button. His cock has shrunk into the surrounding overgrowth, perhaps worried about my understanding of the law and even more, my understanding of custom. Just looking at him, I feel bits of sweaty hair lodged between my teeth.

"You said 'if' and 'may'... I'm presuming that means I don't have to?"

"No, but the Pack will not tolerate grudges or resentments tearing at its fabric. *Misblod ageat sculon ðy læs wyrmsan.* Bad blood must be spilled lest it fester."

"I'll pass," I say and head back to the 7th, chuckling to myself at the thought of August here. August who not only tolerated bad blood but encouraged it, every trifling grievance or imagined slight, so as to keep all his people sniping and snapping at one another. With exaggerated irony, August called it "our happy home," though the compound was in reality a pit fight with company cars.

The Alpha bends down, peering through a window at the sun touching the ragged, tree-lined horizon. A gold disk framed by a valance of orange and purple clouds. "It's almost time," she says, straightening up. Those few remaining Pack still in clothes peel them off, adding them to the neat piles belonging to the wolves in their echelons. Other wolves double-check that the windows are fastened shut. Pack on the floor clamber over one another, noses touching, open mouths clashing, forming a wild chain.

Not Cassius though. He stands stock-still in the corner like a golem carved from the clay of bad blood and petty resentments. Elijah plucks at Cassius's clothes, obviously telling him that he needs to strip, but Cassius ignores him, his eyes focused on Julia, willing her to turn and see his sullen expression.

She might have done it once. It used to be as though she could feel him looking at her, telling her to stop whatever she was doing. And she would, turning to him with a bright and anxious smile.

Maybe she is still aware of him because she turns slightly, offering him an even more decided view of her back while her focus is entirely on Arthur, who arrived late and is folding his clothes, piling them on the table. Then he turns toward Julia, his elegant naked body scarred by the claws of wolves and he smiles at her. Cassius's hands clench into fists.

The Alpha moves in front of Cassius, blocking his view of where Julia makes room for Arthur so that when he sits, his naked hip slides against hers. He pulls his knees up, props his chin on his forearm, turns his head toward her, listening.

The table beside the sofa explodes toward the wall where Cassius has kicked it. Julia freezes, one hand fisted, the other pushing her hair behind her ear.

"Pick it up," Evie says quietly, but since the pack is silent, it's easy to hear.

Cassius looks at her, his lips writhing. Then he torques his body, his shoulder twisted, his fist clenched, telegraphing his attack. I know this, but I don't feel one single bit of protectiveness. Not like I do when some wolf plucks at her sleeve, or sets papers in front of her to sign, or needs a decision about discipline. Or when Poul sticks his nose in her—

Cassius's body slams against the wall, struggling against Evie's forearm at his throat.

—because I know Evie is perfectly capable of protecting herself from those she doesn't like. It's the ones she loves that she is so vulnerable to.

Tiberius stretches and reaches behind him, gathering a Glock and a magazine. With a practiced action—slide, magazine, slide—puts his gun to Cassius's forehead. Evie lets go and Cassius drops into the flagstones of the fireplace, howling in frustration.

At that moment, one sharp ray of light breaks through the window. Shimmering with dust motes and stray wolf hairs, it picks out the details of Evie's body—the slope of her breast, the sharp angle of her hip, the long silk of her waist, damasked with the healed scars.

Standing straight, she turns to her Pack. "*Eadig waþ*," she calls in that particular voice and the resonance scrapes across my skin.

"And be yourself not hunted!" the huge, naked wolfish congregation roars back.

"And be yourself not hunted," I whisper to her, my teeth a dike against the ocean of words I want her to hear.

She moves quickly toward her echelon and my heart beats harder. We are so careful otherwise, but she might sit close to me and I might touch her here in the open, seen by everyone. She picks her way toward the bit of floor that is unoccupied because I refused to have Ziggy's naked, hairy thigh against mine.

"Gamma," she says with a nod toward Ziggy as he moves over.

The light leaking into the room turns from orange gold to purple to gray.

"Remember," she whispers urgently, her head bent near her arm so that even the sharp-eared wolves can't hear. "It will not be like last time." Her eyes run down my torso. "And don't worry about the erection. It will go away during the change. They always d—" Her arm flails out and her body seizes and she starts to fall. I catch her just in time to stop her from tumbling to the floor.

Her head twitches against my chest and her body churns in my arms. I lay her down, pushing her hair back. It starts small, with the dullness in her gold eyes, the ripples riding across skin. Sheltered in the cave of my body, Evie slowly changes: her soft nose lengthening, her beautiful mouth stretching and thinning around the length of her jaw, her bones turning almost rubbery as they bend and lengthen and contract. The tip of a wiry whisker pokes out from her brown cheek.

All around me, bodies are churning, except for two, standing near the fireplace. One of them pointing a gun, eyebrows raised, lips pursed. The other at the muzzle end, wearing a furious, calculating expression and a stretched-out T-shirt from St. Elizabeth's College of Nursing.

I lay Evie down, and because it's too late to hide anything, I curl down around her.

I put my mouth to her neck, feeling the muscles thicken under my lips.

It will not be like last time.

I presume parents are the ones who have "the talk" with their children. I had no parents so I, lucky boy that I was, got to have the talk with August.

There is a place in every Lukani, August had said, and

before he went any farther, I had wrapped my arm around my ribs, my fingers feeling the spot near the floating rib on my left side that felt equally like pleasure and shame.

"*Don't* go looking for it," he'd said as soon as he saw me. "It lets the monsters out."

I dropped my hand and "the talk" was over. I knew better than most Lukani my age what those monsters were. Years went by before I was tempted again, but by the time that moon rose from the North Atlantic, so cold and large and necessary, I was no longer worried that there was a monster inside me. I was now terrified that there was nothing but a big, empty, monster-shaped space.

Cassius yells something at Tiberius, but the sound is already indistinct in my itching ears.

It will not be like last time.

The Great North Pack is not like the Lukani, who came from France to rip up the forests of Canada and make the land safe for cabbages. And though he had never used an ax himself—not on a tree, in any case—August was in his soul a *défricheur*, a clearer of the land. An extirpator of the wild.

With the last of my dissolving agency, I let my arm drop around Evie's waist, sorting through that Alpha scent of the entirety of the Pack for the growing scent of granite and moss that is all her.

It will not be like last time.

Tiny crystals float in front of my eyes and swirl together, blinding me. Bones soften and unknit, tissue unravels, skin tingles and itches as fur erupts. Organs rumble and rearrange themselves and my mind drops, like a dreamer jerking on the verge of sleep.

My ankles narrow and ache, whether from phantom

pain or actual damage, I don't know. Last time, I hadn't known what was happening. I was still dressed, though my pants had fallen off or maybe August had them removed. I still had on the shirt that fell in front of my face so I could see nothing. But as a wolf, I could smell.

It will not be like last time.

I could smell Magnus, hear his ragged sobs. I know now why Magnus had always been able to find me, but I wish that one time he hadn't found me in that secluded beach in the middle of the change.

It will not be like last time.

Terrified, he had run for August, who had me strung up by my back feet, or rather paws, from the single tree of the old compound as a lesson to anyone who might feel inclined to forget who we were.

"Nous sommes Lukani. C'est notre devoir de dompter le sauvage qui nous entoure, comme nous l'avons dompté en nous-mèmes."

We are Lukani. It is our duty to tame the wild without, as we have always tamed the wild within.

I don't know how long I hung there, blindly swaying when the wind or some asshole poked at my body.

The Lukani knew that was not a wolf hanging there. They knew that if August didn't kill me, I would take revenge on everyone who had spit at me, who had jabbed at my genitals, who had made me bleed. They gave me a wide berth. The humans didn't. Magnus tried to keep them away, but he was young, and without me looming behind him lending him power, he had none of his own. August knew he would have to replace the humans once my ankles healed and I was able to walk again, but it amused him to tame the wild with these disposable employees.

It will not be like last time.

Eventually, my ears begin ringing, a welcome change from deafness. The door slams and I move my jaw, trying to pop my ears. Sound and smell begin to overwhelm my brain. Eyes closed, nose stuffed into the crook of the leg that was once an arm, I try to block out as much as I can in order to make sense of what's left. It takes time to identify the soft rhythmic clacking of claws and the infinitesimal creak of the floor. I pick out snufflings as wolves smell one another, the sound of fur shaking.

A damp nose touches mine. *Bop.* I open one eye, then the other. This time when I open my eyes, I realize that we are the last two wolves left in the Great Hall, except for another huge black one still changing under the watchful eye of the small silver wolf, who circles him, shaking out her back leg.

And a beige wolf writhing around inside a baggy shirt that reads St. Elizabeth's College of Nursing.

I try to stand, pushing off with my hands, but forget that I have neither hands nor feet and fall backward on my coccyx. On my tail. I have a tail. Evie starts toward the door, then looks back at me expectantly. I can't follow her. Even through the walls, I can tell that what's out there is too much.

Evie chuffs and closes her jaws around my long nose and pulls, dragging me stumbling and sliding toward the outside and all the chirping and whispering and barking and things that don't make any sound at all, but reverberate through the hollows of my skull.

Scents hit me like physical objects made of damp earth and crushed grass and old char and moldering pine and still water.

Evie licks forcefully at my eyes. Opening them mournfully, I catch the brightness of the stars and the rim of moonlight reflected on the torn veil of low, gray clouds and the flash of a wolf appearing in the ragged tree line who says, "Excuse the interruption, Alpha. The Pack is already running toward the High Pines, where there is news of prey." That is what I understand, though the only sound from his mouth is *Growp?*

Evie sighs and bops her nose to mine. I bop back, understanding that she can't babysit me. I'm grateful that she's not there when I start down from the porch. That first step, as they say, is a doozy. My tail flashes in front of my eyes; the sharp edges of the stairs hit my spine. Finally, I end up face-first on the grass.

With a lurching hop, I pull myself up, my feet planted shoulder and hip width apart. Stupidly, I try to move the front feet first, then the two back ones, hopping forward a few inches before collapsing. I follow with a couple of other combinations that are only slightly better. Finally, I hit on the most reasonable progression of right front and left back forward followed by left front and right back.

Every step I take in the forest seems to release a maelstrom. The scratched surface of the rock, the broken stem of fern, the rapid heartbeat of some small animal I can't see. Wind tells me so much as it sweeps across my fur (Fur!) and tells me its direction and whether it is saturated enough to mean rain. I *feel* north.

Beyond the damp woody edges and white flowers with broad heart-shaped leaves is a rotting log with an alien-looking flower sprouting from it that smells sugary and sparkles in the moonlight. Because my nose is now so appallingly long, I jam it right into the middle of the flower, getting its stickiness all over my muzzle. I slap at it with my long, flat tongue. It is sweet and my tongue is soothing on my fur.

Something uncoils from under the log, long and thin with a bright line running the length of its back. Without thinking, forelegs and hind propel me straight up as it writhes away, whip fast. The less I try to define what is around me, the more I understand of the continuum of life between what is seen and what is spoken.

The path that had been no path at all is now supremely clear to me, like the bioluminescent tide I had seen one night in Jamaica, except more complex. I take my time exploring, circling in ever-wider paths, bumping against new things, though whenever I circle close to Home Pond, I smell Cassius, followed by a changing escort. I catch sight of him once, sullen and furious in the bedraggled, muddy French terry he wore defiantly but no longer has the fingers to get rid of.

I recognize Magnus by the fragrance of juniper and black walnut. He has crisscrossed this place before, sometimes with his echelon, sometimes alone.

Tiberius and Silver are like two strands of a helix, weaving in and out but inexorably bound. Julia and Arthur, though, are always together. JuliaAndArthur, JuliaAndArthur, JuliaAndArthur.

Hardly a minute later, the sun rises, garish and too nosy by half. I stay away from any opening in the canopy, following the scent that is green and earthy and musky and flowering and stony and majestic and wild. Stone and moss. The Alpha is everywhere at once. I imagine her even now dispensing justice and comfort and protection and discipline. I follow a scent that is like earth and woody mushroom and I only now recognize is Ziggy. The 7th moves too quickly for my stumbling steps. In frustration, I throw my head back and howl. It isn't a real howl, just an *oww* suddenly truncated because I run out of breath. Wolves check on me, gray and silent shadows in the trees.

Evie, I want to say but my tongue is long and thin and rests limp on sharp teeth between slashed cheeks. *Where is Evie?*

Eventually, I track the 7th down to where they are quarreling with the 13th over a kill.

My mouth open, I suck in the clean, rich, coppery smell and my stomach rumbles. A female from the 13th shoots me a toothy snarl that almost looks like a smile when I get too close to the hind leg she has dragged off to eat in peace. She lunges at me, then returns to gnawing at the last bit of flesh with her back teeth, her eyes trained on me, until the Alpha barks softly and the 7th begins to move away.

She circles around us, making it clear that we have a mission, and suddenly the 7th is focused and alert, moving as one. Or rather one and a floundering bit. Their noses close to the ground, they stop occasionally at a tree. In the distance, near the southwest perimeter, one woofs quietly. The Alpha trots away, but when I make to follow, Ziggy leaps in front of me, stretching his jaw halfway between a yawn and a reminder that he can fit the better part of my head between his teeth.

The Alpha returns almost immediately, scurrying low to the ground, then bounding twice and racing around the whole 7th. As she moves among her echelon, they crowd close, sniffing at her head and neck. Their back paws prance excitedly in the earth.

They spread out on either side of a rocky hollow, the remains of a dry riverbed. I stay behind, unsure what all the excitement is about, though the wind tells me that there is something with an earthy, musky smell. Animal, yes. Male, I think, but there the similarity to the buck we left behind ends.

Then it crashes through the trees, squealing, frightened, and angry, slipping on the exposed rocks of the riverbed. Sound and smells echo confusingly in the hollow, and Ziggy wags his head side to side, trying to see the thing, only to be blindsided as it charges straight toward him, its upturned nose dotted with mud and grass. Its brown tusks curled around its upper lip.

A fevered excitement spreads through my body: skin prickles, a shiver runs down my spine as muscles contract, and then without thinking, I lunge forward. Armed with nothing but my virgin fangs, I grab hold of its thick, bristled hide at the hump of its back. My bite isn't deep enough, and the feral pig's *(SWINE!!!)* huge head twists and churns, his dull tusk ripping into my skin. He swerves from side to side, trying to shake me, but I hang on, because that is what I have to do to feed my wolves.

A demon in black fur tears from behind a tree and slides under the pig's jaw, taking his throat deep in her teeth, and with a ferocious pull of her jaws, tears it out. The squealing stops though his legs keep churning, slowing until air and earth are warm and damp and heavy with the smell of blood and the 7th opens him up, teeth clacking against the rib cage, claws ripping through the tough hide.

My shoulders relax, the dull throbbing pain at my chest replaced by a much more visceral need, one I would never have admitted to myself before.

There was a reason August sent Cassius and not me to shepherd the hunters. He'd tried that once, taking me with him to a hunt party. I'd been very young and he'd given me a knife, because he didn't want anyone to see me use a gun. I was a kid; my job, he said, was to be "disarming." Then one of the assholes shoots a big cat in the gut, but the guy's tired and wants to go home. August said if I was so worried about it, I could take care of it myself, challenging me. Put up or shut up.

He didn't like it when I came back spattered with blood.

"A *real* hunter"—I remember how cold his eyes went—"keeps his blade clean." It wasn't phrased as a command, but everything August said was a challenge or a command or a criticism to make clear who was the big man and who was small.

An orphaned child with no one else in the world, I obeyed but there was something about watching me lick the gore from that knife that made him narrow his eyes and frown. He never took me again.

I say "something" as though I don't know exactly what disturbed August that day. It wasn't the bravado or the defiance, both of which he could understand.

What bothered him was that I had enjoyed it.

And I enjoy it now: wedged in between furred and powerful bodies, taking still-warm life from this death that we created together.

Once the echelon has taken what we want, the Alpha calls for other members of the Pack to come for any scraps. Ziggy noses around the blood at my chest, his long tongue lapping firmly but gently at the gash, but I stumble back, my lips pulled away from my sharp teeth, a growl rumbling from my throat.

Circling round and round, the 7th lie down, some alone in a tight circle, but more in scattered piles, chuffing and huffing as they pillow their heads on the legs or backs or distended bellies of their packmates.

Evie finishes grooming her muzzle with her front paw, then she stretches back into her haunches and, after one luxurious shake, throws her head back and begins the low resonant howl of evening call. Her ears circle, catching the responses of her Pack floating over the contours of the mountains and valleys, skimming streams and ponds. Only when she is sure that the Great North is safe does she stop, turn around three times, and lie down.

And only then do I lie down a few feet away, full and content.

I have killed for bacon.

Chapter 27

Evie

Constantine clings to the walls of the Great Hall like a gecko.

Even for me, the end of the Iron Moon is hard. It means losing the lightness and connection to the world that comes with being wild. Ears clogged, eyes unfocused, nose dulled, limbs sluggish, head heavy, and torso unbalanced on top of long legs, it's like walking on stilts through mud.

"That wasn't three days," he'd said as he'd struggled into his clothes. It never feels like it since there is no schedule and time is defined by the length of a hunt or measures of a howl. Especially now when the canopy is so thick that the sunlight that struggles through in mottled specks seems barely brighter than moonlight.

After checking on preparations for the Iron Moon Table, that one time when the whole Pack comes together with thumbs and words, I head outside. Constantine's made it no farther than the corner of the Great Hall. He leans against a log end, watching Silver.

She sits in front of the three birches that burned the night the Shifters came to the Great Hall. The bark bubbled brown around the edge of blackened wood, but I would not have them cut down until spring came and we would know whether they survived. They did and put out bright-green leaves and stand here scarred and resilient, just like the Great North.

"*Gehyrað*," Silver says. "Listen."

I turn the gray weathered Adirondack chair to the corner to watch.

The pups who'd been running around Silver stop, their heads bending from side to side, questioning. One of the First Shoes has frozen her bare foot behind her head as she tries to scratch behind her jaw. Another, curled next to his packmate on the grass, stops his gentle gnawing on the other's little, hairless, shell-like ear. There's always a certain amount of backsliding after the Iron Moon.

"*Gehyrað*," Silver says again, this time cupping her hand behind her ear.

A few adults have gathered around too. Some who know what she's asking but who know better than to say anything and two who have not been raised Pack.

Thea pushes back the black cascade of hair from her ear to listen, revealing a pup clinging to her shoulder for balance, its bony, hyperactive tail wagging furiously. Even Tiberius with his freakish senses shakes his head, no.

"*Gehyrað æfter stilnes*," Silver says, prodding them. "Listen to the silence."

I lean back into the chair. I remember playing this game with Sigeberg. No one got it then either.

"Water," rasps Constantine. His voice quavers in the way of someone reluctant to give up the silence of the wild.

"*Gea*, Constantine," Silver says. "Listen if you like. There are no Pack secrets."

He totters toward the edge of the porch, grabbing on to the peeled trunk that serves as one of the roof supports.

Leaning against it, he sinks down, sitting with his knees bent, his bare feet near mine.

"First the water quiets. Then birds molt and become vulnerable and secretive and the noise of spring is followed by the Silence of Summer.

"Do we have time for the story, Alpha?" she asks. "I'll make it short."

I nod and settle into the corner of the Adirondack chair, one foot curled up against the strut, the other near Constantine.

"*Wulfas,*" she says and picks Nils up. "*On ðære wald stearc and grim, alifde ðæt ðæt unasecgende sceolon.*

"In the forest strong and fierce are lives that must be lived unspoken."

Constantine sucks in a deep breath; he stretches out his arms behind him. Hidden by the chair, one hand sneaks around behind my foot, its rough warmth circling the back of my heel, the tendon there, the hard bone at the side, and the soft spot below where the blood runs quick and at the surface.

As with most our stories, the one Silver tells involves the heroism of wolves and the unredeemable shittiness of gods.

"The responsibility for the flow of days was given to two gods: Sol, the goddess of the sun, and Mani, the god of the moon. Like most gods, they were lazy and selfish and thought nothing about their responsibilities and everything about their own power and pleasure. But if Bragi indulges in too much drink, a writer's words come slowly. If Njord lounges by the beach, a traveler is stranded on her voyage. It was different when Sol and Mani dithered around, because then the earth's seasons stopped and life withered.

"The humans were terrified. They indulged in thoughts and prayers, which did exactly nothing.

"Wolves need the Iron Moon to knit the Pack together. To run the territory. To keep the land in balance. While Mani masturbated on the mountain top, there was no crescent moon, no quarter moon, no new moon, and no Iron Moon. While Sol slept, the sands of the desert turned to glass and the trees of the Ironwood withered.

"The Alpha of the Ironwood didn't think and she didn't pray. Instead, she called for her fastest hunters and sent them to chase the laggard gods.

"As soon as Sol and Mani saw wolves coming, they got off their asses and ran. The cycles of the earth started again. Life began and ended. The moon waxed and waned, and wolves could be wild together. For millennia, these wolves did what wolves have always done—kept the balance of life.

"At first Sol and Mani called those wolves Hati and Sköll—Hater and Betrayer—because like the spoiled children they were, they resented being forced to work.

"The wolves of the Ironwood, however, called them by their real names, Háte and Ceald, meaning… Aella?"

Aella looks abashed, caught with her hand up as she rubbed her ear against her shoulder. "I was just—"

"Your hand was raised," Silver says. "So what do Háte and Ceald mean?"

She hesitates, looking around her. "Hot and cold?"

"*Gea,* Aella," Silver says. Tiberius reaches out his curved fingers toward the girl's scalp. She moves her head under his nails, thumping her foot on the ground.

Silver pulls at her smile and begins again. "One night, Ceald could not move anymore. She was after all a wolf, not some mythical creature. Mani was just that, and being deathless and omnipotent, he escaped, happy with his freedom, far from the wolf who had chased him so long. He went back to his old ways, masturbating on mountaintops, spilling more stars in the sky. He drank mead. He played several rounds of *Halatafl*, *Kvatrutafl*, and *Hnefatafl*, even though one round is dull as dirt with only a single player. He kicked comets, and before the first comet found its orbit, he was bored.

"He returned to Ceald, who had changed into skin. 'What do you want, god?' she said, still panting from the millennia spent keeping him on course.

"'Aren't you going to chase me?'

"'*Now* you want me to chase you?' She looked at him disdainfully.

"'Isn't that your job?' he asked, peeved that she'd dared look at him disdainfully. He was Mani, the bright and shining moon, seeder of stars and kicker of comets.

"'No, it's *your* job,' she said, kneading her knotted calf. 'I should not have to hunt you across the skies to make you do it. My *duty* is to make sure the world lives and dies and lives again in time. To make sure that my Pack has an Iron Moon so that they can be wild and together.'

"Mani saw the knotted muscle under Ceald's fingers. He saw a rim of sweat on her dark brow. He saw the depth of her purpose and her love for something that was not herself, and he reached out his hand to his ancient enemy. Under his cool fingers, the knot unknotted. His hand moved up, bringing peace to the still-vibrating length of her bare leg. Then he touched her hip and Ceald felt something beyond peace and reached for him, taking the sharp cold of his body into her own.

"Háte saw his packmate with her god lover and herded Sol, keeping her in place for the longest day, so that Mani and Ceald would have time.

"In time, Mani became one of the few gods who understood that the world did not revolve around him. From then on, he revolved around the world, no longer chased by Ceald but accompanied by her. Hand in hand or hand on ruff. Later, when Háte put off his wild form to take Sol's burning body, too searing for anyone except Heat itself, Mani and Ceald held on to the sky for the longest night.

"After that long day of the summer solstice comes the Silence of Summer, the quiet time while earth's children busy themselves for the coming season of death. After the long night of the winter solstice comes the Silence of Winter, when earth's children rest in preparation for the coming season of life."

Aella squints up at the sky and the sun.

"Are they fucking now?"

"Not until the solstice. Remember, what is important is not the wolf or the god or when they are fucking. What we should take away from this story is that wolves have responsibility not only to themselves and their pack but to the entire balance of life."

Tara calls, announcing the beginning of the Iron Moon Table.

"Coming," I say, my tendon tightening under Constantine's hand. He pulls his hand away and flattens it against his chest.

Chapter 28

Constantine

CASSIUS HAS A LEAN AND HUNGRY LOOK.

I ate well during the Iron Moon. Feral bacon. Leftover turkey. Frog: it looked like it would be cool and refreshing, an amuse-gueule, but it wasn't and I will not make that mistake again.

Cassius clearly ate nothing and falls on the serving platters like a… I'd say "wolf," but it hardly seems appropriate. He always sits in the same corner of the 9th's table, hunched over his food as though it's the only thing that matters, but I see the glint of his eyes as they sweep the room, watching. I see the way he turns his head, listening.

I don't disguise the fact that I'm watching him. He doesn't acknowledge me, beyond a malicious smile. When he is done, two wolves who had been lying unseen on the floor follow him out.

Poul hovers behind the Alpha, and even though I know that when she did what she wanted to, she did it with me, it still makes me angry that he is allowed to touch her openly and I am not. To leave traces of his DNA on her cheek and take hers onto his. Just because he is Pack and she is his Alpha.

Her top lip flickers upward, showing her canine, but then purses tightly, the only sign of her exasperation.

"Why doesn't she like him?"

"Who? Pass the bread."

"Poul, Ziggy." I push the big basket toward him. "Why doesn't the Alpha like Poul?"

He tears off a piece of black bread. When he looks toward the 10th's Alpha, he frowns.

"Before Quicksilver, the noseless dog"—Ziggy spits three times, *puuh, puuh, puuh*—"was our Deemer." I remember the body of the man with the small hole in his chest. The one whose face had been gnawed by the Alpha so he would wander alone for eternity. *Dog,* Tiberius had said, spitting less symbolically, followed by a forceful kick to the spleen.

"Some of the Alphas followed his"—he spits again—"lead. Poul was one."

A dark-red stain seeps across my vision, watching the 10th's Alpha hovering around her, his nose to the face I have held in my hands. His cheek near the ear that has heard my whispered groans. His chin to the velvet mouth that I have tasted.

His very presence marking her like one of the hundreds of No Trespassing signs ringing Homelands, because he is a strong wolf and would fight off any other males who might be interested.

The whole Pack sees him, and everyone knows he sided with the shit who planned to take over the Pack once August's hunters tore its heart out. Tore her out. But the Alpha doesn't flinch as his breath touches her hair.

The membrane covering my eyes ripples in time with the hollow lapping at the walls of my skull. I stumble over the bench, out the door, down the sloping lawn, and to the solace of water that shimmers bright and colorless as mercury.

I stretch out, letting my back absorb heat from planks that have been warmed by the sun and textured by wolf claws, bending my arm to protect my eyes from the too-transparent sky and overly bright sun. The variety of calls that bounded across Homelands when I first came here has quieted. Now it's just the hollow *thock*ing of a woodpecker.

Wolves are nearby. I can't see them or hear them, but I feel them watching from the cool and subtle forest. Before I can ask what they're looking for, a tremor runs from the soil into the timbers of the dock with a heedless thumping louder than that of even the biggest wolf.

"Cassius." I don't move the arm bent across my eyes.

He sits next to me.

"I'm not doing that again," he says.

I recognize an opening salvo for what it is and say nothing, hoping he'll go away.

A boat bumps against the side of the Boathouse.

"I hear you swum all the way to the other side," he says conversationally, trying another tack.

"Swam," I answer less conversationally.

Just because I have my arm cocked over my eyes doesn't mean I don't catch the way his eyes narrow and his jaw tightens. Or the way he manages to corral the tiny twitch at the corner of his mouth into a smile. "That's right, 'swam.' I hear you *swam* all the way to the other side."

Something disturbs the water, sending minute waves into the water plants at the edge. *What do you want, Cassius? What is so important that you would let me chide you like that?*

"Did you hear the cars?"

The bells that had been chiming are now warning tocsins that race across the landscape of my brain. I think about those last meters I swam, Evie's head against my shoulder, pretending she needed to be rescued though we both knew she didn't. Did I hear the road? I have no idea. It was the last thing on my mind.

"I wouldn't know. I didn't make it that far. And just so you know, I've seen you swim. There's no way in hell you could make it that distance, if that's what you're thinking."

He stills for a long time, staring out over the water, then the wood creaks and he leans in close enough for me to feel his breath. "Just so you know, you're not one of them. You never will be," he says, his tone quiet and petty.

My fingers feel the splintering planks of the dock. I'll measure it tomorrow. Tell Sten we need to fix it.

"What do you want, Cassius?"

He knows I meant it rhetorically, but he answers it anyway.

"I'm doing you a favor," he says. "I'd hate to see you humiliated when you find out that the Alpha has no interest in you beyond the fact that you look like her dead husband."

"What?"

"I heard Elijah say it. When he thought I wasn't listening." Cassius's malevolence grows once he sees he's fingered a sore spot. "He said you look more like him than ever. Now that you have the beard."

I touch the edge of my lip.

For winter, she'd said.

I don't know when Cassius left. I only notice the hole left by the absence of the watchers in the woods.

I'm jealous of a dead man. Did he really look like me? Or rather, do I really look like him? When she said I should grow out my beard, was it because it would keep my face warm during the winter or because it would make me look more like John?

"Are you fucking me because I look like John?" I close the door behind me.

It's taken me the better part of the day to find her in her office alone. She is looking between something on her laptop and a spreadsheet on her desk. She makes a mark with her pencil and looks up at me with genuine confusion.

"What?"

"Are you fucking me because I look like your dead mate?"

"I have no idea what you're talking about."

"Elijah says I look like him. Like John. I want to know if that is why you're fucking me."

She closes her laptop and turns around, looking me up and down.

I spread out my arms.

What do you see, Evie?

"I have no idea if you look like John," she says with a shrug.

"How can you not know?"

"*Because that's not the way we think.*" She breathes deeply, her nose flared, her head turned, listening at the door. "I have to sort something out," she whispers hurriedly. "But meet me in my cabin later and I'll try to explain."

Now even I can hear the creaking of the floorboards.

"When?"

"When the moon"—she holds up one hand like a mitten—"is in the Endeberg Notch."

She taps her finger webbing between her thumb and forefinger, and as she does, Poul opens the door. Alpha once again, she dismisses me with a nod.

I do not try to accommodate his girth in the doorframe, punching into him with my shoulder.

"Close it," she says.

The screen door is already closed, so I push the heavy wooden door closed as well. I've come to realize that closing both doors is what she does to signal wolves to give her a tiny modicum of privacy.

"I don't know what Elijah is talking about," she says, opening a narrow closet under the stairs to the sleeping loft, "but he has spent most of his life Offland, and sometimes he thinks more like a human than he does like a wolf." She digs around inside the dark, finally pulling out what looks like a waxed suit bag, the kind of thing that usually holds a tux waiting for those twenty pounds to disappear and wide lapels to return.

I hope it's not a wedding dress.

Evie opens the zipper and reaches in, gently extracting not formal wear but a beat-up old flannel shirt with green and gray and black plaid.

"You want to know what John looked like; I can't tell you. I can't tell you whether his features were symmetrical or the angle of his jaw was square or whether his hair curled." She moves her hands in the air. "I think maybe it did. I know nothing about his eyebrows or the shape of his lips."

Her fingers run along the aged cotton and she brings it to her nose, taking a deep breath, before holding the shirt out to me.

"I am not putting that on, if that's what you're thinking."

"I don't want you to put it on. I'm trying to help you understand what he was like. I don't know if you two look alike, but a wolf knows that you are not at all the same."

After staring at it for a few moments, I take it loosely in one hand. Evie pulls her fingers to her nose, indicating that I should sniff her dead husband's sweaty shirt. I am, understandably I think, reluctant, but she pushes it closer, insistent. *Go ahead.* I exhale, hold it to my nose, and breathe in deeply. Then I shrug and shake my head. It's exactly what I'd expect a man's sweaty shirt would—

Wait.

A second breath and a third and he's there. Not the shape of his nose or the color of his eyes or the curl of his hair. But in my mind, he is there, cool and stony and unchanging.

I close my eyes and breathe in again.

Protective and remote.

A mountain dressed in Beyond Salvation Army flannel.

"Do you see?"

I know she doesn't mean *see*, in that narrow human sense of photons hitting my eyes. This is just one of those ways in which words fail us. I don't *see* him, but I know him. I know what he was like. I feel his strength and I feel his remove.

"Yes."

"John's brother was Alpha. His father was Alpha. He

was born into a pack—the only pack—that had known security for generations. The only threat to their safety was the occasional random hunter. I needed that when I first came to the Great North frightened and angry and alone. I was always grateful to him. Respected him. We were together because we were the two strongest wolves and that is what was expected. You…you are nothing like him."

Stretching out the collar of my shirt, I pull it up over my nose and inhale.

"That's not going to work," she says. "None of us can read ourselves."

"So what am I like?" I ask, pulling the shirt down again. "What was it you say we all smell like? Carrion and iron?"

She leans forward, mouth open, the alae of her nose flared, and breathes me in deeply. A tiny smile plays around the corners of her mouth, then she lets go of the breath with a sigh.

"Steel and carrion. Though for a long time, you smelled like ash. Like land that had been burned over. Now you smell"—she sighs—"nice. Like water and the life at water's edge."

Nice. Like water.

Not sure I like the sound of that.

"And Poul?" I don't like the way I say his name either.

"Poul?" She shrugs, then opens her mouth, her tongue feeling the smooth fronts of her teeth. "Slate."

Iron straps begin to tighten around my chest. "Do all Alphas smell like rock?"

"What are you talking about?"

"John smells like the mountain; you smell like granite; Poul, like slate. It's—"

"And if you hit slate at the wrong angle, it splits. These words are nothing. They are just attempts to describe a thing that can't be described."

"Still, that's some coincidence, don't you think?"

She takes John's shirt back, hanging it carefully on the hanger. "Humans have a lot of ceremonies where they all get together. Leonora says it's because they aren't truly joined the way we are. Anyway, our rituals are mostly private. Quiet. Like the one when I became Alpha of the Great North Pack. Every Alpha has done it: we go to the safe Offland, where we keep our most precious documents and a few things. Very few. But in this safe, in a drawer, in a ziplock bag is our most precious object. We keep it inside a tightly sealed gold box." She screws her hands, her muscles working as she remembers some kind of effort. "I really had to work that thing to get it open."

"So what's inside? Like a crown or something?"

"What use does a wolf have for a crown?" She fits the waxed bag back into the back of the closet.

"I don't know. What use does a wolf have for a gold box?"

"Gold doesn't oxidize. It won't change the scent of the fabric inside. Of the"—she waves her finger back and forth at her neck—"the neckerchief our first Alpha wore when she put on skin and breeches to negotiate for Homelands. When it was all over, she wiped her fingers on it. You can still see the ink stains." She puts her hand to her face. "I laid my cheek against it. Taking a little of her and of every other Alpha that has come before me and leaving a little of myself. It's what we do to substitute for being marked by our predecessor because no Alpha dies of old age."

She leans her cheek against her hand as though still

feeling the frayed piece of stained cloth. "There has never been an Alpha stronger than Ælfrida and *she* smelled like water. Like you do. A mountain is strong, but water will still turn it to sand."

I try to say her name, but those steel bands around my chest are so tight that my voice is broken. I don't care about being stronger than a mountain, I don't care about Poul or John or any of it. All I can hear are her words pinging around my skull, so matter-of-fact.

Because no Alpha dies of old age.

I want her to live until any chance of me surviving her has long passed. I've found a woman who is big enough; now I will move heaven and earth to make sure that the world is big enough for her. I push her against the door, my arms bent on either side of her, the great mass of my shoulders curving to give her protection that she would never admit to needing.

I don't want to make the world safe for fucking cabbages. I want to make the world safe for her.

Holding her head in my hands, I let my eyes run over her face again and again, indulging in the simple, jealous pleasure of knowing what she looks like.

"What are you doing?"

"Looking at you."

She smiles and lifts her chin. "And what do you see, Constantine?"

I tell her some things. Not everything. I tell her about the elegant curve between her forehead and the line of her nose. I tell her about the long arabesque that leads from her narrow chin to the wide back of her jaw, down the sinew of her neck. I don't tell her that the finial is created by the bite marks left by her dead mate.

I tell her about the black brows that bend upward like the wings of a seabird, but I don't tell her how they are so often pulled together in worry. I tell her about the high, full cheeks the color of burnished oak. I do not remind her of the scar she got trying to save a friend who didn't know she needed saving. I tell her about the filigree of tiny curls making their escape to frame her forehead. I tell her about eyes the color of amber. I do not say that like amber, they hold inside them the memory of lost lives.

I tell her about the soft cushion of her lips lined in bronze fading to the mauve of an evening sky at the center. I do not tell her how it pulls me in like a bee to nectar.

Instead, I show her. My mouth rough against her, my tongue pressing through her death-dealing teeth to the silken hollows of her mouth. With my knee, I push her knees apart while my cotton-covered cock presses against the fold between her legs. She rocks against me. Cupping her ass, I pull her up, pushing deeper in my possessed dry humping until her eyes go hazy and she pushes me away hard.

I've seen that look before: the little half smile, the dreaminess around her eyes, but still focused. Her thumb traces the dark line of hair to my waistband. A small thing, the scrape of her finger on my abdomen, until her thumb presses under the elastic tightness, the back of her nail catching on the ridge of my crown.

She smiles at the involuntary jerking, doing it again as her fingers scrape along my back, sliding my boxers down, one hand rubbing along my cock, the other gliding along my ass. She bends her leg, her foot pushing down until I am naked, her knee against my inner thigh.

She writhes against me, a low hum vibrating deep in

her chest. I put my hand on her sternum to capture it and respond with a growl of my own. Her nipple sweeps across the thin skin at the inside of my wrist, igniting a burn that travels up my arm, circling my heart. My hand flows down her breast, cupping underneath, my fingers outstretched. I catch her nipple between my lips, knowing now the perfect balance of pressure and gentleness until she groans and moves, flexing hips against me, leaning hard into the aching ridge. I pull away just enough so I can slide my cock not in but between. She clutches her legs together, forcing every hard needy inch of me closer. Her fingers clutch at my ass.

And when she is nearly there, when her mouth is soft, her breathing hard, and her eyes unfocused, I finally dive in, feeling the powerful ripples of her coming pull out my own.

I watch her sleep and know that what I want is beyond simple lust that can be slaked by a coming or two. This is marrow deep, and no matter how much seed I spill inside her, the need will still be there.

Forever.

Chapter 29

Evie

I KNOW IT BOTHERS HIM.

I can see it in his eyes as I scrub all the places where he has kissed me, touched me, sucked on me, and entered me.

"It's the only way I can do this, have a few moments that are just for us. Beyond this, there is no 'me.' No Evie. There is only the Alpha of the Great North Pack."

What more can I tell him? He knows that we are fighting a losing battle here and that when I call for them to make a sacrifice, they must know absolutely that I have made every sacrifice myself.

It doesn't seem to be enough.

I hand him the washcloth. He stares at it like it's poisoned before looking up like an idea has just occurred to him.

"How about Elijah? He's an Alpha and he's mated to a human."

"You said it. He's *an* Alpha. Yes, he's been fighting challengers for thirty years, and yes, he can handle himself, but *I* was the one who made the decision to let Thea stay, so if things go wrong, I am responsible. I am *the* Alpha. There is no one else above me."

He keeps soaping up the washcloth.

"And when the time comes and you're..." His voice

fades out as he looks at the foamy mass between his hands.

"When I've recovered enough to be fertile again?"

His biceps quiver, his jaw slides forward.

"You'll fuck Poul then?"

"Yes."

"You know he doesn't give a damn about Evie. He only wants the Alpha." He tosses the washcloth into the sink.

"I know."

I'm tired and Thea has gotten hold of a picture she says we need to deal with now. And the truth is no amount of explaining is going to make him understand that a Pack is stability in the middle of chaos. A thing of tradition and our tradition requires strong wolves to mate with stronger wolves to make still stronger wolves.

"Constantine…"

"I'm not going to do this," he says. He bends over, grabbing his clothes, and starts for the door. "I'm going swimming. But don't worry. By the time I'm done, no one will know what I have done. That I have committed the crime of touching the woman I love."

Love?

He's already halfway to Home Pond by the time I open the door. He doesn't turn around and I can't call to him.

I'm not doing well.

He dumps his clothes on the chair at the end of the dock.

Turn around, Constantine.

He shakes out his arms, the arms that have held me and made me feel secure. He stretches out his legs, the legs that have supported both of us when my thighs were tight around his hips and he was buried deep inside me.

See me.

Then he dives off the end and disappears into the cold and quiet where no one can find him.

"Alpha?"

With a sigh, I turn away.

Chapter 30

Constantine

After my parents died, I had been angry. Over and over, I was angry. Angry that they were dead. Angry that they had lied to me. Angry that I hadn't had a chance to confront them about those lies before they died. Angry at being sent to August. Angry at being different, but without knowing exactly how I was different. By the time I was in my twenties, anger had burned through me so often that there was no longer any tinder in my soul for it to burn.

Now there is. I feel the hard, dry knot of things that are hard to disentangle: My fury over being erased. My confusing need for Evie to be both bigger than life and small enough to be mine alone. My anger at myself for becoming one more thing she needs to worry about, when I promised myself I wouldn't.

The wind is blowing hard from the west, bringing with it a wall of gray and projecting bright light against clouds like an old movie theater before smoking was outlawed. Slow and deliberate, I swim back toward the Great Hall. I don't know what I'm going to say to her. Not sorry, wolves don't understand sorry, but something.

The problem is she is surrounded as she so often is: Tara, Silver, and Tiberius. She looks at something on a laptop and closes her eyes and stretches out two fingers on her right bicep.

It's a thing she does, to keep count of her worries.

The back door bangs shut behind Elijah's hulking form. He rolls his shoulders back, then forward again and turns his head, eyeing every wolf in the room, challenging them all. To what I don't know, until I see the woman with the black hair, Thea Villalobos, the Goddess of the City of Wolves, blocked by his bulk.

The Alpha listens to the human, sliding two more fingers next to the two already splayed. The human pulls out her camera and flicks through something with her thumb, then shows the screen to the other wolves. Two fingers emerge on the opposite bicep.

Evie's eyes catch mine, her mouth open as though she wants to say something, but she closes it again. I head out the back.

The air is stiller now, if possible, and pregnant. The wall of black clouds trailing graphite streaks comes closer. A wolf sleeping near the cold frame lifts his muzzle, his mouth open, and tastes the wind. Shaking himself off, he saunters toward the trees.

I follow him.

No longer bothering to hide themselves from me, wolves settle in under the layers of leaves. Some are curled up in the spaces between trunks; some have found relief from the still heat by digging into the forest duff and circling into the cool, damp, fragrant earth.

The sky turns black overhead and the canopy begins to shudder. The wind is strong enough to dislodge even green leaves. A shutter bangs against the Great Hall until someone pulls it closed. Then heavy drops fall, slashing on wood and leaves. Even here protected by the trees, heavy drops come through when the sky opens up. A gray wolf with a dark mask trots over to a beige wolf, shakes himself off, and drops next to her. She opens her eyes but closes them again when his nose touches hers. Her ear rotates, searching for something. She sighs and shifts her body, relaxing again.

That's when I hear the sound of pups barking. Coyotes don't come this close to Home Pond, so they are allowed to wander without adult supervision. Even I can tell they are curious rather than frightened, which explains the benign disinterest of the beige wolf's ear.

I head toward them to see what they've found.

At first I can't tell; they're all gathered around at the far end of a fallen log. Maybe they've cornered a mouse or a rabbit. A spray of golden drops arcs through the air.

"*Rahrp*!" barks a tortoiseshell pup, jumping backward.

A tiny dimpled hand jerks into the air.

When I lean over the moldering tree, I am confronted by the last thing I would have expected to find on Homelands. A baby. Not a pup. A full-out naked baby. He has bronze skin, dark curls, and a look of pure panic in his unblinking black eyes. He lies squashed against a log. He's not hurt. He's not stuck, because I lift him easily enough. The top of his ear is bloody, but when I wipe it away with my thumb, it's nothing, just the marks of pup teeth.

In my arms, he jerks again. I lower my head to his and draw in a deep breath.

"What the hell have you done, Nils?"

I realize how graceless these bodies are. As a wolf pup, he can run, chew, bark, jump. Be out in the rain. Now with this big head, weak neck, arms and legs that move in fits and starts, two tiny, flat, useless teeth, and naked skin that provides no protection from the heavy rain coming through the hole in the canopy, Nils shivers against my chest.

Holding him in one arm, I slowly unbutton my shirt with the other and slide him next to my T-shirted chest, covering him as best I can with the thin layer of flannel.

His fingers and toes are tightly curled, his mouth opens and shuts soundlessly save for a damp smacking. Then he sneezes and his arm flings out in shock. Thunder sounds in the distance.

We're not far from the Great Hall, where his Alpha is, his mother. Nils stares at me, one eye pushed into my torso, the other circling around, confused, four little fingers clinging for support to my arm, a miniature version of Evie's fingers propped on her bicep as she tries to remember what everyone needs.

When I think about it, I probably know more about babies than she does. After all, I've seen human fathers jiggle them up and down, trying to stop them from crying. I've seen human mothers feed them. I even—briefly—saw a father trying to change a diaper on the tiny damp counter between sinks in a gas-station restroom.

The sky cracks again, close like the snap of a wet towel in a locker room, and Nyala breaks into a run toward the Alpha's nearby cabin, followed by the other pups. As soon as they reach the porch, they shake themselves off, then push in through the swinging flap with absolutely no compunction about letting themselves into someone else's home, because it's not a home, it's just one of the stage sets for roles they must play.

Juggling Nils from one arm to the other, I follow them in, stripping off my soaking-wet shirt.

I hang it over the showerhead, next to the brush and shampoo she uses to erase me.

Something scratches at the front door. A wild juvenile a little too large for the pup door is stuck halfway through, his legs scrabbling against the outside until he finally pops through, shaking himself so hard, his back legs slip out from under him.

I push the stiff button on the brass plate to turn on the lights that dot the room with soft, warm light.

From the outside, the Alpha's cabin is no larger than any of the other wolves'. It isn't posh on the inside either. One large room with a kitchen area and tiny bathroom in the back. In the front, a staircase leads to a sleeping loft up above though she has her mattress in the middle of the lower floor. Maybe because she doesn't want to stumble up and down the narrow steps every time her wolves need her.

Next to it is a sturdy sun-bleached blue twill sofa with a flattened pillow to one side. Immediately next to it is a white painted desk with a chipped edge and a faux-colonial side lamp. Where everything else is spare, this is cluttered with two mugs: one holds nothing but a dried tea bag. *I'm not a bitch,* it says. *I'm THE bitch.* The other is made of speckled enamelware and holds pens, pencils, and a ruler. A manila folder with the word *DONE* scrawled across it is next to a large printing calculator and rolls of replacement paper. Another manila folder that says nothing but is full to bursting takes up the middle cushion.

"*Rawp?*" a pup calls from the back, followed by another, and then the whole tiny pack chimes in. They are in the kitchenette. I've never really been back here. Partly because it's farther than the bathroom and partly because there is a small table with two seats that's hard to see without imagining Evie sitting across from the man I know only as an empty wolf skull and a flannel shirt that smells like stony absence.

Aside from that small table and those two chairs, there isn't much: a hot plate, a sink, an electric kettle.

The pups are gathered around, some sitting patiently, staring at the long, open shelf above the counter. Others are propped with their front paws on a lower cabinet, yipping and barking at me.

Hard to imagine what they're so excited about. Dish soap. A stack of kitchen towels. It takes me a minute to realize that the white, blue, and yellow tin that says *Chesty Potato Chips* in fact holds antlers.

I pull it out. "Antlers?"

The pups keep looking at the same place and barking to make clear that they're hunting something better than antlers. I pull down the Chesty Potato Chip can. And there it is: a glass canister with orange sticks like the one that was my puppy pity prize when I first came to Homelands. I now know the cheese chews are about as tender as steel radials but surprisingly tasty. The pups run around in circles, yapping.

Pulling out two, I toss them toward the main room, but the motion disturbs Nils, who jerks, whimpers, and starts to pee again. I aim him toward the sink while he is still low-flow.

"Well, this is certainly not going to work," I tell him, grabbing a couple of dish towels from the shelf above. Something heavy falls to the counter.

There in the middle of the counter with its turquoise and beige boomerangs and round burn marks left by the teakettle is a phone. It has a shimmering red-gold cover and a cursive J set in rhinestone. It is like an alien landing on the worn midcentury-modern Formica.

I feel around the towels until, tucked in the back, I find Magnus's phone, mine, and what must be Cassius's. I'd assumed that they'd been destroyed or were in a distant landfill or locked in a safe, not hidden behind a stack of faded gingham like the key to the liquor cabinet belonging to parents who don't trust the babysitter.

Unlike Julia's glitz, my phone is all business. The case is black, slip-proof, drop-tested, and resistant to pressure, water, blood, bile, and vomit. The phone is called the Titanix Thunderhead. It has a max-power 18,000mAh battery that would have given me fifty days of standby talk time even if the phone hadn't been turned off.

Piss-proof, too, as I discover when Nils startles again and lets out a swallowed cry that sounds like *wrorc* and another little dribble. I aim him back to the sink.

When he's done, I drape a towel over his penis because I no longer trust him. Rinsing off my phone, I push the power button.

I have three bars and only one hand, and that one has been calloused thick by all the hammering and sawing, making it hard to manipulate the little buttons that were once second nature. Finally, I find what I'm looking for.

Twice I watch the video that purports to teach how to rig an emergency diaper with two dish towels (for absorbency) and a T-shirt (to keep it in place). Putting Nils on the mattress, I start my adventure in DIY diapering surrounded by those pups who have suddenly lost interest in the cheese chews.

Endlessly curious, they nose everything, especially the

phone, which Nils has, after all, marked. Then one snuffles at the screen and switches to a video about *Minecraft* skins. "*Hey*," I say folding the towel in thirds, "that is not helping."

"Who are you talking to?"

Between the pups and the piss and the phone, I hadn't noticed the door opening or the pups looking toward it. Or even that one close to me who has dropped his cheese chew and stares at it guiltily.

"*Who are you talking to?*" Evie says, at once furious and despairing. A second later, she barrels into me. I grab her thigh and twist, trying to get her away from Nils. The pups start barking loudly, the baby whimpers, and Evie seems intent on ripping a window into my chest.

I try to protect myself and Nils, whose body has rolled into the indentations made by two enormous adults thrashing next to him. There's a sudden, excruciating pain in my big toe that makes me jump, and Evie takes advantage of it to jam her forearm into my throat.

"*Who. Are. You. Talking. To?*" she demands again, holding my phone with its now-blank screen in her free hand.

With one hand buttressed against her forearm, trying to keep my trachea from being soldered to my spine, I flail around with the other, fumbling to get my thumb to the little spot that will unlock my phone. By the third time, I hit the circle and swipe. After what seems like an eternity, she lets up the pressure on my windpipe and I curl on my side, gagging up my lungs.

"What is it?" she asks, holding up a picture of a wan, cheery woman, diapering a smiling dead-eyed doll.

Things are swimming in front of my eyes, my lungs feel like punctured balloons, and my toe is simultaneously on fire and being crushed by pliers because a pup has inserted her tiny needle teeth into either side of the joint.

Sucking in one discordant breath after another, I jab my finger frantically at Nils. "Dpr!"

My dizziness is joined by a cool tingling, and blood returns to my brain. "Diaper," I repeat and she plucks at the clunky folds of dish towels held together by my T-shirt. "Look."

The phone has gone black again, but I disable the lock before handing it to her. She hesitates.

"Look, Evie. Look at everything." I flick through texts, emails, search history, maps. Showing her that the last call out was to Tiberius the day August died.

Nyala growls deep in her little throat, sending vibrations through her fangs and into my joint. I lean forward, inserting my fingers gently into her mouth. She growls again and tightens her jaws. I suck in a sharp breath through clenched teeth.

"*Liðe*, Nyala. *Liðe*." The pup looks up with her bright, dark eyes, watching as Evie scoots around and rubs her thumb across the pup's muzzle. "Nyala, let go."

Her teeth slowly loosen in an agonizing grinding between the bones.

"Constantine..." Evie says, holding the phone gingerly in her hands, her finger absently tracing circles on the back. "I..."

"Whatever you say, *don't* let it be 'sorry.'"

"I should have trusted you."

"No you shouldn't. You have too much at stake to trust any of us. I have done so many things..." I close my eyes as though that will do anything to erase the draining horror of it all. "I am not a good man, Evie."

She turns her head until her cheek is soft against my hand. “Why didn’t you just bring Nils to the Great Hall?”

“Do you know anything about babies?”

She shakes her head. “Nothing. We haven’t had one since… Since a long time. Do you?”

“A little more than nothing. You clearly had something on your mind.” I cross my arms in front of me and count out four fingers on each of my biceps. “You still do.”

She leans against me, her shoulder brushing mine. Then she pulls down Nils’s lower lip, revealing his two tiny, square teeth.

“How long will he be like this?” I ask.

“Depends. When they’re this young, they don’t understand the change. They don’t know what a trigger is or how to use it to change back. And they don’t have the language to be guided through it, so unless he accidentally triggers it again, he’ll be like this until the Iron Moon.”

She touches Nils’s naked tummy and the little belly button folded like an eye.

“What have you gotten yourself into, *mattalinga*?”

“*Mattalinga*?”

“Little maggot. It’s what we call them because they’re soft and squirmy and they piss wherever they are.”

Even chuckling sends a shock through my toe, and I cross my foot against my thigh to examine the bloody puncture marks.

“Does it hurt?”

“Excruciating. Who knew that puppy teeth in the joint of the big toe could be so painful?”

“You know it is just a—”

“Flesh wound. I know. Doesn’t mean it doesn’t hurt.”

She leans back against my shoulder, smiling distractedly as I rock back and forth, my hand on her calf.

"A hiker saw a gray wolf on the edge of Westdæl," she finally says. "Took a picture. It's not good, easy enough to dismiss as a coyote. Thea is investigating in her official role."

She watches my thumb stroking her wrist for a long time.

"We need that land," she says with a vague wave toward that westernmost peak and the ripped-up range to the north. "The forever wolves won't share with us, and they shouldn't have to. They will also den. Next spring or the spring after, they will start to form a pack of their own. If they wander..." Her voice breaks. "We hoped maybe Tiberius would inherit, but August never had a will."

"Can't say as I'm surprised." August's imagination was profligate when it came to the deaths of others but sterile when it came to his own. Even after he was shot in the neck, he refused to hear any talk of what might happen after his death. "*Après moi, le déluge,*" he'd said.

"Tiberius is going to contact August's mate, Drusi—"

"*No!*"

"What?"

I twist around, grabbing her arms. "*Have you called her, Evie? Have you talked to her?*"

Nils makes an alarmed sound in her arms. "It's the weekend again. Elijah says her lawyer's offices will be closed and we should try tomorrow."

"Listen to me and promise me, *promise me,* you won't try to contact Drusilla."

"We are wolves; we don't make promises. We say what we mean. We need that land, Constantine. Tiberius only wants that. He won't contest anything else."

"Tiberius doesn't know anything about Drusilla. Right

now, the only Lukani who know Tiberius is alive are here. You have to come up with a different way of getting it. Create a shell company that specializes in shale or paper products or something. That's how August bought it in the first place. But do not let Drusilla know about Tiberius. And don't let her know about the Great North."

"Why?"

"It's complicated."

"Don't fob me off with 'It's complicated,'" she says sharply. "I am the Alpha of the world's last great wolf pack. *Everything* is complicated."

I scratch at the old scars on my ankles.

"Constantine?"

"I'm trying to think where to start."

"At the beginning. I find that's usually best."

I don't go all the way back. Some of it is from before I was born, but I tell her what I learned from Otho about how Lukani settlements used to straddle the boundaries between men and the wild. It allowed us to be mostly human but to occasionally indulge our more bestial natures without human interference. As humans spread, eating up the land, they pushed the wild into smaller and smaller spaces. Our settlements, too, and that was when August saw an opportunity to consolidate the Lukani and his own power. He traveled among the settlements, warning that the time of the wild was over. We needed to make a decision: to stay as we were and die or to give up the thing that made us less than human and take the money and power and security that came from being men.

"Before, we were more like the Great North. Women leading, men leading, but at the time August was amassing power, that wasn't going to work with humans who were not used to negotiating with women. So, he said, our men would have to lead and make decisions and the women would…not.

"He had an ally. Drusilla. She was the leader of settlements in the western part of the country, but she tied herself to him. Otho said his sister truly loved August. She went everywhere with him, and while he talked to the men, she 'convinced'—and I use that word loosely—Lukani women that while they would not be the face of power when dealing with humans, they would retain absolute power where it counted most, at home.

"I don't know how long it took. Three years? five? Not that it matters. What matters is that one cocktail party at a time, the Lukani females were domesticated. Those that weren't domesticated were dead."

I don't tell her about my parents. About how I'd always been introduced as Maxima's son. How the older men all had some story about my mother, none of which involved the excellence of her brownies but instead were about the sharpness of her mind and her teeth.

There was something about Drusilla that reminded me of the worst parts of my mother. She was wound so tight. Her clothes were stiff on her body. Her hair was in curls that felt hard if you touched them. The house smelled like bleach and ammonia. Her domestic power was not only absolute, it was tyrannical.

I was there when Mala came, bringing the wild with her, and that was when Drusilla learned the limits of her domestic power, because August, who was a tamer to his bones, was obsessed.

Mala wore clothes only occasionally. Wore shoes never. She bit.

"You?"

"No, Otho, Drusilla's brother. Julia's father."

Mala'd taken off her clothes to shift, and Otho grabbed her hair, telling her to stop. August said nothing. He watched as Mala kicked his brother-in-law in the balls and then bit his hand hard enough to take out a chunk at the base of his thumb.

Otho pulled out a gun, but August...August was like a sleepwalker. None of us existed anymore: not Otho, not me, not Drusilla. Mala was all he could see. I remember it. He said nothing, just touched her cheek. She leaned into it and then he rubbed his face to hers and when he went to the back, she followed. I was a teenager and I knew what was happening. Drusilla followed them into the bedroom, and when she came out, she was another person.

There's only so small you can make women before they explode.

And Drusilla, who had been made *very* small, exploded into something *very* dangerous.

August wanted power, but Drusilla wanted destruction. She traded in the most insidious drugs. She not only didn't care if people died and communities were destroyed; she craved it. Her pain made her need the pain of others. Even August was afraid of her. Mala died in childbirth; August told her that Tiberius died soon after. She killed her own brother for staying with August.

Evie leans against me.

"Do you think Drusilla knows where Homelands is?"

"I know she doesn't. Because if she did, you would be dead."

Chapter 31

Evie

SHIFTING FROM FOOT TO FOOT, CONSTANTINE HOLDS the cold little maggot tucked tight and warm against his body while I open up the Crapton group on WhatsApp.

"Who's Craptin?" he asks.

"It's not Crapt*in*. It's Crap*ton*. As in, we have a crap ton of lawyers. I was tired when I set up the chat group. Obviously not something I want to share with anyone."

Nyala yips loudly. She's got her paws on Constantine's calf. "I'm still pissed at you," he says, but he scoops her up anyway.

"Does Drusilla go by Leveraux?"

"They never got divorced, but I think she uses her maiden name, which is Martel. Drusilla Martel. The last names are all fake, used to placate the humans, so it hardly matters."

I tell them not to make any contact with Drusilla Leveraux/Martel and I use the shouty caps that are the closest virtual equivalent to an Alpha call. Within seconds, the Crapton responds with a thumbs-up emoji, the closest virtual equivalent to submission.

"Keep up, *Wulflingas*." A voice like a muffler malfunction wafts across the stream separating my cabin from the Great Hall.

"I forgot I told Leonora she could bring the class to see

Nils," I whisper hurriedly. It's too late for Constantine to get out unseen.

I sit down, the waistband of my jeans digging painfully into my abdomen. I unzip the zipper, then hold my arms out for Nils. Constantine kisses me quickly, before limping to the chair, a chaste distance away.

"How do eet win is two teefs?" asks Gyta.

"Good question. Did everyone hear? Gyta asked how a maggot eats with only two teeth. Watch the stream, Adrian. That's why Tara bought the regurgitated food. Who has the baby food? Leofric? Don't drop it."

Leonora opens the screen door, holding it for children and pups and mosquitoes.

"Shoes," she barks and our awkward children bump into each other like balls in a pachinko machine, trying to drop their shoes into the old milk crate. They come over to the mattress, eyes lowered for that customary second the presence of the Alpha requires.

Leonora puts her hand on Leofric's back. He steps forward, reaching inside a cloth bag.

"We gotses peas," he says. "And we gotses"—he pulls out another, studying the label—"oatmeal and bananas and we gotses..."

"It's 'we have,' Leofric. We *have* peas. We *have* oatmeal and bananas. Just put the bag on the desk." When Leofric heads over to the desk, Constantine takes the jars, then whispers to him, indicating his shirt.

I can't hear what he says, but Leofric, who had been wearing a Toronto Blue Jays jersey tucked into long johns, comes back pulling the oversize shirt out and letting it fall loose and wrinkled to his thighs. I'm not sure why it matters, but I trust Constantine in this. As Leonora says, the difference between a human child and a wolf in children's clothing is a game of inches.

Soon they are tumbling around me, nuzzling my arm, bopping noses with Nils, licking the bloody cartilage of his ear, teething gently at his feet.

Gyta keeps sniffing around Nils's belly.

"Seegodshiffa'shtnonisbutt," she says.

I look to Leonora, who hesitates.

"One more time, Gyta?"

"Seegodshiffa'shtnonisbutt!"

Opening her quilted bag with a pearl-studded handle, Leonora pulls out a pair of glasses and a handkerchief. With meticulous care, she starts to rub the lenses, which are big and round and exceptionally flimsy. They're not real—wolves don't need glasses—but Leonora uses them as a teaching tool and a way of buying time while she tries to pick apart the words spoken by one of our otherworldly children navigating a tongue that is too thick, teeth that are too flat, and cheeks that are too confining.

After one more concentrated swipe, a look of realization breaks across her face and she sets the glasses on her nose.

"Ah! He has a Shifter shirt on his butt!"

"*Gea*! Seegodshiffa'shtnonisbutt!" Gyta says excitedly.

"Thank you for reminding me, Gyta. Avery, do we have our present for the maggot?"

Avery holds out a log of cloth. Inside are several shirts and dresses, the mismatched culling of whatever was smallest in dry storage. Surrounding them are white cloths.

Then all the wolflings—pups, First Years, juveniles—creep closer, watching me examine the careful cutting and awkward stitching that transformed the wine- and bloodstained damasked linen of hunters into diapers for maggots.

I gather them to me, my pups and children, and they press their faces into mine, taking the comfort that is their birthright. The sense of belonging. The promise of protection.

Leonora is the last to lean in, her cheek cocked to the side, waiting for her turn. Then she trundles the children and pups out of the cabin. Only a few will return to the Great Hall, where they will try to sleep alone on a bed in the paralyzed walled-in air.

The rest will eat a meal of beaver liver and snuggle together under the night trees, snuffling into each other's fur.

"Should I go too?" Constantine stands at the door. "I put the food on the table at the back."

I shake my head, signaling for him to pull the thick inner door closed, so my wolves will give me a little privacy. "I could," I admit quietly, "use some help."

A little smile, a little nod, and Constantine closes the door and heads back to the kitchen, returning with a spoon and a bottle of squash.

Maybe Nils smells it and it makes him hungry. Or maybe it makes him furious to find he's been downgraded from beaver liver to watery orange glop. Whatever the reason, he has suddenly found his voice, an unfortunate amalgam of the high, whiny pitch of a human and the endless lung capacity of a wolf.

When he finally takes the spoon, he gnaws at it with his back jaws, even though he has no teeth there, simply because that's what he's used to. Each mouthful is a struggle, and all I can think is: *Come on, Nils. Can't you do this on your own?*

I stifle a yawn and realize that my back has begun to sag. Almost as soon as I straighten up again, my shoulders curve forward. Then Constantine is there, scuttling behind me, sitting with his feet under my ass and his shins on either side of my spine. Something to lean into until Nils is finished.

Then he reaches around front to take the bottle from me. He touches the front of my T-shirt.

"Did you spill...?"

He looks at the swath of red on the underside of his arm.

"*Evie?*"

"Shh. It's nothing." I put the sleeping Nils down on the mattress and lie next to him.

"It's not nothing," he snarls. He lifts my shirt and stares at the cut, but he doesn't recognize it for the joyous thing it is.

"I will fucking kill whoever—"

"Me, Constantine. I did it."

"*You what?*"

I swallow another yawn. "It's...*complicated.*"

"I've spent way too much of my life not questioning anything because I didn't care enough to wonder why. Now I care. So guess what? You don't get to fob me off either."

Nils burps loudly and settles back in, the awkward T-shirt/dish towel diaper Constantine created drooping low.

"I want to understand, Evie." His hand stretches out like a guardian of pale gold above the gash cut into my skin by ancient tradition.

"Two wolves from the 9th were mated." My hand flows down his arm like water. "So there was a *Bredung*. A braiding. It connects the mated wolves to each other, to the land, and to the Pack. The braid is made from the hide of our deer, tanned by the bark of our oaks." I spread my fingers. "It is drenched with the seed and sex of our mates." He spreads his. "And it is coated in the blood of our Pack."

He looks down at our interlaced fingers.

"Your blood?"

"Yes. My blood."

He looks at the thin slash low on my belly. I think it opened up again when I tackled him. John was Alpha long enough to be covered with the scars of his office. I have only the one. There will be others now that the weather is warm and the blackfly are gone. He lays his free hand across it, like he is trying to mend something that isn't broken.

"It's a good sign, Constantine."

"How is this *good*? You already give them *everything*—your time, your strength, your happiness, your self, and now…now you give them your *blood?*"

"It is what the Pack—"

"*I don't care about the Pack,*" he snaps loudly. "*I only care about you.*"

And there it is, the proof that I can't ignore. He's not pack. Sometimes, I almost think I could forget, but then he says something like that and reminds me of how little he understands what we are.

"Then you know nothing." I stare at his hands, one interlaced in mine, the other on my belly. "To care *only* about one wolf means you are careless of the rest.

Humans... There are so many of them, they can afford to have small, selfish loves. We can't."

I let go of him, pushing his hand away, pulling my shirt down. I suppose I've always known that this was a diversion. The pain tears through anyway.

I straighten the sheet across my shoulders and pillow my head on my bent arm.

Chapter 32

Constantine

SMALL.

I hadn't really thought this through.

In my fantasies of a woman who hadn't been made small, I somehow still expected that I would be her center of gravity and she would fall into orbit around me. When I look at the blood on my hand, I know that's not really an option.

I remember the way Eudemos licked away Magnus's pain when he first changed. When I kneel beside Evie and lift the hem of her shirt, she opens her eyes, tired and wary. The muscles of her torso tighten as I take a deep breath and bend down toward her waist. I am tentative at first—I don't want to hurt her—cleaning the spilled blood smeared by the T-shirt. She is still tense under my hand, and I try to remember the way Eudemos had done it, with faith and commitment that made it seem like a kind of blessing.

Looking at her skin, I take a deep breath and press my tongue to the gash itself, tasting the coppery blood. I try to read her, stroking her, comforting her, loving her in the way a wolf would until finally her body begins to relax. Stroke by stroke, I feel her both coming apart and knitting together under the gentle pressure of my tongue, this unspeakable intimacy, this benison.

Evie eventually falls asleep with Nils on one side. Even in the middle of the summer, the nights can be cold here and wolves don't like to be cut off from the outside, so all the windows are open. I pull the blanket from the back of the sofa and shake it out, letting it settle over the two of them.

A small animal scuttles up a tree and a night bird's wings flap hard in pursuit, pulling fir-scented air in her slipstream followed by a breeze from the north, the lowing of a moose, and a clearing of the sky.

The flap in the door opens and shuts, and a pup sniffs around Evie and Nils with a low whine.

"Nyala," I whisper so she won't wake them. As soon as she jumps up on my chest, my toe throbs in recognition. She turns around and around. I put my hand near her so she has something to cuddle into. Then with a big yawn, she sneezes.

The moonlight breaks through the window and Evie sighs. Putting my free hand gently on her thigh, I feel the pulse of her skin. I smell the forest-infused scent of Nyala's fur. I've been told over and over that wolves and pack and land are one, but words are slippery, and while I heard, I never did understand.

Not the way I do now as I watch the moon clear the trees of the Holm to hit the waters of Home Pond and almost weep for the magic of this place that has turned an island into a home.

In the morning, Evie took Nils with her, along with a bright-pink bag stuffed with the ad hoc diapers, the regurgitated food, and the too-large clothes. Even a maggot belongs to the Pack, and the Pack would take care of him as they did when he had four legs, sharp teeth, and a measure of independence.

The one thing she did not take was my phone. Not first thing in the morning when her foot caught it and sent it sliding across the floor. Not later when I put it into her hand and curled her fingers around it.

Its once-familiar weight now feels odd in my pocket. I take it out and look through the contacts, many of whom are dead: August is listed in my contacts as AAA. Unnamed but always first. Also Antony. Under the D's is a 604 number. Drusilla, the Bitch of Vancouver.

A stick breaks and I cram the phone back in my pocket.

Cassius stands suddenly still behind me. Then he turns and drives something that I can't make out high into a tree. Whatever it is, it's sharp enough to make a pale gash in the bark.

A moment later, I smell the sap bleeding into this wound and another one already beaded with amber.

"They're very protective of their trees."

"'*They're very protective of their trees.*' They don't bother to look any higher on a tree than the height of a raised leg."

"What are you doing, Cassius?"

"Marking a path. If I'm going to be trapped here forever, I need to be able to find my way around."

I realize that at some point I slid my hand into my pocket, trying to disguise the shape of my phone under the shape of my hand.

My thumb feels around, turning it off, so no alerts or alarms will signal to him that there is a line to the world outside, then I slide back into the woods, watching him. Soon, two wolves appear on either side of me, watching, too, until the evening comes and Cassius heads in for Evening Meat.

"I don't trust him," I say to the gray wolf on my right.

She shows her teeth and opens and closes her jaws rapidly, making a soft clacking sound.

"Exactly. You going to movie night?"

Tara makes a little expulsive cough.

"See you there."

Back at the dormitory, I look around for a hiding place. There isn't one, really. The lack of any old stuff makes it hard to hide new stuff. In the end, like a kid at summer camp, I unzip my cotton pillow liner, slip the phone in, put the pillowcase on, and turn it upside down.

You think you know somebody.

From the beginning, I've known Ziggy was the Great North's Number One Werewolf Star Fanboy. I don't know if he's the GNNOWSF because he runs the AV equipment during movie nights, or he runs the AV equipment during movie nights because he is the GNNOWSF.

Either way, he's nuts.

"Bill Nighy is an English actor and Bill Nye is the Science Guy. They are not the same."

"Plug these in," he says, holding a cord out to me. "Then I'll show you."

As soon as I've set up the power strip, I come back. "Look, here they are side by side." Ziggy turns the laptop toward me. "That is the same man. Sickly, they have… light hair and the rims around their eyes."

"Glasses, Ziggy. And he's not sickly—*they're* not sickly—just thin."

I'm not really arguing. I now know it's pointless, given the difficulty Pack have with facial recognition. Strip away sound and smell and feel, and for wolves, it's like trying to separate one stick figure from another.

Once speakers, projector, and screen are set up, I help other wolves distribute the rickety gold-toned party chairs with their bloodstained ecru cushions in rows with ample leg room on either side of the projector tripod connected to the computer.

We toss around large claw-picked pillows on the floor up front and bowls with water and the teeth-shattering sweet potato pucks that wolves like to gnaw. On the short wall to the right of the door is a table with napkin-lined baskets filled with peanut-butter muffins and popcorn. Chipped earthenware jugs are filled with water and iced tea.

There is no swinging door here, so pups jump their paws up on the screen, whimpering until someone opens up. A pup takes the corner of one of the large cushions between his jaws and drags it across the floor. An older wolf drops his cheese chew, clambers to his feet, and drags both pillow and pup back across the floor.

The door opens again, admitting a wolf dragging a slack Nils in his teeth, his legs dragging along the floor.

"Hey!" I grab at Nils and the wolf growls until I smack him in the jaw, not hard, but in the way of wolves making a point. He opens his jaws and drops the baby into my arms.

"How many times do I have to say this: don't carry maggots in your teeth." I smooth out Nils's rumpled and spit-covered shirt. It would help if he complained about the rough treatment but he never does. I suppose he's so used to being carried around by the scruff that it doesn't occur to him that this is not natural. That he should be screaming and crying, not looking up at me with his big, dark eyes and the tip of his tongue sticking out from the corner of his two-toothed smile.

"And just how do you suggest picking him up?" asks Ziggy.

"Arms, Ziggy. Arms."

Ziggy and the wolf exchange glances. The wolf shrugs, then starts to pick something out of his forepaw with his teeth as though to point out the hole in my logic.

I dampen a cloth with some cold water and wash the dirt from the front of Nils's legs and the back of his feet, then drag another pillow over, angled to the side so he can be with the pack but not overwhelmed by the flashing lights on the screen.

Soon, the Meeting Hall is crowded. There's a lot of posturing for the one remaining floor pillow. Magnus gets it until Elijah dumps him out, dragging it away for Thea. Ziggy is once again showing some female his comparison of Bill Nye and Bill Nighy; she lifts her hands up as though to say of course they're the same. Several pups have joined Nils on his big pillow. Lying on him for a moment, then running off. Poor Nils raises his arm awkwardly after them. One juvenile taunts him by waving her tail in his face. He finally catches it and brings it to his mouth, though there is too much fur and it makes him sneeze.

In the third row on the left side, in the chair one over from the aisle sits Poul with his arm around an empty seat.

"Alpha." I nod to Poul and sit down, feeling the warmth of his arm stretched around my back, smelling the scent of his slaggy armpit.

"I'm saving this seat for the Alpha," Poul says, staring at me.

"And if she asks me to get up, I'll get up. Until then, move your fucking arm." I feel the strength, the warmth, and the hesitation in his arm as he tries to decide whether his status is more likely to suffer from giving in to my demands or staying seated with his arm curled intimately around a Shifter.

He taps his finger rapidly on the back of the chair before finally deciding to extricate his arm. Then to make it clear that he's not giving in, he pushes his face close, his eyes boring into mine. I may not be a wolf, but I recognize a dominance play when I see it.

Removing my cheese chew to the hand carrying the iced tea, I rock onto the back legs of the chair and slam forward with fair to middling momentum. Poul backs up, his head raised, trying to stanch the bleeding.

The movie is about vampires and—what else—werewolves. It stars either Bill Nighy or Bill Nye. Even I can no longer tell the difference.

"...first Clan of Werewolves: A Vicious and Infectious Breed, unable to take Human Form ever again...Until he *was born."*

Poul wipes his nose with his hand, wipes his hand on his arm, then looms over me until my knee meets his balls.

Not sure how he got to be Alpha if a seated man can best him without spilling his iced tea.

"Is that your answer then? You will not come with me, so you want me to stay here for you? Like this? Like an animal?"

Poul stomps off to the Deemer, who is in the process of shoving a handful of popcorn into her mouth. He speaks quickly and Silver holds up one finger, chewing carefully before taking a swig of water and saying a word or two. She turns back to the popcorn. Poul shuffles around so that he's in front of her again, his mouth moving more, his finger pointed toward me. I can't hear what's being said, but judging from her expression, the Deemer does not seem to think that who sits next to the popular girl at movie night is a matter for the law.

Poul makes a mistake and jabs an accusing finger first toward Tiberius, then toward Silver. She looks at it coldly, puts her popcorn on the table, and lunges forward, biting him hard with her fanged and salty teeth.

She takes her popcorn back. Tiberius repeatedly smooths his mustache and cropped beard.

Now Poul stands holding his finger, his face bright red and furious. There are no longer two seats together. He thumps back, banging harder against my legs and the skull of the wolf in front of him, who growls, but Poul shows teeth and the wolf lowers his head.

He sucks at his wounded finger, staring at the door until Evie finally arrives. She's trying to do it quietly so as not to disturb the movie, but when she turns away from the snack table, with a sweet potato puck and a glass of iced tea, her expression changes. All her wolves are watching her. Even the pups have stopped fighting. I doubt they understand the middle-school dynamics of the moment, but they recognize the possibility of a fight when they smell it.

"Alpha." Poul stands, blocking me from her view. "I saved you a seat."

I stare straight ahead, still pretending to watch the movie.

"You are a credit to your race. Do you know how to remain so? Keep your eyes on the ground...!"

"Alpha?" Poul says again. "He knows he has to move for you."

"There's plenty of room on the floor," she says. Lowering herself gracefully, she props her head on the hip of a wolf lying like a comma. Another wolf props her head on the Alpha's chest, her eyes slowly rising and lowering in time with her dominant's breath.

Poul limps toward me, nose swelling, sucking on his finger.

"You know she only tolerates you because you look like John," he says without bothering to disguise his voice.

"How would you know, Poul?" comes a voice from the back of the room.

"Elijah told Esme who told Joelle who told me."

Elijah doesn't have the words to confirm or deny but when Thea says, "I told you not to say anything," he drops a paw over his eyes.

Evie looks straight ahead, the iced tea raised to her mouth, her face stony. I focus on the condensation dripping to her lower lip.

"But you're not John," Poul continues. "I am the Alpha of the 10th Echelon of the Great North Pack and you… You. Are. *Nothing.*"

I press my palm against my fingers, and one by one, they crack.

"I know who you are. *You* are the man who plotted with the noseless dog to give the Great North's pups to August. To give your Pack and your Alpha to hunters," I say, my eyes glued to the screen, where interestingly enough wolves are in retreat from a Shifter. "*I* am the man who stopped it."

The room freezes. Poul doesn't breathe, and everyone in the room looks somewhere that isn't at us.

Evie stands stiffly, her palm extended as though she

was hoping to shake hands with someone who has disappeared. Everyone, even the pups, has gone quiet, making the movie so horribly loud.

"The accused has committed high treason against this covenant.

"She has consorted with animals."

Out of the corner of my eye, I watch her. She puts her iced tea on the table, squats down to give the sweet potato to the pup. He jumps up on her knee, his skinny tail wagging furiously until she cups his little face in her hand and marks him. Then she stands and, without looking around, leaves.

"I have saved this coven many times over.

"You have killed your own kind!"

"By the moon, Sigegeat, mute it!"

The door bangs. I extract my legs, making ready to follow her, but Poul puts his hand on my shoulder.

"Get off me."

"Constantine WhateverTheFuckYourNameIs. By the ancient rites and laws of our ancestors, I, Poul Ardithsson, challenge you for *Cunnan-riht*—"

"Stop," Silver says, loudly now. Authoritatively. "He is neither Pack nor table guest; he cannot be challenged for *Cunnan-riht*."

"*Mæþ holmgang*, then."

"What makes you think that if the law doesn't allow you to challenge for fucking rights, you can challenge for honor? Your only alternative is to challenge Constantine to prove himself worthy of the Pack. But, Alpha, if you fight him and he wins, there will be a Thing and the Great North will decide on whether he brings strength to the Pack."

"Like there's any chance he would win," Poul snaps. He takes one step toward the door before Silver's voice cuts through the room, cold and sharp.

"The challenge, Poul Ardithsson, Alpha of the 10th Echelon of the Great North Pack, must be spoken."

Without turning to face me, he starts again: "Constantine WhateverTheFuckYourNameIs. By the ancient rites and laws of our ancestors and under the watchful eye of our Pack and Alpha, I, Poul Ardithsson, challenge you to prove your strength worthy of the Great North. With fang and claw, I will attend upon you the last day of this Iron Moon."

"Down in front," someone yells. "You're blocking the screen."

Neither of us sticks around for the rest of the movie. Poul is long gone by the time I take a seat on the stairs.

Finally, the film howls in triumph.

"Lucian," says a comically deep voice. *"It is finished."*

"No," says another voice, softer, almost gentle. *"This is just the beginning."*

The music builds and wolves begin to straggle out in groups, in pairs, and alone. Many of them stripped down while the credits were still rolling. Like Eudemos. Hirsute and chewing on an antler, he seems half wolf already.

"That shows there's a practical reason for eating them," he says to a female I think is named Eawynn. He taps his throat with a gnawed prong. "A sword through the throat didn't do it, but if Lucian had eaten Bill Nighy, none of it would have happened.

"Did you know he's a scientist too?"

Ah, Ziggy.

"Hey, is Elijah coming out?"

Eudemos puts his head back through the door. "Elijah, you coming?" he says and someone roars out the name of the 9th's Alpha. "Thea's in the bathroom."

"He's coming."

"Maybe the vampires taste gross," says the female. She is carrying, of course, a well-thumbed edition of *Passing the New York State Bar Exam* and has a pencil above her ear.

"You do what you have to. We ate a state trooper. There is no way a vampire tastes worse than a state trooper."

"They've been dead forever," she says and the two of them leap from the porch, landing softly and surely on the ground. "I think they'd taste like humans crossed with roadkill. And dry."

Even in skin, the Pack has no trouble negotiating darkness: the moon is low, there are no porch lights or path lights, only a weak nimbus from one of the windows as Ziggy packs up the AV equipment and holds forth from his trove of obscure and deluded movie trivia.

Elijah moves much more slowly and carefully even though he is wild. Thea, who has her hand buried in the long fur at his shoulders, slides her feet cautiously forward as he pauses at the top of each step. I wait until they are safely at the bottom before approaching them.

"Hello?" she says, turning toward me.

"I need to talk to Elijah."

"You can walk with us to my cabin," she says, tucking her hair behind her ear with her free hand. "Is this about you looking like John? I knew that was going to cause trouble."

Elijah chuffs and scratches at the moldering leaves with his hind legs.

"Not really. Poul wanted to make me angry. I shouldn't have let him, but I did and now I have to fight him. I've fought...a lot...but never tooth and nail."

"I think it's fang and claw."

She stumbles on a rock, but before I reach out to help her, Elijah darts forward and she steadies herself on his shoulders. She is a small human and he is a large wolf, but still I like them together. They add strength to each other, even if it isn't the kind of strength the Pack understands.

"I'm not afraid of working or fighting or getting hurt, but for the first time in my life I'm afraid of losing, because for the first time in my life, it means something. If I lose, Poul is still the strongest unmated male. Ev... The Alpha doesn't like him, but she will not go against Pack traditions for her own sake. Not like she did for you."

Elijah gazes at Thea, the woman who smiles toward him but not at him because it's too dark and she's too human.

"If I win," I continue, "then at least she has a choice. I want her to choose me, but whatever else happens, Poul will no longer take it as his right to sniff around her like she's his personal fire hydrant."

I know I'm talking too fast and saying too much, so I take a deep breath. "All I'm asking is to give me a chance to give her a choice."

Elijah moves to Thea's front, his muzzle at her chest until she squats down. He pats his head against the underside of her chin and she lifts her head back, eyes closed while Elijah opens his enormous jaws, fitting them to either side of her vulnerable throat. She is motionless except for a few thin strands of hair that bend to the current of his breath. When he moves away, one fang traces a gentle line down until it catches on the leather braid at her collarbone.

Then he plants himself in front of me, his head cocked, looking expectantly, though if he thinks I'm going to stick my throat between his jaws, he can go—

He jumps up, grabbing the front of my shirt between his fangs and pulling me down. Next he rubs his muzzle against my cheek. First one side, then the other.

"Do you understand?" Thea asks.

"Uhhh." I watch her pull the flashlight from her belt. "Tell me he's saying yes."

"He's saying yes."

"Just wanted to make sure."

Thea trains the bright beam on the steep hill in front of her.

"Can I ask you something?"

She points the flashlight down.

"If you had this all along, why didn't you use it?"

"Hurts their eyes," she says, grabbing hold of a branch and pulling herself up.

I stand at the base of the hill, watching the light and the woman and the wolf until in the middle distance, a door closes.

Chapter 33

Evie

THAT'S WHY WE HAVE LAWS AND CUSTOMS IN THE FIRST place.

I drop my jeans and shirt over the back of the Adirondack chair at the end of the dock.

Sometime, somewhere, some ancestor did a bad thing and fell in love with the wrong wolf.

Holding my nose, I jump in, the water a frigid slap against my overheated skin. I spread my body out across the surface so the water at my back lifts me, the wind at my front caresses me. I paddle slowly toward the other side.

I don't know what happened to that ancestor, but probably that strong wolf found out and challenged the wrong wolf, and in the end, the wrong wolf was defeated. The difference being that was a pack challenge, and pack challenges are about submission, not death.

This was where I made myself small so I could sink down where no one would find me, except Constantine, who found me and saved me. There was something sweet about it, the worry on his face, as though he imagined that I was the kind of wolf who might conceivably need saving.

Why did he have to do this? I know he doesn't like Poul, but couldn't he have pretended to offer him the respect due him as Alpha of the 10th? I've put up with so much shit from Poul... Why couldn't Constantine have done this one thing? My love always has to be so encompassing. Couldn't he have lowered his eyes and let me keep this little love that's all our own, just us two?

Pulling my legs in and wrapping my arms around my knees, I make my body small again and sink deep into the water, my wolf's metabolism letting me stay there for a long time. On my second time down, the water around me ripples around me, above me. I know who it is circling around me, just like he did when he was looking for me before.

Breaking through the surface, I swim as best I can for the Holm. Constantine moves faster and is already there.

"Did he challenge you?" I ask, squeezing the water from my hair.

"Yes."

I shiver as the cool air of the summer evening hits my damp skin.

"Don't say it, Evie."

"You have to apologize to him."

He shakes his head. "I will not apologize to him."

"You have to apologize, Constantine. If you were Pack, you could submit. At its heart, a challenge is bravado. We are all in this together. We don't *want* to destroy one another. But you are not Pack, this is not bravado, and Poul does want to destroy you. He doesn't have to, but you embarrassed him: you called him a traitor, you made him bleed. And he will."

"He won't be the first person who's tried to kill me."

"*Not wild*. You were almost killed by a *pig*. Fighting wild means getting close. It means lashing at a mouth filled with more teeth than you thought existed moving at speeds you can't see. It means fighting someone who knows what you are going to do before you do. We are hunters to our core. For us, fighting is just a hunt with fewer rules."

He reaches out his hand the way he has before, like when he wants to comfort me. "Don't… Don't touch me," I say and pull away, rubbing my arm with my knuckles.

"You were the one who said 'sorry' was a hard word for wolves. Pity and regret. Well, I don't pity him and don't regret what I've done, so how can I apologize?"

Looking across the water, I pull at one of the strands of my hair, stretching it out long. The lights of the Great Hall are out now, wolves dispersed across Homelands, some in cabins, most among the trees.

"I've never said no to a fight, Evie. I'm not going to start now. Not with him."

I let the strand go, watching as it pops back into a tight spiral.

"Then he will kill you. And I will have to watch."

Chapter 34

Constantine

THERE'S NOT GOING TO BE MUCH OF ME LEFT TO KILL BY the time Elijah is finished.

At the end of each day, I limp back to the end of the dock, licking the blood from my fur and wondering, as Evie said I would, at the number of teeth a single wolf has. I try with my tongue to poke at my own, to figure out exactly how many there are, but it's inexact. In the end, I only count thirty-eight or forty-two, a figure that is hundreds short of what Elijah seems to have.

Either way, Elijah still manages to tear through my hide, and now my body is crisscrossed with wounds, both raw and healing. Aggression isn't enough. Claws aren't enough either. Jaws are really everything. There is a vicious immediacy to fighting wild that no amount of street skirmishing can prepare you for. There is no such thing as "arm's length." When Elijah rushes, I have no choice but to meet that rush with my chest. When he attacks, it is fang against fang, ringing hollow through my jaw and into my skull.

I have tasted his saliva. I have felt his teeth and tongue against mine. He has tasted my blood.

Rushing, jumping, confusion… Even the posturing is very, very painful.

Then there is the change. All the cuts and bruises then

stretch and tear again. Gashes in my loin become rips as my hips straighten out. Anything that managed to clot starts to bleed again.

Still, pain is the best teacher. And I've become more adept and graceful. This time, I manage to whirl around on my back feet, keeping Elijah in front of me so instead of a gash on my thigh, I have one on my cheek. It hurts more, but at least it means that I wasn't caught from behind again.

We practice in what I had thought was a huge abandoned sandbox, though I suppose the lack of other playground equipment and the variety of blood spatter should have tipped me off.

Curious wolves have started to watch. A few have even offered to spar, seeing me as a cheap date, because while there is no gain if they win against me, there is no loss either. Wolves of various levels of competence have started lining up for a practice run. I take them all on, because I learn something from each one and because I never say no to a fight.

There is one wolf who never comes.

Poul passes by, his teeth chittering fast like an angry squirrel, but since he has jaws like the grill of a monster truck, it's not as funny as it should be. Elijah always stops when he is near. Maybe there are wolves who will tell him what I am like as a fighter, he says, but maybe not. Anyway, there is a world of experience that cannot be expressed by words.

Traditionally, Elijah says, challenges are held on the last day of the Iron Moon. The subordinate wolves fight first. They tend to be more cautious and circumspect. A lot of posturing overseen only by the echelon's Alpha. But by the time the higher ranks fight—the Alphas, Betas, Gammas—the aggressiveness increases and so does the audience.

"Blood sells," Elijah says, picking at something in his teeth that had earlier been attached to my foreleg and is now bleeding profusely from my bicep. "The biggest draw for a long time was when Varya fought Kieran for insulting Thea. You know him? The brindle wolf with the scar through his eye? I never understood why Varya, who had always hated humans, tore open a wolf's face over one. Still yours... Got it." He spits the piece of my hide out. It has a bit of fur attached. "Still yours has sex, xenophobia, and a high probability of death...so, you know, what's not to like?"

There is another wolf who never comes.

I rehearse that last time I sat with her on the Holm, watching the water streaming down from her collarbone. Picked out by the moon, it gleamed like lightning on her tawny skin, and the truth is, at that moment, I was so tortured by thirst, I would have done whatever she wanted if she would let me lick the water from her breasts, suck it from her nipples, slake myself inside her.

Then she scrubbed her arm with her fisted hand, like she does when she's cleaning away any trace of me, and I couldn't.

As the days pass into weeks and the wolves decide that I'm not a walking casualty, that there is a chance, however slim, that I might not die in the first two minutes, they begin to whisper suggestions, making it clear that not all of the Great North sides with Poul simply because he's one of them. Tiberius tells me to walk off the paddock several times, measuring it with my feet for the dips and rises that will tell me if I'm getting too close to the wall.

A female from Poul's own echelon says he twisted his left hind ankle and is still stiff.

Järv tells me to jump in as soon as the fight between the 11th's Gamma and Beta is over so I can take the western edge and the sun will be at my back.

"But piss first," Ziggy adds. "Once you've entered, you cannot leave until the fight is over. If you do, you are a coward and outside the protections of the law. For wolves, submitting is acceptable, but running away never is."

I finally see her on the first evening of the Iron Moon. With blackfly season over, the Pack spreads out on the grass that rolls down from the Great Hall to Home Pond. The sounds of crickets and katydids meld with quiet conversation and gentle snufflings as Homeland and Offland wolves greet one another. A loon glides through the air, skimming through the purple-gold surface of Home Pond and almost, but not quite, going under. His voice is hollow as he calls to his mate.

That's when she leaves the Great Hall, closing the door behind her.

After giving the traditional blessing, she sits not with us but with the 9th. She says nothing to Elijah and he doesn't bother her. Even Cassius has the grace to keep his mouth shut while he digs divots in the grass with a stick.

I don't see much of her once we are changed either.

People have heard about the wolf sighting, and as much as the Great North has tried to spread rumors that it is a coyote, the photograph has gone viral under the hashtags #ADKWolves and more ominously #ADKTrophies.

I hunt with the 7th, then lope through the High Pines where the tree-darkened days meld into the bright moonlit nights, all of it infused with my own cool gladness.

There was a birthday many years ago when I imagined I'd reached the pinnacle of happiness. I had waffles and sausages and goose and cake. My mother had given me all the crispy skin. And most of the chocolate frosting. I'd gotten all the toys I'd wanted. I was full. I was happy.

But the next day, I was empty. The Deluxe Li'l Wizards Magic Set had trickery but no magic: hiding balls and coins in plastic compartments. The dart gun either jammed or the dart failed to achieve more than the velocity of a laden swallow and dropped a few feet in front of me. The parachute, on the other hand, never deployed and the paratrooper fell fast and hard to the ground.

The cracklings and chocolate did a number on my intestines.

It is, I think, what Evie was trying to tell me with the cup. Stop trying to fill up the empty spaces and shatter. Open yourself up to everything around you—the smell of the black earth under a balsam pine, the feel of moss and cold water, the motion of a breeze sliding through guard hairs and rustling through leaves.

The only thing that's the same is a goose, which had no cracklings but was fatty in that late summer way and delicious.

Midafternoon of the final day, I hear Tara call the start of challenges. It takes me a while to make it down from the

High Pines but I miss only two minor skirmishes. From the tussle between the 13th's Kappa and Iota over their rank within the echelon, I trot around the largely deserted paddock, watching how wolves slash with teeth that can and do rip open faces. How they charge suddenly, banging chest to chest. How they leap to the side, leaving slavering jaws with nothing but air. How they submit.

With each successive bout, the paddock becomes more crowded. By the time it arrives at the challenge between the 11th's Gamma and Beta, it is very tight. I growl at wolves to give me space. I don't need them blocking my leap into the arena. As soon as the 11th's Gamma submits, I jump in, not even waiting for the combatants to leave. The Beta won, but as she pulls herself over the side, blood drips down her back leg and she makes it to the top of the paddock wall with trouble before dropping to the other side.

Claiming the western end, I do everything I've been told to. I walk back and forth across the paddock again to feel any changes in the earth under my feet, the gouges made by wolves who fought earlier. Chuffing repeatedly, I gauge my distance from the walls by the reverberations in the air.

More echelons descend from the woods, vying for places. The 10th has taken up its positions on the eastern end. The sun is still too high, but even so, their pupils are constricted. It won't take long before it is right in their eyes. In Poul's eyes.

Elijah is behind me, snapping irritably at wolves who dare take up places he has reserved for the 9th.

Pups run around snapping at ankles and tails, yelping excitedly at seeing so many adults together and wild. A wolf gently takes a pup by the scruff and sits it on the top of the paddock wall where it lands splay-legged before getting to its feet and strutting back and forth. Evie bares her teeth and the wolf quickly retrieves the pup, pulling him back off.

My eyes catch hers and she looks away, but not before I've seen that she's hurting. I hate myself for being the cause of it, but I am tough and prepared and I will win and he will get his fucking nose out of her ear once and for all. Please, Evie. See me. Know me. Have a little faith in me.

Speaking of the devil, Poul leaps into the paddock on the east side. I watch him land, checking to see if his ankle is still stiff.

I'm grateful to see the 7th crowding in at the western side, at my side, next to the 9th. Everyone is here and yet…

Something is bothering me. Something in the vast continuum between what is seen and what I can't put into words is wrong. I run around the paddock, trying to focus my mind on what it could be. Evie is here, so is Magnus, and Ziggy and Elijah.

So what's wrong?

Evie takes her place on one side, opposite Silver. Both stand at the front so they can see everything and make sure the few laws that govern a fight like this are followed.

Tara barks once, warning us to take our places as she will soon announce the beginning.

Silver rubs at her head with a paw; an ear pops up.

Gehyrað æfter stilnes. Listen to the silence.

"Don't just pay attention to what's there," Otho once said. "Pay attention to what's missing, because the man who doesn't bring a gun to a meeting like this has a sniper on the rooftop."

Racing back to where the 9th is arrayed, I jump up, my feet on the paddock wall, craning to see over all the wolfish bodies of Elijah's echelon. I know them now; they've all come to watch their Alpha train the Shifter. I see them all. Elijah growls, warning me to get back down.

I snap at him, then round the paddock, looking carefully at every side. More wolves snarl at me, sensing panic, and maybe it smells like cowardice. Like weakness. Unfortunately, I don't have the words to tell them otherwise. To ask them: with the entire 9th here, with *all* of the Great North here, where the hell is Cassius?

At that moment, Tara howls. Poul squares up. Silver stares at us, her ears straight ahead. I look at Evie one last time. Not so long ago, I would have stayed and I would have fought and I would have won for you alone, Evie. It took me a long time, but I finally understand that there is no you alone. There is you and all the multitudes you contain, or there is nothing.

I head back to the corner, then run full out, clearing the paddock wall and landing on the backs of wolves. They part like the water, snarling and growling and stunned as I run flat out, sniffing until I locate that bitter, resentful smell, following it toward the Great Hall, then into the woods.

The door to my dormitory bumps in the wind. My skin chills even though it is summer and I am covered with fur. Inside, my mattress lies tipped on the floor and my pillow has been clawed open.

I hear you swum all the way to the other side.

Poul howls triumphant from the paddock.

Looping deep into the woods, I break into a run, negotiating the gothic tangle of roots in the spruce, leaping over an orphaned boulder softened by bright-green moss, pushing through the thickets of low bushes with their powdered blueberries that the Pack will pick soon.

They've started after me, Poul and a handful of wolves from the 10th. They don't bother to disguise themselves or their passage, because I have forfeited and am now outside the law.

Splashing through the slow summer streams and the pitcher-plant bogs, I follow his scent. In the bushes behind the Boathouse, I smell where Cassius must have lain hidden, changing into his skin while the wolves were distracted by my spectacle.

When I break through the tree line, I see him, a speck across the water, his fingers wrapped around the paddle of a canoe. It won't take long before there will be nothing left but a gentle slipstream skirting the Holm.

Tearing along the dock, I pick up speed toward the end. Wolves at the paddock have started to notice, and just as I launch myself into the water, Evie's stunned eyes catch mine.

Sorry, sorry, regret and pity.

My legs bicycle desperately, frothing water into my nose just barely clearing the surface. This is not swimming; this is speed walking with a head cold. Coughing and churning, I leave off following Cassius directly, paddling my legs as fast as I can in a direct path toward the Holm so I can run faster for that little while at least. I make land right near the spot where my hesitant hand first touched Evie.

There is no way Evie could have seen Cassius from the paddock. I try not to think what she is imagining. I love you enough, Evie, to not love you alone. It's never been clearer to me as I pull my bedraggled body out of the water and race after Cassius so close to getting away, carrying with him my cell phone, the Bitch of Vancouver's number, and bad blood that has festered too long.

I make better time running through the Holm until I reach the southern side that isn't properly land or properly water, just weed-choked shallows with painfully sharp sedges at eye level and a thicket of buckthorn that puncture my paws.

Cassius has slowed down, too, though. He uses the canoe paddle as a walking stick, jamming it into the sludge, then pushing against it, extracting one foot after the other.

It's not an easy place for humans, but it isn't an easy place for wolves either. The ground is uneven and tricky to negotiate. It's also hard to distinguish scents because everything is masked, camouflaged by the thick smell of decay and sphagnum. Worst of all, there is too little cover. There are a few bushes without enough leaves and no trees at all except for a couple bleached and skeletal remains.

"Did you hear the cars?"

He must have heard about cars somewhere and squirreled the information away. I'm not sure he can hear in that form, but I certainly can in this and know we are too close to the world of men. I try to keep low, but it doesn't help. Cassius sees me, and as soon as he does, he moves faster. Reaching into his pocket with his free hand, he pulls out my phone and pushes the power button. I find myself praying to the moon for a dead battery, but no, because it has a max-power 18,000mAh battery, it has fifty days of standby talk time even without turning it off, and because I'd wanted to prove to Evie that I would never do anything to hurt the Great North, I'd unlocked it.

Cassius holds my phone with his free hand and swipes at the screen with his thumb. Since he knows I'm here, I try to make up time, pushing off with my back legs, bounding over and over to try to clear the deep mud.

A truck roars past on a distant, invisible road. It's so catastrophically loud to me, but Cassius still doesn't hear. Distracted by the phone, he moves more slowly. I can almost feel him searching through my contacts.

Mud stings the thousands of tiny flesh wounds I've been accumulating during these weeks when I trained so hard so that I had a chance at a place in the Great North. That's gone now. No point thinking about that now. I just have to keep slogging forward while Cassius takes floundering steps through the loin-high bog, one hand holding the phone to his ear, the other tracing wide balancing loops through the air.

He alternates between panting and yelling. I can hear the panic, but I'm having trouble making out the words.

I bound forward again, but this time, I land in a deep sinkhole of mucky water up to my shoulders.

And Cassius...Cassius who could have kept on, Cassius who is within earshot of the road, Cassius who could have found help from humans, turns around because he has no real purpose. He is still that same golem carved from the clay of bad blood and petty resentments, and now he sees a chance to act them out on my helpless body.

My nose just clears the surface, blinking at Cassius silhouetted in the bright sunlight, that oar held high. He slaps the surface over and over. It hits me, too, but the bog absorbs enough of the force to protect my bones. I keep my head pressed to the side, trying to shake away the thickness enveloping my head and body and threatening to drag me down.

With every blow, he yells his hatred of wolves, of Julia, of trees, of the Alpha, of Arthur, of Lorcan, of Elijah, of Constantine...and for the first time, I realize he has no idea who is foundering in the mud in front of him. To him, I am just another gray wolf in a pack that is full of them.

As soon as the time for fighting begins, Otho said, the time for thinking is long over. So when my back leg finds a stone sticking out from the side, I grab the ledge with my front paws and push off with my hind paws. Scrabbling awkwardly up, I don't bother to catch my breath but instead lunge at his leg and sink my teeth in, feeling the grinding of bone against fangs. It's a better bite than I had for the feral pig. Cassius tries to shake me, then starts to hit at me with his paddle, but I hang on like a burr on fur in this sinkhole in a roadside bog, not because anyone told me to, but because I know I have to.

Even when he raised the paddle high. I feel the air eddy as it starts down, then it hits my shoulder and my front legs give out, but I don't let go.

Cassius lashes at me with his oar, hitting again and again.

Then I hear it, wolves coming. I had a head start and am a better swimmer, but they are still coming. This time, it isn't Poul and his posse, howling for my blood. Cassius has never hunted with the pack, so he doesn't know the tiny sounds they make so as to not alert prey.

The pack is wary this close to Offland. Now even Cassius can hear the blare of the semi horn to the south, and he knows wolves won't kill a man on the shoulder of a county road. He turns the paddle to the side and swings it down with everything he has. As the snap of the bone resonates through my head, my jaw opens because I can't help groaning and Cassius immediately squelches away toward the road, where the first thing this shit will do is tell everyone about this forest strong and fierce and these lives that must remain unspoken.

My front leg is useless, blood and mud thicken in my brain, buckthorn drills through my paws, but it doesn't matter. Coiling the muscles in my hind legs, I take one last leap.

When he falls, the open sky is reflected in his terrified eyes and finally he knows.

"Constantine? But you're one of—"

And with one crushing bite, I rip out his throat.

Because I am not one of you.

His body flails, hands grabbing at my muddy fur, viscous bubbles turn bright red at the hole in his neck, his rasping gurgles slow then stop, and eventually, his body stills, his head falling empty-eyed to the side while his tongue lolls from his mouth, covered in blood.

The hours that follow are made from odd and horrible memories interrupted by excruciating pain when ripped skin and broken bones are pulled apart as they find a new shape. If my voice actually functioned, I'd be screaming, but it doesn't, so I don't.

I can't see anything, hear anything, move anything, smell anything, but I am blessed with the ability to feel not only the physical pain but the even more exquisite agony of what I've lost. There I was, after all that work, ready to teach Poul a lesson and prove myself strong enough for the Great North, big enough for Evie, and I blew it.

I can't move either, not consciously anyway, but some involuntary twitch moves my body forward a little and I feel something warm. I replay Cassius's last moments, especially his final bubbling exhalation to reassure myself that there is no way he could have survived. I'm not such a stranger to death that I would make that kind of mistake.

Then I know who it is. Blind, I know it's Evie. Deaf, I know it's Evie. Unable to smell, I know it's Evie. Dead, I would know it was Evie.

I collapse against her, feeling pain combined with the helpless coming together of our changing bodies until finally when I take a breath, I make out granite and moss, and as always, Pack.

"Constantine?"

"Mmm-mmm."

"Can you walk?"

I try to lift my hand against the bright early morning sun until my shoulder reminds me. Not that hand.

The other one is hardly better.

Evie sits beside me, her head to the side, pulling her fingers through her hair.

"'S Cassius?" I manage to croak out.

"Dead, yes," she says and bends her head again, finger combing the other side. She doesn't offer to help or anything as insulting as that, but she does watch carefully as I struggle to get up, pushing with my one working hand and my wobbly feet. She stands next to me, the still blood-smudged oar clasped under her arm, still combing her hair, pretending to ignore my flubbed first step and every flubbed step after until we reach the place where Cassius left the canoe. Evie holds it steady while I fall in. She ignores my swallowed scream as my collarbone separates. Pushing free of the mud and weeds and bushes, she paddles around the edge of the Holm.

Huddled deep in the hull, my throbbing arm propped on my leg, I watch the water go past and then the Holm. There's a bloody bone there and Cassius's boot. In the back, Evie sees the direction of my eyes.

"Don't worry," she says. "We saved you some."

Chapter 35

Evie

"That's a flesh wound. That's a flesh wound. That's a flesh wound. And that..." Constantine groans loudly as Tristan pokes his collarbone. "*That* is not a flesh wound."

He pokes some more around Constantine's bruised and bloodied body.

"Nothing broken here," he says, digging his finger between his patient's ribs and wiggling it. "But I bet it's painful as hell, isn't it?"

"Fugyer, Trisin," Constantine spits out through gritted teeth.

I suggest that Tristan try for a slightly sunnier manner, a suggestion I immediately regret it as he launches into some strangely threatening human song about sunshine.

"But if you leave me to love anoooooother/You'll regreeehhht it all someday."

At the upper left quadrant of Constantine's bruised torso, Tristan pokes a few times and the pain makes Constantine gag.

He snaps off his gloves. "Ruptured spleen."

Constantine will need a few days of bed rest so I bring my laptop and papers. Wolves have been coming in and out of Medical for two days, and I don't bother to hide what I'm doing here. When Constantine sets his beaten and punctured hand on my knee, his finger searching out my skin through the holes in my jeans, I feel lighter for it.

"Tristan," chokes yet another despairing voice from the door.

"As much sweetgrass as you can manage and call me in the morning," Tristan shouts from the back as he has with every choked and desperate wolf who has come to his door.

"Isn't there anything stronger?"

"Ah, Julia," Tristan says, appearing from the back. "Hold on a second."

When he returns, he is holding a sponge basin. "You could just vomit him up."

With a tight shake of her head, Julia hiccups.

"You ate twice as much as anyone else," I tell her. "No one would think less of you."

After a few more convulsive swallows, Julia stands high, presses her hand tight against her stomach, and says through gritted teeth, "But I would, Alpha. I would."

She leaves in a cloud of sweetgrass-scented air.

Poul claimed that having run from a challenge, Constantine is no longer protected by the law, but Silver was very definite that as he didn't run from cowardice, the challenge was not forfeited, just postponed. She gave Poul the option of calling it off, but he refused.

A day or so later, Poul passed me in the hall and put his nose to my ear. I elbowed him in the intestines and told him that whatever he smelled there, it wasn't for him, and if he stuck his nose in my ear again, I would eat his testicles.

He still wouldn't call it off, because his interest was

always in the status that came with being the Alpha's companion. Not like Constantine, who goes along with "all the Alpha crap," as he calls it, because that's the price that comes with loving me.

"You were upset when he challenged me last time. Why not now?"

I don't tell him that it's because I believe now. I believe his love is good for me and for the Great North. I believe that if—when—Poul loses, there will be a Thing with for-speakers and against-speakers and the Pack will decide whether Constantine brings strength to the Pack. And I know, as I look at his battered body, that the answer will be yes.

I also know that Poul will lose because not only will Elijah give him all the advantage of his long years of fighting, but I will too.

"Because this time, I know you will win."

Epilogue

Constantine

It's just a rock, a chunk of granite tumbled by ice and circumstance down from Canada to play its part in Homelands. Who knows how many thousands of years ago it came to rest here. Long enough for lichen to soften its surface, moss to colonize it, a treelet—a tamarack—to sink its roots into a fissure. A damselfly to sun its lacy wings on top. A fox to give birth underneath.

After a long day poking through the sphagnum and sedges and muck of that patch of wetland where Cassius died, I lean against this rock, my fellow refugee, and wipe the mud from my phone against my jeans.

Even though I can't see her or hear her, I feel her here. I hold the phone up, so Evie will know that I've found it, then with a sweep of my thumb, I hit Last Number and hold the phone to my ear.

"So where is Cassius?" says the familiar voice as soon as she hears me.

"He's dead."

Somewhere on the other side of the continent, ice swirls against crystal while she takes this in. "Hmm. And where are you now?" she says, trying to sound casual, though I feel the hunger in her voice.

My collarbone hurts, but I don't want Evie or Tristan

to suspect I am in pain and change their minds about the advisability of letting me be wild.

"Let it go, Drusilla," I say, hooking the thumb of my free hand through my belt loop to reduce the pressure. "They're all dead. You got what you wanted. You—"

"*Don't,*" she snaps. "They are not *all* dead." A door creaks on her end. "And don't you dare presume to know what I wa— *I said stay out,*" Drusilla yells away from the speaker.

There is a sharp crack at the other end of the line, and when Drusilla speaks again, her voice is calmer as it always is when she's hurt someone. "So tell me where the mutts are, Constantine, and let me let you live."

I hear a rapid-fire clicking and picture her, tapping at the mirror glaze surface of her desk, waiting impatiently for my answer, but I have nothing left to say to her. She knew who I was, but she knows nothing of the vast, uncharted land between who I was and who I am now.

The Titanix Thunderhead pops and crumples in my fist. A few pieces dribble from my hand as I remove the battery and fold the SIM card. I set them on the boulder.

"She doesn't know," I tell Evie as I pull off my shirt.

When the last of my clothes are folded in a neat pile next to the broken black case, I lie down, surrounded by the dry whine of the dog-day cicadas and the buzzing of bees at the nearby milkweed. A phoebe trills, then sings *fee-fee-fee* high among the shifting leaves of the lacework canopy. The black wolf lays her jaw on my shoulder as I give in to my wild. She will watch over me until I can join her.

Another of the lives that must be lived unspoken in the forest strong and fierce.

About the Author

Maria Vale is a journalist who has worked for *Publishers Weekly*, *Glamour*, *Redbook*, and the *Philadelphia Inquirer*. She's a double RITA finalist whose Legend of All Wolves series has been listed by Amazon, *Library Journal*, *Publishers Weekly*, *Booklist*, and *Kirkus Reviews* among their Best Books of the Year. Trained as a medievalist, she persists in trying to shoehorn the language of Beowulf into things that don't really need it. She lives in New York with her husband, two sons, and a long line of dead plants. No one will let her have a pet. Visit her online at mariavale.com.

Also by Maria Vale

The Legend of All Wolves

The Last Wolf

A Wolf Apart

Forever Wolf

YOU HAD ME AT WOLF

First in the Wolff Brothers, an exciting new series from *USA Today* bestselling author Terry Spear

Private investigator and gray wolf shifter Josie Grayson is on an important mission: find evidence to prove that the man staying at the Silver Town Resort faked his death for the insurance payout. When her partner is sent home sick, Josie needs to find a new fake lover in order to keep her cover intact—and the handsome wolf shifter and ski lodge owner Blake Wolff seems interested in the role...very interested.

"Delicious...a thrilling good time."

—*Fresh Fiction* for *All's Fair in Love and Wolf*

For more info about Sourcebooks's books and authors, visit:
sourcebooks.com

WOLF UNDER FIRE

New from *New York Times* and *USA Today* bestselling author Paige Tyler is the action-packed, international series STAT: Special Threat Assessment Team

Supernatural creatures are no longer keeping their existence secret from humans, causing panic around the globe. To monitor and, when necessary, take down dangerous supernatural offenders, a joint international task force has been established: the Special Threat Assessment Team.

STAT agent Jestina Ridley has been teamed with former Navy SEAL and alpha werewolf Jake Huang. Jes doesn't trust werewolves. But if they're going to survive, she'll need Jake's help.

"Unputdownable... Whiplash pacing, breathless action, and scintillating romance."

—International bestselling author K.J. Howe

For more info about Sourcebooks's books and authors, visit:
sourcebooks.com